COMING HOME

A Cold Shivers Nightmare #5

by
D Glenn Casey

www.dglenncasey.com

The novel, *Coming Home* is a work of fiction. Names, characters, places and incidents either are the product of the author's imagination or are used fictitiously. Any resemblance to actual persons, living or dead, events, or locales is entirely coincidental.

Copyright © 2022 by D Glenn Casey

All rights reserved. No part of this publication may be reproduced, stored in a retrieval system or transmitted in any form or by any means, electronic, mechanical, recording or otherwise, without the prior written permission of the author.

ISBN: 979-8-8348539-5-4

Cover design: D Glenn Casey
Cover art: innovari @ depositphoto.com

Other works by D Glenn Casey
(All titles available in ebook and paperback)

The Chronicles of Wyndweir
The Tales of Garlan - Prequel
Wicked Rising ~ Book One
The Wrath ~ Book Two
(coming soon)
The War For Wyndweir – Book Three

A Cold Shivers Nightmare
Beware The Boogerman
Shattered Prisons
Crossing The Veil
Demon Hunter Academy
Coming Home

Campfire Stories
Darius James: Monster Hunter
(coming soon)
Sister Clarice: Vatican Demon Hunter

Other full-length novels
Into The Wishing Well
(coming soon)
The City Of Time

My Amazon Author page

My writer's blog
www.dglenncasey.com

Table of Contents ~ Coming Home

Chapter 1 – A Hunting We Will Go..................................1
Chapter 2 – Catch And Release....................................12
Chapter 3 – Coming Home..18
Chapter 4 – A New Baby Brother...................................33
Chapter 5 – Can't Fool An Old Demon..............................43
Chapter 6 – Trouble Comes To Town................................52
Chapter 7 – A New Orphan...65
Chapter 8 – The Old Bat Puts Up A Fight..........................72
Chapter 9 – Breaking The Bad News................................88
Chapter 10 – The New Girl..94
Chapter 11 - Captured...107
Chapter 12 – A Bit Of Air Sickness..............................115
Chapter 13 – Having A Blast.....................................126
Chapter 14 – The Interrogation..................................140
Chapter 15 – Getting To Know Brother............................147
Chapter 16 – Don't Mess With Goblins............................153
Chapter 17 – Hell Hath No Fury..................................164
Chapter 18 – A Message From Above...............................172
Chapter 19 – Calling An Old Friend..............................182
Chapter 20 – Going To Get Mom...................................194
Chapter 21 – The Mission..202
Chapter 22 – A Friend Comes To Town.............................222
Chapter 23 – Feeding The Prisoners..............................235
Chapter 24 – Andy Comes To Town.................................251
Chapter 25 – We Have An Alien Problem...........................268
Chapter 26 – Chopping Down A Tree...............................277
Chapter 27 – A Trip To Warmer Climes............................291

Chapter 28 – The After Action Report..................................308
Coming in late 2022...317
    Sister Clarice: Vatican Demon Hunter
Other books by D Glenn Casey..325

COMING HOME

A COLD SHIVERS NIGHTMARE #5

Chapter 1 – A Hunting We Will Go

"I don't like it, Tito."

"Shhh! I thought I heard something," hissed Tito.

Don't you shush me, you jerk! When you said you wanted to do something exciting tonight, I didn't know you meant low-crawling through the dirt and grass!

It was just after midnight and these two explorers had decided to see if any of the rumors they'd heard were true. Creeping through the tall grass, they could see the metal building in the distance. It sat alone, in the middle of a field, lit up by the full moon. There were some lights shining through a couple of windows, but the area appeared to be quiet.

"C'mon, Lisa," said Tito, as he began crawling through the grass.

"I want to go home," whispered Lisa. "When you promised me a fun time tonight, I didn't think you meant crawling on my belly, through the mud and bugs!"

She didn't get an answer because Tito had already moved further away and she couldn't see him anymore.

Oh, why in the world did I allow him to talk me into this? When we get home, we are SO finished!

She raised up just a little to see his location, but the grass reached so high that she couldn't see anything.

Just as she thought about calling out to him again, the door to the building opened and a large man stepped out and she dropped to her belly in the grass.

"All right, you two mangy mutts, time to get out here and do your business," yelled the man.

Lisa raised up to scope out the situation and she saw a huge brown dog come racing through the door and into the grass. Following close behind him, a little wiener dog stopped and looked up at the man.

"Buster, mind your P's and Q's when you're outside. You know the sheriff is just looking for a reason to vaporize you."

Buster yipped at the man and bounded off the porch and into the grass. Now our two explorers weren't only trying to stay quiet and hidden in the grass, they were also trying to keep the dogs from discovering them.

By this time, Lisa had lost Tito completely. Hidden somewhere else in the field, she had no clue where he went.

She heard a howl go up and it sounded like something that she did not want to meet. Staying as quiet and low as she could, she thought of backtracking her way out of the field and back to the truck.

"Oh my God!" yelled Tito.

Lisa did not know what caused his outburst, but he sounded terrified. Then she heard the wiener dog yipping, but it sounded like his yips were getting a lot lower in tone.

"Whachu got, Buster?" yelled the man.

Another growl sounded across the field of grass and she heard the second dog somewhere else close by.

Turning tail and running seemed like a good idea, but then she felt a presence behind her. Turning around, she came face-to-face with the biggest, meanest looking brown dog she had ever seen in her life. When she went to move away from him, he growled and took a step toward her and she got the message.

Don't take another step!

As she looked at the dog, she saw glowing red eyes, but the thing that caught her attention the most were the fangs that looked like they were as long as her forearms. That was probably an exaggeration, but to her wide eyes, they sure looked that long.

She heard a commotion to her right and glanced over her shoulder just in time to see the man come off the porch and run into the tall grass. He ran strangely. One could describe his gait as loping. She realized she had to be seeing things when the man changed into a werewolf.

There is no way I just saw what I think I saw!

She heard the large dog watching her growling, causing her to turn and look him in the eyes. The look in his eyes said the dog did not want her watching what happened on the other side of the field.

She stood up straight and could see Tito about thirty yards away and he had a large black dog staring him right in the face. Even from this distance, she could feel the fear coming off of him.

The black dog looked bigger than the truck that he had driven here tonight. She could not believe the size of the dog. This dog appeared bigger than a horse.

That's just not right.

Looking for the man, who changed into a werewolf, she saw him raise up out of the grass, standing on his back legs. He looked back and forth between the two of them and she could see his yellow eyes glowing in the dark.

"If I were you, I wouldn't move a muscle, either of you," growled the werewolf. "I have called the sheriff's department and they are on their way right now."

"Please sir, we will just turn around and go home," whined Lisa.

"I'm sorry, but the time for turning around and going home has long since passed."

Lisa grew tired of standing in one position and she went to shift her weight, which caused her to take a step back and the dog in front of her barked and snapped at her.

"Like I said, don't move a muscle! That is Bosley and he is a Hell hound. There is nothing he would like more than to drag your butt back to Hell and present you to his master."

Lisa looked into the red eyes of Bosley and she knew in her heart that he was exactly what the werewolf said.

A freakin' Hell hound!

As they stood there, she could hear a siren in the distance and it was getting louder and closer. Obviously, the werewolf was not kidding when he said he called the sheriff. Within a minute, a sheriff's SUV pulled off the highway and came down the dirt road and parked near the building at the edge of the tall grass.

When the door opened, Lisa saw the law man get out. Or to be more precise, the law woman. She was a tiny lady, only about five feet tall and skinny as a rail.

She stopped at the edge of the grass and looked at the scene in front of her. Her gaze shifted back and forth between the two explorers and the two large dogs that were guarding them.

What surprised Lisa the most was her gaze passed right over the werewolf, without stopping and giving him any consideration. As if she was quite used to seeing a werewolf on this piece of land.

She walked into the field and stopped next to the werewolf and said, "Hey Bill, looks like you caught a couple."

The werewolf just growled and she reached over and patted him on the shoulder.

"You go on in the house and I'll take care of this. Cal is on the way and he's going to back me up."

"Yeah, like you need backup," growled the werewolf.

Then he turned and loped across the field, back to the building and through the open door.

"Now, what to do with you two?" said the law woman. "My name is Deputy Debbie and it will be my pleasure to place both of you under arrest."

"Ma'am, if you just let us get back to the truck we will leave this area and never come back," offered Lisa.

"I'm sorry, but it's too late for that," said the deputy.

The deputy made her way to Tito and when she got there, she said, "You have got to be kidding me."

She was shaking her head as she pulled her handcuffs off her belt and stepped behind Tito and cuffed him. As she did that, Buster leaned in real close to Tito's face and a large glop of drool landed right on Tito's nose.

"Buster! Back off, buddy!"

Buster backed up a few inches, but he still kept his nose right there in front of Tito, looking like he was ready to chomp his head right off.

"Now, just stand right here or Buster will make you wish you hadn't moved."

They could hear another siren in the distance and it didn't take long for another sheriff's SUV to pull in behind the first one. When this law man got out of the vehicle, Lisa saw a big man.

He walked over and stopped next to the deputy and said nothing at first. He just did the same thing she did when she first got there, just looked back and forth between the two explorers.

"So, how do you want to handle this deputy? Let the hell hound drag them back to Hell or maybe just let Buster eat them."

"Oh geez, Cal! The last time we let Buster eat anything, it took him three days to pass it. We could just shoot them and bury them in the field. No one would ever find their bodies."

Cal looked back and forth and shook his head.

"I'm not feeling it, Debbie. I'm not in the mood to dig a couple of graves tonight."

"Wuss. You didn't say that last week."

"That was last week."

"Hey," said Debbie, "does your unit still smell like a dead skunk inside?"

"Yeah, Earl can't figure out what it is."

"Do me a favor, then. You take this guy. He peed his pants and I don't want him in my truck."

Cal took a step to the side, looked down and laughed.

"Yeah, I can take him."

"You peed your pants?" yelled Lisa.

Cal took Tito by the arm and started leading him out of the field and back to his truck. Deputy Debbie turned and made her way across the field toward Lisa and Buster walked right along beside her.

When they stopped in front of Lisa, Buster moved over and bumped his head up against Bosley, knocking him out of the way. Then, he tried to do the same thing to Lisa that he did to Tito. He got right in her face and she could see the drool was ready to fall.

She reached up and put a hand on his wet nose and pushed him away.

"Oh, no! Get your wet mouth away from me!"

Buster pulled back and looked at her like he had no clue what to do with her.

"Uh oh, Buster. Looks like she's on to you," laughed the deputy.

"Well," said Lisa, "I figure that if they were going to eat us, they would've done it before you got here."

"Yep, she has you figured out, buddy. There will be no fun with her tonight."

The deputy reached out and took Lisa by the arm and started leading her out of the grass. Lisa could hear the two large dogs moving through the grass behind them.

As they walked out of the grass, Lisa looked over and could see Tito sitting in the backseat of the other deputy's truck and she saw his eyes go wide with terror.

She looked behind her and saw Bosley coming out of the grass, but she didn't see Buster. Then, she saw a little black wiener dog come scampering out of the grass.

The deputy walked her over to the truck and opened the passenger door and asked, "Am I going to have any trouble with you?"

"No, ma'am. I've had just about all the excitement I can stand for one evening. This will be the last time I ever let that idiot talk me into doing something like this."

The deputy motioned for her into the front passenger seat of her truck.

"Aren't you going to put handcuffs on me?"

"Why? Do I need to?"

"No, deputy. I was just asking," said Lisa as she climbed into the truck.

As she sat down, the door to the building opened back up and the man stepped out onto the porch, this time wearing a bathrobe.

"You two mutts get in here right now!"

Both dogs ran across the open area and the hell hound bounded through the door, while the wiener dog stopped and looked up at the man and yipped.

"Yeah, Buster, you did good tonight."

Just then there was a loud crash inside the building and the man yelled, "Bosley! Knock it off!"

Then he looked down at the wiener dog and said, "Go get him, Buster!"

Buster barked and ran through the door, followed closely by a large growl that was probably heard for miles.

The deputy walked over to the man and asked, "How are you feeling, Bill?"

"Debbie, I'm doing pretty good. The doc was right when he said that I'd feel much better once the full moon came around."

"That's good to hear," said Debbie. "We need you strong and healthy to keep those two under control."

"Sometimes, I wonder if it's all worth it."

Debbie laughed and said, "It's worth it to me and definitely to my daddy."

She looked around and then said, "Well, I guess I'll head back to town and take care of these two. You take it easy and get some rest."

He reached out and patted her on the shoulder as she turned and headed back to her truck. She climbed in and was getting herself situated when she looked over at Lisa and sighed.

"Seatbelts, young lady. Safety first."

Lisa reached around and pulled the seatbelt around and fastened it. She watched as the deputy started the truck and did a quick turnaround in the driveway and headed back to the main highway. She caught one last glimpse of Bill as he shook his head, then turned and went inside and closed the door.

Chapter 2 – Catch And Release

Pulling up outside the department a couple of days later, Debbie sat in her SUV, thinking about how the morning was going to go. She had two young people locked up in the secret basement cells. Remember, those secret basement cells don't exist. It was time to turn the two monster hunters loose, making sure that they would never return to Prattville. Like she had done many times before.

As she walked into the department, Cal was sitting behind the counter finishing up a bit of paperwork and she said good morning to him.

"Any trouble out of our guests?" asked Debbie.

"No, not a peep out of them," said Cal.

"Well, I guess I'll go downstairs and see how they're doing."

She walked back past the regular cells and stopped in front of a set of lockers. Reaching out, she twisted one of the combination locks back and forth a couple of times and then stepped back. A second later, some metal rods snapped up out of the cement floor. There was a grating sound as the lockers swung out from the wall. When fully opened, there was a set of stairs going down into the basement under the building.

As she walked to a heavy steel door at the

back of the basement, she placed her hand on a glass panel on the wall and it lit up, reading her palm print. After it recognized her, she heard a couple of heavy thunks and pulled the door open.

She flipped the lights on and it took a few seconds for the florescent lights to come on, illuminating three cells on the left and four on the right, with a bathroom at the far end on the left. Cells two and three on the left were occupied and as was cell number four, on the right at the far end.

Some of the cell occupants stirred from their sleep as the light flickered on. As she walked down the aisle between the cells, she looked into cell number two and said, "Good morning, Billy Ray. You ready to get out of here?"

The big guy stood up off his cot and stretched and looked at her, smiling his big grin.

"Of course, deputy. I feel much better this morning."

"Is there any way I can get you to stop acting the way you do and having me throw you in this cell?"

"Well, gee, deputy, I don't know. Whatever would you do for fun?"

She looked at him and then reached out and placed her thumb on the scanner pad on the door of the cell and it popped open. Billy Ray stepped out of the cell and she had to crane her neck to look straight up at him.

"You know," said Billy Ray, "maybe I just enjoy our little interactions."

Debbie laughed and said, "Get out of here!"

Billy Ray didn't have to be told twice as he turned and headed out the door and up the stairs.

They could hear Cal say, "Try to stay out of trouble for at least one day."

Debbie stepped to the next cell and looked in to see Tito curled up in the corner of his cell, sitting on his mattress with his knees pulled up in front of him.

"Morning Tito, what seems to be the problem?"

He just looked at her, but said nothing. He had a look of terror on his face that she had seen many times before. Such as every time she stuck monster hunters in these cells, right next to whatever monster was in lockdown.

She shook her head and walked down to the fourth cell on the right and its door was wide open. She stopped in the cell's door and looked in. Lisa was stretching and trying to wake herself up.

"Good morning, deputy," said Lisa with a smile.

"Good morning to you, too. Did you get a good night's sleep?"

"Well, I did finally get to sleep after Billy Ray changed back to human and stop terrorizing

Tito. Before that, it was pretty loud down here. I finally had to step out there and ask Billy Ray to keep it down and he did."

Lisa stood up and stretched again and then said, "Thank you for not locking the door. I needed to visit the restroom a couple of times."

"That's okay. We could see that you would not be any trouble at all. Are you ready to get out of here?"

Lisa stepped out of the cell and looked across and saw Tito and said, "I am and I'm sure he is, too. Looks to me like I'm going to be doing all the driving home."

The two of them walked back over and looked at Tito, still sitting on his mattress and could see that it would be a long time before he ever thought of coming back to Prattville. Lisa stepped into the cell and put a hand under one of his arms and helped him off the bed. With her support, he could shuffle out of the cell and toward the door and up the stairs out of the basement.

They stopped at the counter and Cal slid a couple of papers across the counter to them and Lisa looked at them and then signed one of them. She slid one in front of Tito, but he just stared down at it, as if he did not know what he was looking at. Lisa finally coaxed him to pick up the pen and scrawl his name on the bottom line.

Debbie got them turned and headed out the

door, but before they reached the door to the street, it flew open and an enormous man walked in, dressed in the Sheriff's uniform.

He was blocking their way out, looking down at both of them with the meanest look he could muster. He even growled at the two of them, causing Tito to take a step backwards, trying to hide behind Lisa.

Lisa looked up at him and asked, "What kind of monster are you?"

Debbie laughed behind her and said, "He is the worst monster of all. He's the Sheriff and one hundred percent human. Oh, and he's my daddy."

"Debbie! Why are you always trying to undermine my authority?"

"Because it's fun," said Debbie with a giggle.

The sheriff looked at the two hunters and growled, "Are we ever going to see you two in this town again?"

Tito could only mumble and nobody could understand what he said.

"No sir, you won't have any trouble from us ever again," said Lisa.

"Good, make sure it stays that away."

Sheriff John stepped out of the way and let the three of them pass through. Out on the sidewalk, it surprised Lisa to see Tito's truck parked in one of the parking spaces outside the department and not in some impound lot.

Debbie handed her the keys to the truck and

she went over and unlocked the door, helping Tito into the passenger seat. After getting him buckled in his seatbelt, because *safety first*, she turned and looked at Debbie.

"I am sorry for letting him talk me into coming here, but it has also been an interesting experience."

She stopped and looked around, seeing the quiet little town's streets coming to life. She took a deep breath of the clean, fresh air and let it out slowly.

"To tell the truth, deputy, you have a nice little town here. It's a shame I can't come back."

"Never say never," said Debbie. "And please, call me Debbie."

Lisa reached out and shook her hand and then walked around, got in the truck and started it up. As she drove away, the entire town could hear Lisa yell, "Omygawd, Tito! Couldn't you wait until we get home?"

Debbie laughed to herself and stood there, watching them go. She wondered how long it would be before she saw Lisa again. Something in the back of her mind told her it wouldn't be too long.

Chapter 3 – Coming Home

Sitting in one of the rocking chairs on her front porch, Debbie sipped a cold one and thought about the day's events. The night was quiet; the birds having gone to sleep a couple of hours ago and with Bosley moved back in with Bill and Buster; she didn't have to worry about the Hell hound destroying her house.

She still could not get over how easily Lisa accepted the fact that monsters exist and she was okay with it.

She took another sip of her beer and watched as a shooting star moved across the sky just above the horizon. As she sat there, getting ready to make a wish, her attention became more focused on the star and she realized it wasn't what she was thinking.

Especially with the star slowing down and moving just over the treetops a couple of miles away. She knew it wasn't an airplane or helicopter because she had seen it coming down from too high up and at a speed that would have been unheard of.

Jumping to her feet, she ran into the house and grabbed her keys and then back out to her truck and took off toward where she saw the light coming down. With the hour of the night, she didn't run into any traffic, but still she raced with her lights on.

Running down Old Highway 42, she searched the skies whenever there was a break in the trees and she wondered if she was just chasing after a meteor.

The answer to that question came about a mile later when she saw the light floating above the trees just to the north. Based on its direction, she had a pretty good idea where it was going.

She hit the gas, rocketing to race car speeds and then slammed the truck into a power slide, flying off the asphalt and down a dirt road that went through the trees.

A couple hundred yards in the trees gave way to a clearing and she had every belief the vehicle was heading towards that meadow.

As her truck slid to a stop, she jumped out and ran around in front, with the headlights shining brightly behind her and her blue and red spinners flashing off the surrounding trees.

Within seconds, the lighted craft came over the trees and hovered over the meadow for a few seconds, looking like the inhabitants were trying to decide if they should set down there or not. She waved at them and after a few seconds, they decided to land.

She watched as the craft, about the size of a passenger airliner, settled down on three legs that extended from the underside of the craft. She could feel the hairs on her body standing up as the static electricity in the air increased.

After the craft settled down, whatever it was

using for power must have shut down, because the static in the air lessened and dissipated.

As she waited, Debbie wondered if she should have called for backup. But she put that thought out of her mind quickly.

As she wondered if the craft's occupants were going to come out, a ramp lowered from the underside with stairs.

She took a few steps towards the craft, stopping about halfway between her truck and the ramp. And waited.

After about a minute, she could see someone coming down the steps. They moved cautiously and stopped about two steps up. From what Debbie could tell, this occupant was a female, having quite a feminine shape. From the light behind her, it was hard to see the alien's face.

Two things stood out about this visitor. First, she stood about six feet tall. And the other thing was her bright blue skin. Debbie could feel her heart in her throat as she realized who this might be, but she didn't want to get her hopes up.

The woman on the stairs looked past her, at her truck with its spinning red and blue lights and Debbie could tell she was looking at the emblem on the door.

"Yes, I am a deputy with the Prattville Sheriff's Department," said Debbie.

The blue woman took two more steps, reaching the ground and she looked at her.

"I wish to speak to Sheriff John Dinkendorfer," said the woman.

"Mom?"

"Debbie?"

It took less than two seconds for the two of them to cross the space between them and wrap their arms around each other.

"You've come back!"

"And you've gotten big," said her mom.

"Well, not really that big. I guess I didn't inherit any of yours or dad's genes for height."

As they embraced each other, Debbie saw another being step into the light at the top of the ramp and she could tell this was a male and probably younger than her.

"Who's that?"

Her mom turned and looked and said, "Oh, that's Jaxon."

Her mom motioned the man to come down and when he reached the bottom of the steps, she pulled a device from her pocket and clicked a button, causing the ship to disappear.

"Where did it go?" asked Debbie.

"It's still there, but invisible."

Debbie looked at her and then the young man and said, "So, I guess you want to see dad?"

"That would be good."

She led them back to her truck, getting them in and situated and then drove back out of the meadow, onto the highway and back to town.

As they drove, the young man in the back seat stayed quiet, not saying anything. Her mom couldn't stop talking, asking questions about Debbie's life and what it'd been like since she left.

Debbie answered all of her questions, but never got to ask any of her own about what her mom's life had been like since she left the planet.

As they drove through the quiet streets of Prattville, her mom looked around and commented that it didn't look like much had changed at all.

"No, mom, it's the same town it was before you left."

After a few seconds of silence, Debbie could hear her mom crying and she reached into the center console and pulled out a couple of tissues and handed them to her.

"I'm sorry," said her mom, "I just missed so much, being gone for so long."

"You had to leave, mom. If you hadn't left, who knows what would've happened?"

"I know, sweetie, but I wasn't there for you as you grew up. There is no way I can tell you how sad it makes me feel to know I missed the last twenty years of your life."

Debbie pulled the truck to the side of the road and turned off the engine.

"Like I said, you had to leave. It was hard on dad and me at first, but we knew why you had to go."

Her mom looked at her and she could still see the tears in her eyes.

"But now comes the hard part," said Debbie.

"What's that?"

Debbie just pointed out the passenger window and her mom turned and looked.

"Oh," said her mom.

Right in front of her was the house she had fled twenty years before. Debbie could feel her mom's resolve beginning to waiver.

"Well, you wanted to see him."

"Yes, but now I'm not so sure. I guess I should ask, does he have someone else?"

"No, mom, he doesn't. He hasn't even dated another woman since you left."

Her mom looked back at her with wonderment in her eyes.

"Not even after all these years?"

"No, he always said he was married to the most perfect woman in the galaxy and any other woman would be a letdown."

Her mom looked at the house again and whispered, "Oh, John."

"Well, shall we go in?" asked Debbie.

The three of them got out of the truck and began walking up to the house. There were lights on in the downstairs part, so Debbie knew her dad was still awake.

As they walked up the sidewalk, she couldn't help but wonder who this Jaxon was behind them. He had said nothing, not even one word.

Debbie gave a quick tap on the door and opened it, stepping inside followed by her mom and Jaxon.

"Dad, you here?"

"Yeah, kiddo. I'm just popping some popcorn, getting ready to watch a movie. Want to join me?"

"Well, yeah, but..."

John was standing in the kitchen with his back to them and when he turned around, the bowl of popcorn in his hand fell to the floor. He stood frozen in one place, looking like he was trying to figure out how to take his next breath.

"Celia?"

"Hi, John."

She took a couple of steps towards the kitchen and he became unfrozen. They threw their arms around each other and hugged each other tight. John looked like he would never let her go again.

"When?"

"About twenty minutes ago, in the meadow just north of Johnson's farm," said Debbie as she moved past them to get the broom and dustpan and clean up the popcorn on the floor.

After she finished with the popcorn, she started a pot of coffee and told her mom and dad to sit down. Jaxon stood off to the side, looking like he was completely out of place. He was dressed in the kind of silver space suit you would expect to see on a 50s sci-fi TV show.

With the coffee finished, she grabbed four mugs and set them on the table and sat down, motioning for Jaxon to sit down in the empty chair. After he sat down, Debbie took a good, hard look at him. He didn't have the same blue skin her mom did. As a matter of fact, he looked rather human.

"I don't even know where to begin," said John.

"I do," said Debbie. "Mom, why don't you tell us who this is?"

Celia looked at Jaxon and then back at Debbie. Then she looked at John and took a deep breath and said, "This is my son, Jaxon."

"Wait, what?" asked Debbie. "Your son?"

"Yes, he is my son."

"You cheated on dad?"

John said, "Debbie! Stop that!"

"What do you mean, stop that? You spent the last twenty years being faithful to her, never once cheating on her and now you find out she has a son who was obviously born after she left here."

"I couldn't really expect her to not meet somebody else," said John.

"You didn't!"

They both looked back at Celia and she was just looking down at the table. Then she looked up at them and they could see her eyes were misty again.

"Yes, Jaxon is my son and … he is also your son, John."

"What?" gasped John.

John looked across the table at Jaxon, trying to figure something out.

"How could this possibly be?"

"Oh…," said Debbie. "I get it now."

She looked at Jaxon and asked, "And Jaxon, how old are you?"

The first words that Jaxon had spoken since he came to this planet were, "About twenty years old, in Earth years."

"I still don't understand how this could happen," said John.

"Well, dad, when a man and a woman meet each other and they like each other …" said Debbie.

"Knock it off, Debbie!"

"Well, isn't it obvious? She was pregnant when she left here."

John's eyes whipped back around to Celia and she just shrugged and gave him a half smile.

"It was a few weeks after I left here that I realized I was pregnant," said Celia. "By then I was on the other side of the galaxy and had no hope of coming back here."

"See dad," said Debbie, "perfectly logical explanation."

She turned and looked at Jaxon.

"I guess you're my brother."

He just smiled at her and said, "I guess I am,

sis."

"You speak pretty good English for this being your first time here."

"That's because of mom. Most of the time she wouldn't speak anything but English. She was always planning on us coming back here."

John was looking at him and finally stood up and held out his hand to his brand-new son. Jaxon stood up and took it and when he did, John pulled him into a bearhug.

"Glad to meet you, son."

John just looked him up and down, trying to gauge what kind of man he was. Like Debbie, he had no outward appearances of being half alien and half human. But he was pretty sure there were some alien tendencies below the surface.

"He has been bothering me for the past ten years to come to earth and meet you two," said Celia.

John and Jaxon sat back down and Debbie looked at her mom.

"So, are you finished running from the hunters that were after you?"

Celia looked down at her cup of coffee and picked it up and took a sip. John and Debbie both knew she was trying to avoid the question. Debbie looked at Jaxon and he just looked at her, not wanting to answer the question, either.

"Mom?"

"No, Debbie, I am not finished running."

"So, this is just some sort of pit stop?" said

John. "Just a brief side trip to say hi?"

She looked at John and he could tell she was struggling to keep from crying.

"The hunters know nothing about Jaxon. My intention is to drop him off and leave, so he can be safe here with you."

"And what about you?" asked Debbie.

"I could look out for myself, Debbie!"

"So can I, mom!" said Jaxon.

She looked across the table at him and shook her head.

"I brought you here to hide you."

"So where is your ship right now?" asked John.

"It's still in that meadow just north of Johnson's farm," said Debbie.

"No, it isn't," said mom. "I sent it to the far side of the moon and it's hidden in a dark crater. There was too much chance of it being discovered in that meadow."

"How are you planning on getting it back here?" asked John.

"With this," she said, pulling a small device out of her pocket.

John reached over and took the device from her fingers and looked it over. It had a couple of buttons on it and looked almost like a remote for a garage door opener.

"So you just push one of these buttons and it comes right back here?"

"Yes."

He took the device and handed it across the table to Debbie and said, "Deputy, why don't you lock that up in the safe down at the department?"

She took the device and stuffed it in her pocket.

"Sure thing, Sheriff."

"What?" said her mom. "Give me the device, Debbie!"

"What device?"

"Debbie! You don't understand how dangerous these hunters are!"

"Celia, you seem to have forgotten what this town is full of," said John. "We have seen our share of dangerous."

"Jaxon! Help me out here!"

"With what?"

"Oh, you people are incorrigible!"

"What does incorrigible mean?" asked Jaxon.

"It means we're hopelessly beyond reform," said Debbie.

"Oooo, I like that," said Jaxon. "I'll have to remember that one."

Celia looked at the three of them and they could tell she was becoming infuriated. Her usual blue face went right past pink and straight to purple.

"None of you understand what you're getting into!"

"No, mom," said Jaxon, "it's you that

doesn't understand. I am sick and tired of watching you push yourself from one end of the galaxy to the other, trying to keep me safe and alive."

"Please, Debbie, give me back the remote," pleaded Celia.

"Not going to happen, Celia," said John. "And I'm with Jaxon on this. We are tired of seeing you run. Maybe it's time to stop and make a stand."

Celia sat back in her chair, folding her arms across her chest, realizing she was going nowhere.

"Mom, you never explained why you're running in the first place," said Debbie. "Why are these hunters after you? Why are they trying to kill you? What did you do?"

"I did nothing more than be born."

"They want to kill you just because you were born?" asked Debbie. "That's pretty harsh."

"It's not that simple," said Jaxon.

"Enlighten us," said John.

Jaxon stood up and walked around the table and placed his hands on his mom's shoulders.

"Dad, sis, mom is royalty on our planet. Her mother and father were the rulers back home and my uncle killed them to take the throne. Mom was still a young girl, but uncle would have killed her, too, if not for a group of loyal followers, who spirited her away from the planet."

"So how much time do you think we have before the hunters get here?" asked John.

Celia mumbled, "Probably only a week. Maybe even just a few days."

"Well then," said John, "I suggest we get a good night's sleep and start making plans in the morning."

"Good idea," said Debbie, as she stood up and pulled her keys from her pocket.

"Jaxon, I have a couple of extra bedrooms at my place and I think you should probably stay there."

"Absolutely," said her brother.

On the way home, she and Jaxon stopped at the department. She had to unlock the door because Cal was out, making one of his rounds through the town.

"Just wait right here while I take care of this device."

She disappeared into the back and when she came back out, Jaxon pointed to a safe near the far wall.

"Isn't that the safe?"

"It is, but mom probably knows the combination to it, if she still remembers it. She could also try to get Mabel to open the safe, but I think that's highly doubtful. I put the device somewhere no one is going to find it and use it to make a clean getaway."

"Good thinking. I don't think mom is going

to give up trying to get off this planet and lead the hunters away."

After locking up, she took her new brother home, taking the long way to show him some neighborhoods of Prattville. Even though it was dark, he spent most of his time looking through the windows at everything and asking questions about the people there. It was obvious Celia had kept no secrets about the kinds of people that called Prattville home.

Chapter 4 – A New Baby Brother

It had been a long time since Debbie sat on her porch and had company sitting with her. The last time was when Cindy was visiting after they had rescued her from the Boogerman.

Now, she sat there with a brand-new brother, whom she had met just a couple of hours ago. As they sat there and sipped on their cold drinks, hers a beer and his a soda, because he was still underage, they got to know each other better.

"So, tell me more about your planet," said Debbie.

"Loiria?"

"Loiria? That's a beautiful name for a planet. Much better than Earth."

"Well, names can be deceiving. Compared to this planet, it's a hellhole. This planet is a paradise by every meaningful comparison."

"This planet is not a paradise in every way. It has its problems," said Debbie.

"You don't know problems then," said Jaxon. "The surface of Loiria is so hot that the entire population lives underground, because of the proximity to our star. We can only go above ground if we are wearing protective gear, even after night has fallen. If we ventured above ground without it, we burst into flames within one minute. That says nothing of the Kraynoks."

"Kraynoks?"

"They're hard to describe," said Jaxon. "There's nothing like them here on Earth. The closest thing I could think of is, picture a large, hairy spider the size of your truck, but with the head of a rabid dog. They have fangs about a foot long and are quite proficient at using them. They have killed many Loirians when caught above ground."

"So, the Kraynoks don't have any problem surviving on the surface of the planet?"

"No, they are quite comfortable in the heat."

"Okay, so everyone lives below ground. What is your society like?"

Jaxon took a sip of his soda and thought of how to put it.

"There are only a couple of million Loirians on the entire planet and we live under a ruling class, of which, mom was born into."

"So, if mom is next in line as the rightful heir to the throne of Loiria, does that make me a princess of Loiria? Am I in line for the throne?"

Jaxon laughed and said, "Well, yes and no. Yes, you would be considered a princess of Loiria, but being as I am the firstborn male, I would move in front of you."

"Well, that's not fair," said Debbie.

Jaxon laughed again and said, "Don't get too worked up about it. They would never accept me as their ruler, either. On account of both of us being half human."

"They wouldn't accept a half-breed, huh?"

"No, they would probably just kill us."

"That's good to know, just in case I ever find myself on Loiria. I'll know to defend myself."

"I'd say that after this is all over, I could take you to Loiria for a visit, but I hope I never see that planet again."

"So, if mom has been running from the hunters all this time, how did you ever visit Loiria?" she asked.

"We made a stop there once, when I was about ten. Those still loyal to her family hid us. She wanted to see if there was any way to take the throne from her uncle. We were there for about six months, Earth time and when it became clear it was hopeless, her supporters begged her to leave. She didn't want to, but she also didn't want her uncle to find out about me."

"That totally sucks," said Debbie, "but I can assure you, Earth has had its own share of power struggles. Lots of killing just to sit on a throne."

They sat for a few more minutes and then Debbie took him into the house and showed him to his bedroom. After getting him situated, she went into her own room and crawled into bed. Before her head was on the pillow for five minutes, she was sound asleep.

Tonight's dreams featured alien hunters, ray guns and she and her mom fighting off every attack. No matter how many hunters they killed, there always seemed to be a lot more.

Waking up in a cold sweat, Debbie almost reached for her gun she kept between the mattresses of her bed. Her dreams had ended with her facing an alien hunter, in a white space suit and a helmet that had a mirrored face plate. He had come at her with a wicked looking two foot blade at the end of a four foot long staff, making the whole thing about six feet long.

When she looked down at her hands in the dream, all she had to defend herself was a pocket knife.

The hunter started advancing toward her, slashing the blade through the air and each time he swung it, it made a buzzing sound.

When he jabbed it straight at her was when she jerked up in bed. She could still hear the buzzing in her head as she tried to catch her breath. The buzzing just wouldn't stop.

Then she realized it was her phone on the nightstand that was buzzing. She grabbed it and saw it was a text message from her dad.

> *Your mom and I are going*
> *to the diner for breakfast.*
> *Want to join us?*

She jumped out of bed and texted back they'd be there in thirty minutes. Grabbing her robe, she went to Jaxon's door and tapped. Not getting an answer, she quietly pushed the door open, hoping she was not going to find him doing something twenty-year-old Loirian males do.

The bed was empty, but looked slept in.

She stepped to the top of the stairs and looked down and saw the front door was open. When she went down and looked out, she saw him sitting in a rocker, watching the sun come up.

When she reached out and put a hand on his shoulder, he jumped. She laughed to herself at being able to sneak up on him.

"Hey brother, what's up?"

"Damn, sis! Don't do that!"

"A little jumpy, aren't you?"

"Well, if you had hunters trying to kill you every day of your life, you'd probably be jumpy, too."

"Ehh, I've had worse."

He settled back down in the chair.

"Watching the sunrise, huh?"

"Yes. Back home, this is something we never would see."

"Hey, mom and dad are going to the diner for breakfast. I told them we'd meet them there in about half an hour."

"Great, I am hungry."

"I'm going to grab a quick shower and then we can leave."

After she finished with her shower and went back to her room, she heard Jaxon taking his own shower. She got dressed in her best uniform.

This was going to be the first time her mom and Jaxon had seen her in uniform and she wanted to look her best. Sharp creases and polished boots. Just like the Army had taught her when she was a military police officer.

She went downstairs and sat on the porch and waited for Jaxon. Feeling the sun on her face, she realized just how special it would feel to her brother.

When he came out, she couldn't help but giggle. He was wearing the same silver jumpsuit he had arrived in.

"What? This is normal, everyday clothing on Loiria," he said.

"I think you're adorkable," she said with a laugh. "Maybe after breakfast, we can get you something a little more Earth-like."

As she drove them into town, she thought about seeing how he'd handle her driving like a race car driver, like her dad always accused her of, but then remembered Jaxon was used to flying around the galaxy in a spaceship.

When they reached the diner, they found John and Celia sitting in one of the back booths and there was no daylight shining between either of them. John was leaning over, kissing Celia near her ear, when their children walked up.

"Hey, get a room, you two," said Debbie.

"What? I can't help it if your mom and I are still madly in love. And last night was ama ..."

"Hey, hey, hey! I don't want to hear about your wild monkey sex session either!"

"What's the matter, sis? Sex is a normal part of being alive."

"Yeah, well, you were raised by mom. I was raised by dad and I'm going to be paying for it for the rest of my life."

"So, mom," asked Jaxon as he and Debbie slid into the seat across the table, "does dad still have it where it counts?"

"Jaxon! I raised you better than this," she whined.

Celia got flustered and when that happens, she can't maintain the human look of her skin and it reverts to the blue. And with this conversation, there was a lot of red mixed in the cheeks.

That was when Carrie walked up to take their orders. Her eyes went wide when she looked at Celia.

"I'm sorry, I'm sorry," moaned Celia, trying to cover her face with the menu.

"Don't be," said Carrie. "That is a lovely shade of pink. With the blue of your skin and eyes, you look stunning."

"Carrie," said Debbie, "this is my mom, Celia, and this is my brother, Jaxon."

After breakfast, Sheriff John walked into the department, lighter in his step than usual. And whistling a merry tune.

Mabel looked up from her paperwork, over the top of her glasses.

"What's got you in such a good mood?"

"What, I'm not allowed to be in a good mood?"

"It's just a serious change of pace for you. You might hurt yourself."

He sat down behind his desk and started looking at the reports Cal had left from the night before, but couldn't wipe the grin off his face.

Then he started whistling again.

"Alright, sheriff! What's going on?"

"Nothing, I swear," he said without looking up from the paperwork. Then he mumbled, "It's just that Celia came home last night."

"What? I didn't hear that!"

He looked directly at her and said, "I said Celia came home last night!"

"What! Celia? Your wife has come home after ... how many years?"

"Twenty."

"Twenty years and she's come home?"

"Yepper. Debbie saw her spaceship landing, went and found her and brought her to the house."

He went back to the paperwork, fully cognizant of the fact she was just staring at him.

"Yeah, well, I guess that would put you in a good mood," she said, going back to her own work.

Then John mumbled, "And she brought my new son."

"What? I didn't hear ... young man, if you don't start speaking up, I'm going to come over there and rip your arms off. And you know I can do it!"

The sheriff sat back in his chair, looked at her and sighed.

"Yes, I know you can do it, you mean, old woman. I said she brought my new son with her."

"Your new son? How in the world did that happen?"

"Well, as Debbie explained it to me, when a man and a woman love each ..."

Mabel stood up, her eyes glowing red and she growled.

John sat back and looked at her.

"Calm down, you old bat. I guess Celia and I had a rather healthy sex life before she left ..."

"I don't want to hear about your nasty sex life!"

"Funny, that's the same thing Debbie said this morning at breakfast. Apparently, Celia was pregnant when she fled the planet. Jaxon, my son, was born not too long after she left."

Mabel sank back down into her chair, trying to take it all in.

"Oh, and that isn't all."

"What, you have a new daughter, too?"

"No, thank God! One is enough. Evidently, the hunters that were after Celia twenty years ago haven't given up the chase. Her plan was to drop Jaxon off and then leave, hoping they would follow her. But Debbie and I confiscated the device she was going to use to call her ship back, because, well ... she's finished running."

"Okay."

"So, under no circumstances are you to give her the device locked up in the safe."

"Umm ..."

"What?"

"I was just in the safe half an hour ago. There's nothing in there but the usual papers and such."

"Hmm? I guess Debbie didn't think it would be safe in there. She probably hid it somewhere else."

"I wonder why she'd think that."

John mumbled under his breath, "Probably didn't trust you to not give it to Celia."

Next thing he knew he was being popped upside the head by the wet sponge she'd had sitting on her desk.

Chapter 5 – Can't Fool An Old Demon

Hazel Godwin was standing at the kitchen sink, getting some things ready for breakfast and paused when a couple of powerful arms wrapped around her from behind. The kiss of two cold lips on her ear caused her to shudder and moan.

"Oh, you old demon. Stop that or you won't be getting any breakfast."

"Mmmm, I could survive without breakfast for one day," said Lowell, her husband.

He had jet black hair and stood more than a foot taller than her.

"Well, I need something to eat after last night," she giggled, "so unhand me, you scoundrel."

He laughed and kissed her again on the top of her head. She sighed as she leaned back against him, but then went back to preparing breakfast.

"Did Chester bring back my flood lamp yet?"

"No, sweetie. He called yesterday and said he'd have it back here today."

"That boy is always borrowing my tools just when I'm fixin' to use them."

"Oh, give him a break. He needed it for work."

"He works for the police department. You

would think they'd have plenty of money lying around to buy their own damn flood lights."

She sighed and said, "You know he always brings things back, usually cleaner and in better condition than when he borrowed them. Besides, I think he just comes out to borrow things to have an excuse to visit."

"A boy shouldn't need an excuse to visit his parents," he said gruffly.

"Oh, sit down, you old coot. Your coffee is going to get cold."

Then she felt him tense up and stop breathing.

"What?"

She looked back over her shoulder and could see he was looking out the window, which faced the back field. She looked and couldn't see anything through the early morning darkness.

She heard him growl his deep demon growl and saw his eyes turn red. For this to be happening, something bad was coming.

"Call the sheriff," he growled, as he walked to the back door of the house. He reached up above the door and pulled down his 12-gauge shotgun and checked it for ammo. It was loaded and ready for anything.

"Lowell?"

He turned and looked at her, his eyes burning right into hers. She was sliding into full-blown terror now.

"Don't you come out here! And call the

sheriff like I said!"

He pulled the door open and stepped out, pulling the door closed behind him. The sky was just beginning to lighten and she could see him through the window as he made his way into the field.

He stopped when he was about fifty yards away and looked back. She could see he was looking right at her and she got the message. Running to the living room, she grabbed her phone and hustled back to the window while she was dialing. She wasn't dialing the sheriff, though.

As she waited for the call to connect, she began watching her husband again. He was just a little further out when the call connected. And went straight to voicemail.

Oh god!

"Chester, this is mom. Something's going on out here. Your dad is in the field and he sees something I can't see."

Just then, Lowell came to a stop and raised the shotgun. She could hear him yelling at someone, but she couldn't see who it was.

Then the shotgun erupted. Twice.

"Oh god, Chester. Something is out there and ..."

"I don't know who you are, but you picked the wrong place to land your spaceship!"

Twenty yards in front of him, Lowell could

see two beings in silvery, white suits, standing shoulder-to-shoulder and staring at him. They had helmets that looked like motorcycle helmets with mirrored face shields.

One of them held out a small tube, about a foot long and it slammed outward, becoming about six feet long, with a two foot long blade on one end. The other spaceman, a couple of inches shorter than his partner, did the same thing.

When Lowell got a look at the two blades, he knew he had seen enough and pulled the trigger. The shotgun exploded with a load of lead shot, hitting the taller alien in the chest, but the shot just bounced right off him.

He fired again at the other alien and got the same result. He could see the suits were some kind of armor.

The first alien ran a few steps forward at an incredible speed and swung the bladed weapon, knocking the shotgun from Lowell's hands, sending it helicoptering into the long grass.

Then, in the blink of an eye, the alien twirled the weapon in its hands and slammed the blade through Lowell's gut. The long blade sliced through the demon's body and came out his back.

Lowell was lifted off the ground like he was nothing more than a rag doll, but being a demon, he didn't hardly feel the blade in his body.

He changed immediately and six-inch claws

extended from his fingers and he slashed at the alien, catching him across the shoulder, ripping a hole in his suit.

The blade had some sort of force it emitted and Lowell found himself not able to push himself off it. It was also draining his life force and causing a huge amount of pain.

He roared as the pain intensified and swung his claws again, this time catching the alien at the neck and removing his head.

The other alien screamed as he saw his partner lose his head and moved forward, swinging his blade, catching Lowell just under the chin and removing his demon head.

As the head bounced down along the ground, he heard a woman scream in the house, across the field. Looking at the house, he began walking toward it.

Hazel screamed when she saw her husband decapitated. She still couldn't see what was out there, but it had just killed Lowell.

Clicking off the call with Chester, she dialed 911 and almost immediately got an answer.

"Prattville Sheriff's Department. What is your emergency?"

"Cal, this is Hazel Godwin! There's something out here at the farm and … oh god … it just killed Lowell!"

"Hazel, lock your doors! I'm on my way!"

"Please hurry!"

She laid the phone down and ran to the back door and made sure it was locked. Then, running to the chest of drawers in the living room, she pulled out her 9mm pistol and slammed a magazine in and charged it.

She took refuge at the recliner, Lowell's favorite recliner and knelt on the seat, her arms resting over the back. She carefully aimed her gun at the back door of the house.

Cal ran out of the department and jumped in his truck, tearing out of his parking space and heading west as fast as the vehicle could go.

Cal reached over and turned up the volume on his vehicle radio. He could hear Hazel's phone was still connected. Then he heard what sounded like a door being blasted off its hinges and then a fusillade of shots from a gun.

He tried pressing harder on the gas pedal, but it was already on the floor.

"Faster you piece of crap!" he muttered.

Hazel was sighting down the barrel of her gun, hoping the back door would remain closed. She heard some heavy boots stomping up the steps outside and then silence.

Then the door exploded inward, its pieces slamming across the kitchen. She couldn't see anything, but she saw something walking on the debris of the door. The broken glass crunched under the invisible boots.

Squeezing the trigger, the pistol erupted in her hands and she could see the bullet hitting something that looked like an energy field. Firing again and again, she watched as the bullets had the same effect. The fourth shot just hit the wall near the door.

She saw some of the glass on the floor near the chair she was hiding behind, get stepped on by some invisible being and she fired at where she felt they were. The bullets were just bouncing off whatever was there.

After a few more squeezes of the trigger, the gun just stopped firing with a click.

Then Hazel gasped as a two-foot long blade slammed through the back of the chair, through her chest and out her back. She could feel it was sucking her life-force from her body, draining her energy.

A shimmering being came into view and she looked at the covered face of an alien. She struggled to breathe as the faceplate on the helmet changed and allowed her to see the blue face of the alien behind the glass. He was just staring at her as her life was ending.

She gritted her teeth and said, "My Chester is going to make you pay for this."

Then her head fell forward and her eyes closed.

The alien pulled his blade from her body and then retracted it. Looking around, he saw nothing else he needed to worry about and headed back out the door.

In the distance, he could hear a siren and it was getting louder. Figuring it had something to do with him, he headed back into the field. Stopping to reach down and grab his partner's head, he laid it on the body and pressed a button inside the helmet. The headless body and head disappeared from the ground.

He stood up and looked at Lowell's body, looking at the long claws and then at the demon's head a few feet away.

What the hell are you?

Reaching up under his chin, he pressed a button inside his helmet and disappeared from the field. A minute later, the invisible space craft lifted off from the back of the Godwin's property and started floating across the sky. On his viewscreen, he saw a vehicle approaching the farm at a high rate of speed with red and blue lights flashing on its roof.

A few minutes later, the space ship passed quietly over a small town and he saw another vehicle, with the same red and blue lights get on the road heading out of town, toward the farm he had just left.

Well, there goes the element of surprise.

"Sheriff John, you out there?"

John rolled over in the bed while Celia snuggled up against him, her blue arm thrown over his chest. He reached for the radio on the nightstand.

"Yeah, Cal," he said with a lethargic voice. "What's up?"

"Sheriff, I'm out at the Godwin place. I think you need to come out here."

John rubbed the sleep from his eyes and sat up, hearing Celia moan slightly.

"I'll be right there."

Sitting on the edge of the bed for a moment, he looked over his shoulder at his lovely blue wife and felt a ripple of fear wash over him. He didn't know for sure, but whatever Cal was calling about most likely had to do with her.

He got dressed as quietly as he could and snuck out the door, completely unaware that Celia was watching his every move through half-closed eyes.

Rolling down the main drag through town, he looked around and saw no activity at all. Not a single person or monster was out on the streets and for that, he was grateful.

He didn't turn on his flashers until he got to Main Street and then headed west, out of town and to a horror he wasn't quite ready to take on.

Chapter 6 – Trouble Comes To Town

"Deputy, you awake yet?"

"Yeah, sheriff."

"Hey, I need you to come out to the Godwin place and …"

She waited for a moment for him to finish and when he didn't, she said, "I'm sorry, sheriff. I didn't get that last part."

After a couple more seconds of silence, the sheriff came back with a shaky voice, "I need you to bring Jaxon with you. I think he might be helpful here."

"I'll … we'll be there as fast as we can."

"Try to keep the speed down, young lady. I don't need you scaring the locals as you blast through town."

Debbie stepped out of her bedroom and tapped on Jaxon's door. He called out to come in and she found him sitting on his bed, reading a sci-fi space adventure.

"These writers really have a lot to learn about space and traveling through it."

"Yeah, I'm sure they do," she said. "Hey, dad called and said I needed to get out to a place on the other side of town. Something's happened out there and it doesn't sound good."

Jaxon just looked at her and she could tell the idea scared him the hunters might already be here.

"The thing is, he's asked me to bring you with me, saying you might be of help. I'll be ready to leave in five minutes."

"I'll be ready, too."

After they got dressed and out the door, Debbie did as her dad had asked and kept the speed down until they got through town and on the highway toward Hobart. Then she let the horses loose and screamed the rest of the way there.

As they came over a small rise, she could see several cop vehicles in front of the old farmhouse and two of them belonged to her dad and Cal. The others were from Hobart.

Pulling into the long drive, she parked behind Tom Jeffers' cruiser and felt an odd skip in her heartbeat. She knew that now was not the time to be thinking about him, but she couldn't help it.

As they approached the house, she could see Cal and Tom were out in the field investigating something.

Her dad stepped out the back door of the house and motioned to the two of them.

She motioned to all the cars and said, "I'm guessing from this level of response, this isn't good."

"No, deputy, it's not."

Then he looked at Jaxon and said, "I normally wouldn't ask something like this of a civilian, but there are things in here that I think you can answer. But, I need to warn you, it's not pretty in there."

"Dad, hunters have hunted mom and me since the day I was born and we've killed a few of them together. I've seen a lot of things that weren't pretty."

"You know, it actually saddens me to hear that from you."

He motioned them inside, warning them to watch where they stepped. They had most of the evidence marked off, so they should avoid disturbing it.

Before they could walk up the steps, Chief Handley stepped out the door and looked at the two of them.

"Chief, this is my son, Jaxon. I think he'll be able to give us some valuable insights into what happened here."

Jaxon held out his hand and the chief shook it. Bart looked at John with a question in his eyes.

"I thought you had a daughter and that was it."

"It's complicated," said John, "and something I'd be happy to discuss with you at another time."

Bart looked at Debbie and asked, "Does she really need to go in there?"

"Oh, you did not just suggest I can't handle what's in there," said Debbie, looking him directly in the eye.

"All I'm saying is this is really bad," said the chief.

"So was the Boogerman, but I didn't seem to have any trouble taking him down."

"Umm," said John, "I believe it was Buster, Bosley and Buttercup that took him down."

When she whipped around and gave him the evil eye, he held up his hands and said, "But you did quite a bit of the legwork."

The chief stepped aside and let them into the house. When Debbie saw the destruction, she felt a small bit of terror, but it was nothing compared to how she felt when she saw the covered body laying over the back of the recliner.

She noticed the 9mm shell casings laying on the ground, along with the pistol that had been dropped by whoever was under the white sheet. Walking around all the marked shells and the broken glass, she knelt down and lifted the sheet.

When she saw the face of Hazel Godwin, she felt like her heart was being torn out of her body. Hazel had been one of her teachers in grade school and the one that most understood her. To say she was one of her favorite teachers was putting it mildly.

She felt her dad put a hand on her shoulder and ask her to step back. He reached over and lifted the sheet off Hazel's body and then looked at Jaxon.

"Some sort of blade killed this woman, as near as we can figure. Have you seen anything like this?"

Jaxon stepped forward and knelt down, looking at Hazel's face first. He closed his eyes for a second, knowing she had died terrified and most likely because he and his mom had come to Earth.

He looked at the slice in the back of the recliner, running his fingers over the edges of the tear. Then he stood up and walked around the other side and looked at Hazel's back.

"Hunters," he breathed.

"You're sure?"

"Yes," he said, looking at his dad. "A weapon that is a favorite among the hunters killed this woman. It's called a Rocun blade."

He held his hands up and said, "It has a blade about this long, attached to a shaft about four feet long. But that's not the worst of it."

"It's worse than what we see here?" asked the chief.

"Yes, sir, it is."

Then he stopped and looked at the sheriff, wondering how much he could say in front of the chief.

"It's okay, Jaxon," said the sheriff. "He knows about monsters and aliens and such. You can say whatever you need to."

"The Rocun blade is a weapon that is banned in quite a few corners of the galaxy. But, the hunters have never been ones to worry about the rules. They will use any weapon they can get their hands on and the Rocun blade is their favorite."

"What makes it so bad?" asked Debbie. "I mean, it's just a blade, right?"

"No, sis, it's not just a blade. It is a weapon that is made to keep the victim alive for as long as possible. While the victim is impaled on the blade, it sucks the life force out of them and transfers it to the warrior using it. And it is not a painless process. The victim only dies after every ounce of energy has been drained from their body."

He could see the horror in his sister's eyes. She was having a hard time taking a breath. Then she looked down at the body of Hazel and a tear rolled down her cheek. She reached out and ran the back of her fingers over her old teacher's face.

"And I thought we had monsters here in Prattville," she whispered.

John took the white sheet and began draping it over the body.

"Back away, sweetie," he said as softly as he could.

After he covered Hazel, he moved Jaxon and Debbie away and back into the kitchen. He pointed to the empty casings and some of the deformed slugs laying on the floor.

"What do we know here, son?" asked the

sheriff. "She obviously hit something, but we've accounted for every bullet she fired, including the two holes in the window over there. I don't mind telling you, Hazel was an excellent shot. If she had something in her sights, she hit it."

Jaxon crouched down and looked at two of the slugs. He could see how they were flattened on one side. He just hung his head and shook it.

"She hit what she was aiming at."

"And yet," said the chief, "every bullet we've found looks just like that. If she hit what she was aiming at, where's the blood? Where's the body?"

Jaxon stood up and looked at the chief.

"They equip every hunter with a suit and helmet that act as a suit of armor. Though they look no more protective than these jeans I'm wearing, they can stop just about anything you shoot at them."

"Is there nothing that can get through their armor?" asked Debbie.

"Sure, there's one thing. A Rocun blade."

"Which is the one thing we don't have in our armory," said the sheriff.

"So, what do we do?" asked Debbie.

The chief spoke up and said, "First thing we do is take a walk into the field."

They all followed him out of the house and started walking across the field. Tom and Cal were busy marking off evidence, of which there wasn't much. Just the body of a beheaded demon.

Tom gave Debbie a half-smile as they walked up. She tried to return it, but she was still aching from seeing Hazel.

"What do you got out here, guys?" asked the sheriff.

"Well, it's apparent Lowell got attacked," said Cal, "changed into a demon to fight back and it didn't end too well for him. There is a shotgun over there and we found a couple of spent shells."

Jaxon crouched down to get a look at the body. He could see the gash in the demon's body going all the way through. He lightly ran his fingers over the edge of the cloth of Lowell's shirt.

Debbie leaned over and asked, "Why do you do that?"

"Do what?"

"Touch the wound or the surrounding clothing?"

"Oh, there is a residual energy the Rocun blades leave and I can feel it. This energy feels quite different from the one in the house, but I'm going to assume that's because he was a demon and she wasn't. She wasn't, was she?"

Debbie felt a catch in her voice when she said, "No, she wasn't."

"Run your fingers along this tear," he said.

She reached down and lightly ran her fingers along the edge of the cloth and almost jerked her hand away. Gasping, she found it hard to breathe.

"You can feel it, too. We have the same mother and father, so our abilities are probably the same."

"What am I feeling, exactly?"

"You sure you want to know?"

She looked at him and he could tell she wasn't so sure, but then nodded.

"You're feeling the mixture of two energy fields. The one the Rocun blade generated and … the one his life force left behind in the fabric of this garment."

Debbie closed her eyes and tried to keep the tear from running down her cheek. She was unsuccessful.

"Oh, Lowell, you and Hazel didn't deserve this," she whispered.

Cal looked at the sheriff and said, "Take a look at his right hand, or more specifically, the claws on his right hand."

John crouched down on the other side of the body and pulled a handkerchief from his pocket and picked up Lowell's right wrist.

There was something crusted on the claws. Something blue.

"That's Lorian blood," said Jaxon. "Obviously he got his claws into one of them."

Then Cal said, "Okay, now look at this."

The three of them walked across the small area of trampled grass and Cal pointed to the ground. There was a significant stain of blue on the ground, enough that it hadn't completely dried up.

"And then, right over there," he said, pointing a few feet away.

There was another stain of blue blood on the ground, this one a bit smaller.

Jaxon stood there, looking at the larger stain and then walked over and looked down at the smaller one.

"Okay, Jaxon," said his dad. "Give me a guess. I don't care if it's a wild guess, an educated one, whatever. Let me hear what you think."

Jaxon looked at the two stains again and then said, "He caused a serious injury to one hunter. And by serious, I mean the hunter probably lost an arm or a leg. That larger stain is probably where the body fell and this smaller one is probably where the severed limb fell."

Then he crouched down and looked at something on the ground next to the smaller puddle.

"See this?"

John, Cal and Debbie leaned over to see what he was pointing at. It looked like a small, silvery piece of glass.

"Okay, a piece of broken glass," said John. "There's probably a ton of it in this field."

"That is not a piece of ordinary glass. This is from the face shield of a hunter helmet. And if I were to amend my earlier statement about it being a limb the hunter lost, I would say he lost his head."

"Well," said John, "knowing demons the way I do, I can assure you, he would have gone for the head if he had any chance to do so."

"Well, I think he had the chance."

John stood back up and looked around.

"There was no doubt the hunters were here. But where are they now?"

"Okay, John," said the chief, "it's time to bring me into the loop here. Obviously, you know something I don't know."

"Walk with me, Bart."

The two of them began walking away from the group, toward the trees. It took a couple of minutes, but the sheriff told the chief everything that had happened over the past couple of days.

"So," said the chief, "we don't have a monster problem here. We have a galactic problem."

"That's about the size of it."

Then John looked down and then called Jaxon over. He pointed to a small depression on the ground and asked if it was significant.

"Oh, probably," he said as he looked around.

The chief called Tom over and had him flag the depression, as Jaxon started moving back toward the trees. After a few seconds, he called out there was another one. Tom marked it, too.

"I'm guessing there's one more, either there or there," Jaxon said, pointing in two opposite directions.

It took less than five seconds to find the third depression.

"Their craft settled down right here and it was facing directly at the farmhouse. What I don't understand is the shuttle craft would have landed under a cloak of invisibility. How would Mr. Godwin know it was here and come out to investigate? If he hadn't done that, the hunters probably would have left him and Hazel alone."

"Demons can see in wavelengths the rest of us humans can't," said Debbie. "I'm sure he looked out to the back of the field here and saw something strange and came out to take a look."

"That extra sight cost them their lives," mumbled Jaxon.

"Okay, we need to get out of this field and wait for Teston to send down their CSI," said the chief. "We've probably trampled the place so much they're going to raise holy hell."

"You're calling in Teston on this?" asked John.

"Well, no, you are. They will expect all kinds of warnings from you if you call. And I can't very well put Chester on this."

They started heading back to the house when they heard a large V-8 engine screaming down the highway. It was at least a couple of miles away, but it was plain as day someone was flogging those horses.

"Shit!" said the chief. "Tom, get up to the house now and keep him out!"

Tom took off at a full run, praying he'd get there before the car pulled into the driveway.

Chapter 7 – A New Orphan

The rest of them were about halfway back to the house when they heard some yelling out front. Debbie knew exactly what it was and she began running to head off trouble before it got started.

Rounding the corner of the house, she found Tom trying to keep himself between Chester and the front door of the house. Chester was just as adamant about getting in there.

"Chester, I can't let you in there. Chief's orders," said Tom, as he tried not to get physical with the department CSI.

"This is my parent's home! I have every right to go in there!"

Debbie ran up and put herself between Chester and Tom, placing her hands on his chest. He stopped struggling when it was her, as he looked down into her eyes.

"Please, Debbie. I need to get in there," he said, trying to keep his voice from breaking.

She reached up and placed both her hands on the sides of his face and he could see she was also fighting the tears.

"Chester, please stay out here. You don't want to go in there right now."

He stopped pushing and stepped back against the side of his car. Without warning, his knees gave out and he slid down, sitting on the ground next to the front wheel. His hands came up to his face and he leaned forward, trying to keep it together.

Debbie sat down next to him and put a hand on his arm.

"She called me," he cried into his hands, "but it went straight to voicemail. She sounded so scared and I wasn't here to help her."

Then he looked at her and asked, "And my dad?"

The look on her face told him everything he needed to know. It soon became very real to him that he was now alone in the world.

As the two of them sat there, the sheriff and chief came walking around the house. Chester was on his feet in a heartbeat and standing in front of the chief.

"I want to do the investigation!"

"Chester, you know damn good and well I can't allow that! I'm sorry, but you're going to have to take a back seat on this one."

"They were my parents!"

"Yes, they were and for that very reason, I can't allow you anywhere near this case."

"Who's going to do the work?" he demanded.

The chief glanced over to see John was on the phone and Chester saw that.

"Prattville? You're telling me the sheriff's department is going to handle the crime scene investigation? They call me when they need a

CSI!"

John got off the phone and walked over.

"No, Chester," he said, "I just called up to Teston. Their CSI will be here within the hour."

Chester was trembling out of a mixture of pain, sorrow and rage.

"Go home, Chester," said the chief.

He looked at the chief and said, "I'll be in the lab at eight. I want to see the reports as soon as they come in. I may not be allowed to be on site, but I'm pretty sure I'm within my rights to see what Teston finds out."

"Okay, I can allow that, but don't come back here. Don't make me have you cuffed and put in a cell until this is done."

Chester turned and walked around his car and got in. The engine rumbled to life and everyone kept their eyes on him. As he slowly turned the car around and headed back out onto the highway, he stopped and they could see him looking at the house. The grief was written all over his face.

Then, he slammed the gas pedal to the floor and left black marks for a hundred yards down the asphalt.

The chief looked at John and said, "I assume you told whoever in Teston what it was they would be looking at."

"I talked to Dean Cartwright and he will take care of that."

"I don't think I know Dean."

"Yeah, you do. He was there the night Cindy was taken. Him and his tiger."

"Oh, right."

"He knows our little world down here because he's part of it. Whoever he sends will know what they're walking into. I also told him to tell them to work out of your lab. It will keep Chester involved and hopefully out of here."

John looked over at Debbie and Jaxon standing next to each other. He started tapping his thumb on the buckle of his belt, looking like he was forgetting something.

Debbie read his face and then a light bulb went on in her head. Pulling her phone, she dialed a number and waited for it to pick up.

"Jake? Hey, I need you and Randy to go to dad's house and stand guard ... my mother ... she's back in town and it appears the hunters that chased her away last time are back and have already killed two people ... the Godwins ... thanks, guys."

She hung up the phone and looked at her dad.

"I'd love to see those hunters try to get through those two boys," she said with a forced smile.

"Okay," said her dad, "can you stay here until the CSI is finished? I'm going to send Cal home."

He looked over at Cal and nodded. The deputy turned and headed to his SUV and left the property.

"Sure," said Debbie. "Give Jaxon a ride back to town."

"I'd like to stay if I can," said Jaxon. "I'd like to see what you do around here."

"It will not be very interesting, bro. I'm going to be sitting on my butt, waiting for the CSI to get here and then wait for them to get finished with their work. Besides, when those two big boys show up at the front door, mom is going to be wondering what's going on, especially when they put her under house arrest. I think she is going to need you more."

"Okay," he said, shifting his gaze to his dad, "but let me help in any way I can. I know these hunters, having dealt with them before. I know what to look for."

"You've already proven that, son," said John. "But your sister is right. There's no reason for you to stay here. Let's go."

He looked at Debbie and then at Tom, who was standing just a few feet away.

"I'm sure I don't have to tell you two to keep it professional while you're here."

"Daddy ... err ... sheriff!"

"At this moment, sir, any relationship I have with Deputy Debbie is in the background. This," Tom said, gesturing toward the house and field, "is more important than that."

John nodded and then leaned over and kissed Debbie on the cheek.

"Be careful. Keep your eyes open. If they can be invisible, we don't know where they are."

"Yes, sheriff."

John and Jaxon got into his vehicle and left the property, leaving just Tom and Debbie standing in the front yard. She walked over and leaned up and kissed him on the cheek.

"Thanks for that," she said.

"I meant what I said. Something tells me this is going to be a lot worse than the Boogerman."

He looked at her and then cocked his head.

"So, you have a brother. And your mother is back in town."

"Yeah," she said with a slight nod. "Let's sit down on the porch and I'll fill you in on the latest family drama."

Celia answered the door and looked up to see two of the largest men she had ever seen. Well, since she got back to Earth. Both of them had large wooden clubs dragging on the ground behind them.

"Boys, what brings you two by?"

Jake tapped his brother's shoulder and said, "I'll stay out here and keep watch."

He walked back down the steps and took up a position in the yard in front of the house. And changed into a very large ogre.

She saw that and then looked at the other one.

"Come on in, Randy and tell me what's going on."

Chapter 8 – The Old Bat Puts Up A Fight

That morning, as all the deputies and sheriff were at the Godwin place, no one noticed the ship that flew slowly over the town, heading to the east. No one could've noticed it because it was invisible. Well, demons might have noticed it, but there were none out.

There were some monsters that could feel it, though they didn't know it. There was a feeling that went through their bodies they just didn't understand.

Mabel was one such person.

As she was walking across the street, heading for the department, she felt a sense of foreboding that caused her to stop in her tracks. Never mind that she had come to a complete stop in the middle of Main Street.

Gasping for a quick breath, she stopped and her eyes glazed over as she felt a sense of danger more powerful than she ever had before. She was completely frozen with fear, not looking around, not looking up or down.

"Mabel? Are you okay?"

She shook her head and looked to see Kelly standing next to her. The young nurse was on her way to work at the hospital when she saw Mabel standing in the middle of the road.

It took a second for Mabel to realize what was going on and she just smiled.

"Oh yes, a bit of déjà vu, I believe."

When she went to take a step, she found herself a little unsteady on her feet. Kelly reached out and took her arm and helped her out of the road. Walking with her to the door of the department, it surprised Mabel to find the doors locked.

"That's strange," she said, as she pulled her keys from her purse. "There's usually somebody here."

"I don't know," said Kelly, "but Randy and Jake got a call earlier to go to the Sheriff's house and they lit out like a couple of cats with their tails on fire."

"I wonder what's going on?" asked Mabel.

"I was thinking you could probably tell me."

"Sorry, I'm just getting in and I don't know."

Mabel got the door unlocked and Kelly pulled it open for her and they stepped inside. The department was empty and Mabel came to a stop inside, looking around. This was totally unusual and she wondered if it had anything to do with Celia.

She walked over and set her purse down on the desk and sat down, still in the slight stupor from earlier.

"Are you sure you're okay?" asked Kelly.

"Oh yes, guess I'm just feeling my age."

"Oh, come on," said Kelly, "you're not nearly as old as you try to tell people."

Kelly looked up at the clock on the wall and

said, "Well, if you're sure you're okay, I need to head out and get to the hospital. You call me if you need anything."

"You run along, deary and don't worry about me. I'll be fine."

Kelly leaned over and kissed her favorite ex-teacher on the cheek and turned and headed out the door.

Mabel sat at her desk, staring straight ahead, trying to figure out what was wrong with her. She knew she was feeling something, but she did not know what it was.

Maybe it's exactly what I thought and has something to do with Celia.

Unbeknownst to her, the invisible spaceship was still hovering over the town. Its only living occupant had been staring down at her from his view screen. After seeing the second woman walking away from the building, the alien picked up his blade, reached up underneath his helmet and pressed the button.

In a flash, he appeared standing in front of the desk, behind which sat the old lady that he'd been watching.

She jumped up as soon as he appeared and she knew immediately this had everything to do with Celia. She knew she was looking at one of the hunters they had warned her about.

In a metallic, computerized voice, the being asked, "Where is the criminal, Celia?"

"Who? I'm not sure I know who you're talking about."

As soon as she said that, the alien lifted his Rocun blade and pressed a button on it, extending it to six feet long, its two-foot blade still covered with blood.

Mabel took a step back when she saw the blade and the alien brought it around and pointed it right at her.

"I ask again," said the alien, "where is Celia?"

"Why don't you go get back in your spaceship and get out of this solar system?" said Mabel. "You do not know what kind of trouble you're stirring up here."

The alien began advancing toward Mabel and she could feel the energy of the blade as it was coming toward her. And that was all she needed to know.

Doing something that she had not done in over twenty years, she transformed. If anyone were to describe her, the best description would've been a miniature Cthulhu. But, even being smaller than the dreaded, ocean-dwelling monster, Mabel grew to eight feet tall. She had two sturdy legs and four massive arms with clawed hands at the end of each. Her monster look grew even more terrifying with the three-foot long tentacles hanging from the lower part of her face and blazing red eyes sunk deep in her head.

The alien jabbed the blade straight at her chest and all he got for his troubles was a right hook upside the head. Catching a right hook with your head is usually a pretty bad idea, but when it's delivered with two right hands, it's doubly bad. If she had hit a human like that, they would have been looking behind as their head would have been spun completely around.

As the hunter went to shake off the effects of the punch, or punches, she pounced on him, driving him backwards. Trying to keep his footing, he swung the blade and one of her left hands grabbed the shaft and clenched it. Then a couple of her tentacles reached out and wrapped themselves around his neck and he could tell she was going to squeeze the life right out of him.

He struggled to get away from her and realized she was much too strong. With every last bit of effort he could muster, he reached underneath his helmet, squeezing his gloved finger past her tentacles and pressed a button.

In a flash, he disappeared from her grip, leaving her snarling at the empty air in front of her. She let out a roar that could be heard for miles.

Swinging her head back and forth, her burning red eyes searched for the attacker as her tentacles slapped each side of her head. She knew he would not give up that easily.

As she turned looking for him, he reappeared behind her. The flash caused her to spin, but not quick enough. The hunter brought his blade up and into her chest, driving it all the way through her body.

As he drove her to the ground, working the blade back and forth in her chest, his face plate cleared and he looked down at her.

"What the hell are you?"

She roared again, trying to get her claws on him, but the blade had some kind of energy that was sapping her strength. Quickly, she became so weak she wasn't even able to raise her arms.

One of her tentacles lashed out and smashed the clear faceplate of the alien's helmet and tried to drive inside to get at his face. But even that became impossible, as she could feel her life force being drained from her body.

Within a few more seconds, her arms fell limp at her side and her eyes closed.

The alien yanked the blade from her body and stood back, watching as the beast crumpled to the floor. As he looked down at her, trying to figure out what she was, he nodded a couple of times toward her. She had put up more of a fight than anyone he had ever come across in his many years as a hunter.

Then he pressed the button in his helmet and flashed out of sight.

Kelly was about halfway to the hospital when she heard the roar. Knowing exactly what it was and who made it, she turned around and ran full speed back to the Sheriff's department.

Rushing through the doors, she cried out as she saw the beast laying on the floor in a growing puddle of blood. Black blood.

Dropping to her knees next to Mabel's head, she pulled her phone from her pocket and called the hospital. She ordered an ambulance and they needed to come prepared for a monster.

After she hung up, she reached out and ran her hand over Mabel's brow and she could tell her favorite ex-teacher was slipping fast.

"Hang in there, Mabel. Help is on the way."

Debbie was sitting on the porch with Tom, filling him in on her family affairs. She had just told him about her mother and her new brother and how they had been fleeing from hunters for the past twenty years.

She was just about to say something when she heard the roar. It was a roar she hadn't heard in over twenty years, but instantly knew exactly who it was. And if she made that much noise, it wasn't good.

She jumped up, without even saying goodbye to Tom and ran to her truck and jumped in. Spinning her tires all the way back out to the road, she slammed on the brakes and dropped into Drive and pointed herself back to town.

Tom just had to watch her go because someone still needed to be there when the

Teston CSI showed up. But, even he knew something terrible was going on back in Prattville.

Debbie's Blazer's hit top speed within seconds and she didn't care who was going to see it. She needed to be back in Prattville yesterday, not ten minutes from now.

She was going so fast she caught and passed her dad and brother like they were driving a horse and buggy.

"What the hell, Debbie!" shouted the sheriff on the radio.

"You didn't hear that?" she yelled back.

"No, and you better slow that damn thing down!"

"Something's happening to Mabel!"

She did not lift her foot even one centimeter off the floor and she could hear her dad pressing his foot down, too. She left him in the dust, but she knew he wanted to get back there faster than she did.

As she flew up the hill, past the Manning farm, her lights and siren warned everyone to get out of the way. Within seconds, she slammed on the brakes and skidded to a stop just outside the department. Jumping out of the truck, she pushed her way through the small crowd outside the building. A small crowd that was getting larger by the second.

Running through the doors, the sight of

Kelly kneeling over Mabel, who was still in her beast form, caused her heart to crawl into her throat. Seeing the young nurse crying, played with her mind, telling her their beloved dispatcher was gone.

Debbie's knees were shaking as she made her way across the room and dropped down next to Mabel.

"No no no," cried Debbie. "This can't happen."

She looked over at Kelly and asked, "What?"

"I don't know," cried Kelly. "I saw her on the way to work this morning and something spooked her. But I don't know what."

A few seconds later, they could hear the sheriff's siren approaching the department and then his Blazer skidding to a stop. Two sets of footsteps came running through the doors and Debbie looked up to see her father's face go completely white.

He looked like he was about to fall over and Jaxon reached out and grabbed him, helping him to sit down in his chair.

Then he came over and crouched down next to Debbie and asked, "Who is this?"

"Mabel," moaned Debbie.

"Mabel? You mean that sweet lady I met yesterday?"

All Debbie could do was nod.

Jaxon reached out and ran his fingers over the edge of the wound and then dropped his head.

"You really didn't need to do that," said Debbie. "It's quite obvious what happened here."

"That's not the only reason, Debbie. Not only can you feel the energy left by the blade, but you can also feel the essence of what happened here."

Debbie reached out and ran her fingers over the edge of the wound and gasped as images flooded her mind of the battle that Mabel had fought. She didn't really see images. It was more like feelings and emotions and rage.

The sound of the ambulance screeched to a stop outside and a couple of EMTs rushed through the door with a gurney. Ordering everyone to move back, they went about trying to lift Mabel, but being totally human, they struggled.

Kelly stood up and told them to stand back. Then, she changed into an ogre just as big and bad as her two brothers. Reaching down and with as much tenderness as an ogre could muster, she lifted the body of the beast and laid it on the gurney.

Within seconds, the EMTs and Kelly pushed the gurney out the door and loaded her into the back of the ambulance. The men jumped in and headed for the hospital, leaving Kelly standing in the middle of the street, her big, green shoulders bobbing up and down.

Debbie stepped up next to her and put a hand on her arm. When the nurse turned and looked at her, they threw their arms around each other and cried. Jaxon came walking out and just stood away from them. He didn't think it was strange at all to see his sister hugging an ogre and both of them crying their eyes out.

He looked around and saw a much larger crowd of townsfolk gathered. He could tell they felt the same way these two ladies did.

After a few seconds, Kelly reverted to her human self and Jaxon walked over and handed her a handkerchief, which she used to dry her eyes.

"I need to get to the hospital," she cried.

She turned and began jogging around the corner, heading for work.

Jackson mumbled, "Sis, I don't think dad's doing very well, at all."

She looked up at him and nodded.

"He won't be. He and Mabel have been together ever since before he became Sheriff. She was one of his teachers when he was a kid. Even mom is going to start a Loirian wail when she hears."

She turned and headed back into the building and he followed. Their dad was sitting in his chair behind his desk, just staring at the pool of black blood in the middle of the floor. They could barely tell he was breathing at all. His face was still white and he didn't even acknowledge them coming back in.

Debbie walked around and knelt in front of him, taking his hands and said, "Daddy, go home right now. You should go be with mom."

He finally snapped out of his funk and looked at her.

"Nobody's checked on her?" he asked.

"Daddy, Kelly's brothers are there and if a hunter had showed up there, we would have known about it. Please go home and be with her."

Just then, Cal came running in the door. He was dressed in sweatpants and a t-shirt because he had already gone home and was prepared to go to bed.

When he saw the pool of black blood in the middle of the floor and knowing who it came from, he almost had the same reaction as the Sheriff.

"Cal," asked Debbie, "can you watch the desk for a few minutes while I take daddy home?"

"Uh ... yeah, no problem."

"Come on, dad," said Debbie as she held out her hand. "Let's get you home."

Jaxon and Debbie got him up from his chair and took him out to her SUV. After getting him in, she and her brother took him home.

Pulling up outside the house, there was a sight that, at any other time, Debbie would have laughed. It was quite comical. Ogre Jake was standing in the front yard, wearing nothing but a pair of Spandex shorts and a huge club laying over his shoulder.

As they walked up the sidewalk to the house, Debbie told Jaxon to get their dad inside. Then she walked over and stood in front of the big green guy.

"How are you doing, Jake?"

"Nothing happen," growled Jake. "Very quiet."

"Quiet? You didn't hear the roar about an hour ago?"

"Heard. Not know what it was."

She dropped her head and looked at the ground.

"What was it, Debbie?"

She looked back up, with tears in her eyes.

"It was Mabel. They attacked her at the department."

Jake looked like he was going to fall down. His knees were shaking so much. His breathing got raspy and the club fell to the ground with a large thud.

Finally, he sank to his knees and let out a roar almost as loud as Mabel's. His eyes slammed shut as he screamed at the sky. He didn't stop until he felt a tiny hand settle down on his large hand.

He opened his eyes to see Debbie standing in front of him, her hand on his, with tears streaking down her cheeks.

"Who did it?" growled Jake, just as his brother came running out the door of the house.

Randy ran over and put a hand on his brother's shoulder.

"It was the hunter that's been chasing mom. He was gone by the time we got to the department."

A low, rumbling growl came from Jake's belly and his eyes turned red.

"Hunter die," growled Jake.

"Yes, when we find him, he dies."

She patted his hand again and then looked up at Randy. Nodding, she headed into the house, leaving the ogre brothers to stew in the rage that was building in their hearts. She didn't want to be anywhere near them if they found the hunter because it was going to be messy.

Her dad was sitting in his favorite chair, just staring straight ahead. Celia was kneeling next to the chair, holding his hands, resting her cheek on his lap. Debbie could see the tears running over her blue cheeks and she just knew her mother was blaming herself for what had happened.

She walked over to the kitchen and found Jaxon trying to figure out the coffeemaker. Debbie gave him a quick lesson and then said she needed to get back to the department so Cal could go home.

"I'll come with you," he said.

"No, Jaxon, you won't. You stay here with them and watch over them."

He looked over at his parents and shook his head.

"What am I supposed to do? I don't have any idea how to help them through this."

"Just be here, brother. Just be here for them."

He gave a slight nod, but she could tell he was quite uncomfortable with this.

"If you send Cal home, you will be all alone there."

"He needs to go home to get some sleep. I'll be fine. I would actually pity any hunter that walks in there right now."

"Be careful."

She leaned up and kissed him on the cheek.

"Don't worry. The boys are going to be out front and they will watch this place."

Then she turned and walked over to the chair. She leaned over and kissed her mom on the cheek and then did the same to her dad.

"It didn't have to be this way," whispered her mother.

Debbie knelt down and put a hand on her mom's cheek.

"No, it didn't and those hunters are going to find out why they shouldn't have done this."

She went to stand up, but her mom reached out and took hold of her hand.

"Please be careful, Debbie. I came here to bring Jaxon, but I also came to see you. I don't want to see you get hurt."

Debbie kissed the back of her mom's blue hand.

"I will be careful. You stay in the house with daddy."

She got up and then said, "I love you, mama."

She looked at Jaxon and said, "You, too."

Then she hustled out the door and was on the road in less than a minute. And driving slowly because of the tears in her eyes.

Chapter 9 – Breaking The Bad News

Standing in the open space of his ship's bridge, the hunter hunched over the control station of the craft. He was still feeling the effects of having Mabel grab him by the throat, but he was more than thankful he had survived it.

But surviving that confrontation was going to be a snap compared to what he was about to do.

Looking behind himself, he stared at the body of his partner, laying in pieces on the floor. Taking care of the body was a straightforward task. Just stick it in the incinerator and burn it to ash.

Reporting his death to the commander was an entirely different story. This kind of failure was likely to result in him laying on the floor next to the beheaded hunter in front of him.

Realizing he couldn't put it off any longer, he pushed a couple of buttons on the console and turned to face the open space. Within seconds, his commander's hologram appeared in front of him.

"Karg, give me some good news," said the shimmering female apparition.

"I truly wish I could, commander. We have met with resistance and we have suffered a loss."

He could see her eyes go dark with anger and was glad she wasn't there in person.

"Being as how there were only two of you on this mission," she growled, "can I assume the loss you refer to is my brother?"

"Yes, commander," he said as he pointed to the floor behind her.

When she turned and saw the body of her brother, she gasped. Spinning back around, her eyes were full of fire and she directed the heat squarely at Karg.

"How did you let this happen?" she yelled.

He hesitated for a few seconds before speaking up.

"He died a hero, fighting against something neither of us had seen before."

"This planet is full of nothing but weak humans! Surely you can handle a few humans, can't you, Karg?"

He reached up and removed his own helmet and she got a look at the marks around his neck.

"What in the hell?" she muttered.

"Commander, these humans are not nearly as weak as they have led us to believe. There are some things about them I don't think we've been told."

She turned back around and stared at the body of her brother. She was going to be lucky if her father didn't have her executed as soon as she returned to Loiria. He didn't appreciate failure in any form. But losing his son was going to enrage him more than she cared to imagine.

As she gazed upon the body, she said, "In a few hours, I will send another shuttle down to your location."

Turning back around, she glared at him and said, "Don't fail me again, Karg. Be ready for them when they arrive."

Without waiting for a reply, she ended the transmission, allowing him to breathe again. After he could get his knees working again, he hauled the dead body to the hatch in the side wall and dumped it in. He could hear the flames consuming the body before he could even close the hatch.

Ursula stared at the darkened screen for a moment, trying to keep her rage from destroying the ship. When she had finally calmed herself a little, she turned around and looked at the three hunters on the bridge with her.

Two stood at perfect attention, awaiting her orders. The third was sitting in a chair behind them. Sitting didn't really describe what he was doing. He had one leg slung over the arm of the chair and looked to be quite disinterested in anything going on around him.

She looked at the two and gave them orders to find Captain Jorgen and prepare a shuttle for their journey to the planet. When they left the bridge, she looked at the third one.

"You know, it wouldn't kill you to show a

little more respect when you're on the bridge."

"Yeah, but what fun would that be?"

"Your cousin was just killed on this hellhole of a planet and you think this is funny?"

"Your brother was an idiot and I know you agree with me on that. Make no mistake, I shall avenge his death, but he was still an idiot. Kind of like his father."

Her eyes grew narrow as she said, "Do not talk in such a manner about my father, your king."

"Oh please. You know damn good and well you think Andrakus is a blood-thirsty tyrant and it would be better if he died."

She stared at him, trying to decide if she should just kill him where he stood or admit he was right about her brother.

"Just make sure you don't get anymore of my men killed, Durz."

"Hey, I will look after myself. They are grown men and can defend themselves. By the way, what would you like me to do with Karg?"

"As soon as you feel he has surpassed his usefulness to you, cut his head off."

"That's a little extreme, don't you think?"

"Did you not see what he allowed to happen to Drok?" she yelled. "I want him dead! He is never to set foot on this ship alive again … ever!"

"Okay, I can do that. Now, if you don't mind, I'm going to get some sleep before we head down."

Without waiting for a reply, he spun on his heels and headed out of the bridge, leaving her to stare daggers into his back. He didn't really give a rat's ass what she thought, though. He was a free-lancer and she wasn't really his commander.

As he walked into the shuttle bay, he saw Jorgen and the other two hunters checking the shuttle over. He thought the captain was an even bigger idiot than his cousin. The other two were just junior hunters and hadn't really proved themselves yet.

As he walked to the ramp, he called out, "Try to keep it down out here. I'm going to get some sleep before we head down."

He giggled to himself as he went up the ramp, having seen the look on Jorgen's face. He had no respect for Ursula and had even less respect for Jorgen.

He heard one hunter ask Jorgen, "Just who the hell does he think he is?"

The captain shushed him and said, "He's one of the best hunters in the galaxy."

"I know that, but he doesn't have to be such an asshole."

The other hunter said, "When I get to be as good as him, I'll be a bit of a jerk, too."

"Yeah, right," said Jorgen. "If you live that long."

Durz moved through the shuttle and found a quiet, out-of-the-way cubby hole and laid down to get some shuteye. It took him less than a minute to go from closing his eyes to snoring. Just one more thing that solidified his reputation.

Chapter 10 – The New Girl

When Debbie returned to the department, it surprised her to see Cal was finishing cleaning up the puddle of blood.

"You didn't really need to do that," she said. "I was going to call Flo and have her send a cleaning crew over."

"S'okay Debs. I needed to keep myself from flying off into a fit of rage."

She walked over and patted him on the shoulder.

"Go home. Try to get some sleep. Why don't you come in a couple of hours later tonight? I'll hold down the fort for you."

"Why would I do that?"

"With what happened out at the Godwin place and this here, you've put in more than your share of hours."

"Debbie, we don't punch a clock around here. We work when we have to. I'll be in at six, as usual."

She forced a smile as he turned and headed for the door. She knew she had made the right choice when she suggested he come to Prattville and talk to her dad about a job.

She walked over and sat down at her desk and just stared at the spot where Mabel had fallen. Cal had done a complete job on the floor and there was no sign of the blood.

She looked across the room at Mabel's desk and could almost see her ghost sitting there. Her rhinestone glasses would be down at the tip of her nose as she read through a report. A cup of steaming coffee would sit on the desk near her left hand.

Debbie could feel a tear about ready to begin its journey down her cheek and she reached over and pulled a tissue from the box on her desk.

She looked at the clock on the wall and saw that it was time for her to make a round through the town, but with no one else in the building, she knew she couldn't leave.

She prayed Prattville would not need her out there on the streets today. She wasn't sure she'd be able to do her job satisfactorily.

Looking around the empty office, she could feel the loneliness press in on her. Right then, she would have welcomed the company of Billy Ray in one of the cells downstairs.

It was then she realized they were going to need someone to take over Mabel's duties. Though the attack had just happened a couple of hours ago, the office was still going to need someone for the department to function as it should.

Running names through her head, she settled on the only one she could think of. Pulling a file out of her desk, she flipped it open and reached for her phone. Taking a deep breath, she dialed and waited.

"Hi, Lisa? This is Deputy Debbie in Prattville."

Less than three hours later, Debbie was standing out front of the building, talking to the few people that wandered by, when a dusty, rusty Volkswagen Beetle pulled into a parking space.

Debbie could see it was crammed full of boxes and bags, leaving little room for a driver. But there was a driver and they pushed the door open and climbed out.

Lisa ran around the front of her car and ran straight into Debbie's arms and hugged her.

"I'm so sorry, deputy. I can't believe what happened to Mabel. She was so nice to me when I was here."

Debbie just squeezed her and then pulled away.

"I just knew if I called you, you'd be the one to take the job."

"Are you kidding?" asked Lisa. "This has got to be one of the most fascinating towns in the entire country."

"Let's head inside and I'll show you what you're up against."

As they turned to go into the building, Debbie said, "Nice, classic car. I bet Earl could get that Beetle all cleaned up and running like new."

"If he touches one speck of dirt on that car,

I'll kick his butt."

Debbie looked at her with surprise.

"It's my papa's car. Well, it became my car when he passed away a couple of years ago," said Lisa in a soft voice. "It looks exactly as it usually did when he was alive."

"You're right," said Debbie as she put her arm through Lisa's. "We won't let him touch anything but the engine."

Over the next hour, Debbie took Lisa around the office, showing her what her duties would be and where she could find everything.

About the middle of the afternoon, Debbie left the building to make a run through the town. She made sure Lisa knew how to work the radio so she could call for anything.

Driving through the streets of Prattville, she saw the people wave as she went by, but could feel they didn't have the usual smile or joy behind the gesture. Word had spread from monster to monster before noon and by now, every vampire, werewolf, demon and goblin within fifty miles knew what had happened.

On one of the back streets of town, she sat at a stop sign, just staring straight ahead, her mind lost in a haze. She had her arm resting on the open windowsill of her Blazer and just about jumped out of her skin when a hand settled down on her shoulder.

"Shit! Sorry, deputy. Didn't mean to scare you."

"Billy Ray! Please don't do that to me right now!"

Looking up into the big man's eyes, she could see he was hurting like the rest of the town.

"I'm sorry," she said. "I shouldn't snap at you like that."

"That's okay," he said. "Anything that gets your mind off what happened earlier and gets you back to beating on me is just fine with me."

She forced a laugh and said, "I hope you know I don't beat on you because I like it."

"I know that," he said with a grin. "Hey you can get out of the truck and throw me to the ground and handcuff me. I mean, if it will make you feel better."

"I'd love to," she said with a slight laugh, "but maybe next time."

Just then, her phone rang and she answered.

"Yes, mama … sure, I'll be there … hey, set another plate because I'll be bringing someone … love you, too."

As she hung up, she looked at Billy Ray and said, "I have to get going. You're a good guy, Billy Ray."

"Hey, don't be spreading rumors like that around. I have a reputation to uphold."

She laughed and said, "I'll see you around. Take care."

As she drove away, she looked in the rearview mirror and saw Billy Ray watching her drive away. She really meant it. He was a good guy. He just got a little wild sometimes and needed to be corralled.

Just about dinnertime, she swung by the department and picked up Lisa. She warned her it was now time to tell her dad what she had done. Lisa let out a small gasp when she realized the sheriff hadn't even been told about her coming to Prattville and taking the job.

"I'm beginning to think this might not have been such a good idea," said Lisa.

"Hey, like I told you before, he's just a big teddy bear. Don't let him intimidate you. Mabel never did."

When they pulled up out front of the house, Lisa giggled and asked, "What's that?"

"That is Jake. He is an ogre and he has a twin brother inside. They actually have a younger sister who terrifies both of them."

They got out of the truck and headed up the walk toward the house and Debbie guided her off the sidewalk to meet Jake. Jake held out his big, meaty hand and it surprised Lisa to find out how gentle he was when she shook his hand.

"Everything still quiet around here?" asked Debbie.

"Yes, deputy. Nothing happen here."

The deputy nodded and turned to lead Lisa into the house. As they walked into the living room, Debbie was heartbroken to see that her father was still sitting in his chair, looking like he hadn't moved since she left. Her mother was in the kitchen, working on dinner and she could tell she was just trying to keep it together.

"Daddy, you remember Lisa? I called her earlier to see if she wanted to come down and take over for Mabel."

For the first time in what was probably hours, he looked like he snapped out of the funk he was in and looked up at them. She could see a bit of anger in his eyes, but also a lot of sadness.

"Daddy, I had to call somebody. You're here at the house and Cal had gone home for the day. We need somebody at the department for days like today."

Almost immediately, she saw her dad's expression soften and he nodded slightly.

"I know, baby. I just wasn't ready to think about this."

Then he pushed himself up out of the chair and sounded like every joint in his body was creaking and cracking. She was right. He hadn't moved since she left that morning.

After he got up, he stretched his body to work out the kinks and then looked down at Lisa.

"Lisa, welcome to Prattville," he said as he held out his hand. "We're happy to have you."

After they shook hands, he said he was going to change clothes and walked out of the living room.

Debbie walked into the kitchen, followed by Lisa, to introduce her to her mother. Celia was in her normal blue hue as she stood at the stove, stirring the spaghetti sauce.

"Mama, this is Lisa. She's going to be working at the department and I asked her to join us for dinner."

When she turned from the stove to face them, Lisa looked up at her and smiled, holding out her hand. Celia took her hand and then remembered she was still blue.

"Oh, sorry."

"Sorry? For what?"

Debbie leaned in and said, "She worries sometimes about presenting herself as blue, which is her normal color. She's an alien."

"Don't be sorry," said Lisa. "You're lovely just the way you are."

This caused Celia to blush again, her cheeks getting purple when the redness spread across them.

Lisa looked at Debbie and said, "So, if she's alien, that means you're half alien."

"Yes, it does."

There was a sound behind them and Debbie looked to see her brother walking into the kitchen.

"And this is my brother, Jaxon."

When Lisa turned around to meet him, the look on Jaxon's face was impossible to miss. He had that deer-in-headlights look when he looked at her. When she held out her hand, he didn't even notice.

"Jaxon, Earth to Jaxon."

Lisa smiled as he finally snapped out of it.

"Oh, hey, my name is Jaxon. And who are you?"

"Umm, I'm Lisa," she said with a little laugh.

"Oh, that's right. Debbie just said that."

Debbie shoulder bumped Lisa and said, "He's half alien, too and just arrived on Earth a few days ago. I don't think he knows how to talk to women yet."

"Aww, sis! Come on, give me a break."

"Really? You just came to Earth for the first time?"

It was clear he was still stunned by the sight of this beautiful young woman in front of him. It took him a few seconds to answer her.

"Jaxon," said Debbie, "why don't you tell her a little about your adventurous life, while I go outside and talk to Jake and Randy?"

Debbie turned and walked out the door and down the steps. The two ogre brothers were still standing in the front yard, but only Jake was in his ogre form.

"Hey boys, do you think Kelly would like to have a roommate, even if it's just temporary?"

"Don't know, deputy," said Randy. "She has a couple of extra rooms, but are you sure that young lady will be comfortable living with an ogre?"

"What are you talking about? Your sister is an angel."

Both the brothers looked down at her, like she had said the most horrendous thing she could have possibly said.

Jake popped his brother in the shoulder with his fist and said, "Angel of Darkness, maybe."

They both started laughing and Debbie put her hands on her hips and looked up at them.

"Don't you be talking about your sister like that."

"We still remember how she treated us when we were in the hospital a few weeks ago," said Randy.

"Hey, that was your own fault. You were told to be careful when you went out looking for him and what did you do? You let the Boogerman tear you a new backside. So, you deserved everything she gave you."

Jake scrunched up his ogre face and asked, "You ever want to let your pops give you a sponge bath?"

"Uhh, no. That wouldn't be my first desire."

"Now you see how we feel," said Randy.

"Anyway, I think Lisa and Kelly will get along just fine."

"Call her and see what she says."

Debbie stepped away from the two and

pulled her phone out of her pocket and dialed Kelly's number. After talking to her for a few minutes and making arrangements, she went back inside the house. She almost had to laugh when she saw Jaxon and Lisa sitting at the kitchen table, face-to-face and getting to know each other.

She walked over and put a hand on Lisa's shoulder and said, "I've found a place for you to stay, if you like."

The younger woman looked up and said, "I trust your judgment."

"It can just be temporary. You might decide you want to get a place of your own later."

"We'll see how it goes," said Lisa.

"Dinner's ready," said Celia.

John came walking back into the dining room and took his usual seat, as Debbie helped her mom bring the food to the table. It was almost comical to watch Jaxon make sure that he and Lisa sat next to each other.

They spent dinner with a lot of talking. Some of it was John making sure Lisa knew what her job entailed. By the time dinner ended, the sheriff was quite satisfied that Debbie had made the right choice.

Debbie took two heaping plates of spaghetti outside to the brothers, which necessitated Jake changing back to his human form. It would've been a comedy of errors if he had tried to eat spaghetti as an ogre.

After dinner, Debbie drove Lisa back to the department to get her car and then follow her to Kelly's house. When they pulled up out front, Kelly came hustling out of the house to meet them.

"This is Kelly, the sister of Randy and Jake," said Debbie.

"Hi Kelly," said Lisa as they shook hands. "I hope this isn't an imposition."

"Are you kidding? Having a roomie will be one of the best things about having you here."

Lisa stepped back and looked at her and said, "Are you sure she is the sister of those two big guys back at the house?"

Kelly laughed and asked, "You've met my brothers, have you?"

Debbie said, "Don't let her fool you. She can be a mean, old troll sometimes."

"Debbie! Trolls are smelly, brutish animals. I am nothing of the sort."

Debbie laughed and said, "That's not what your brothers say."

"Oh well, who listens to those two, anyway?"

Then Kelly turned and led them into the house and it instantly enamored Lisa with what she saw. The house looked as if one of the most expensive interior decorators had decorated it.

"This is beautiful," she said as she looked around.

"See Debbie, a troll wouldn't have such a

nice place."

Debbie leaned over and put an arm around Kelly's shoulders and said, "I know and I hope you know I'm kidding."

Kelly took them to the back of the house and showed Lisa the bedroom that would be hers and then the three of them went out and emptied the Beetle of all the boxes and bags.

As soon as it was done, Debbie made her excuses and left the two of them to get better acquainted. She drove back to her parents' house to pick up Jaxon and head back to her place.

For the next couple of hours, everything seemed quiet, but she knew it was hopeless to think that maybe the hunters had changed their minds and left.

Nobody has that kind of luck.

Chapter 11 - Captured

Racing through the woods and fields just south of Prattville has a certain appeal. Lots of hills and creeks to jump. There was no better way to spend a summer afternoon.

Bobby Wolfsbane twisted the throttle grip on his dirt bike and shot up and over Lyle Creek, landing hard on the other side. To call it a creek was being generous. It was more like a rivulet. Maybe even a trickle. But it was ten feet deep at the point Bobby launched himself, so it could have been the Grand Canyon for all he cared.

After landing the jump, he tore along the single track that cut through the woods and aimed for the meadow a few hundred yards in.

As he broke through the trees, he was shooting for the trailhead on the far side of the clearing and gunned the Husqvarna engine and felt it leap forward.

Then he felt it stop.

Instantly.

Which had the unhappy effect of sending him catapulting over the handlebars and tumbling through the dirt for the next twenty yards. Being the tough kid that he was, he bounced back up and looked back at his bike.

As he walked over and looked down at it, he was dumbfounded. The fork was completely torqued and bent backwards, as if he had hit something very solid. The front wheel had been tacoed and spokes snapped all around the rim.

"What in the hell!"

He went to grab the handlebars and banged his shin on something.

"Ow! Sonova ...!"

Reaching down, he could feel something that felt like a fat, round tube angling up from where his motorcycle laid crippled, to some place over his head. He reached up and his hand hit something smooth and cold. He felt an electrical energy flowing through the invisible object as he ran his hand over the surface.

As he tried to figure out what he had found, he heard a snapping sound and then a motor somewhere about twenty feet away. Stepping backward, he moved cautiously, not knowing where he'd run into another hard, invisible surface.

As he got a few more feet away, he saw a ramp come down from out of thin air. A ramp that obviously went up into some kind of craft. When he saw the man in the silver spacesuit coming down the ramp, he dropped to his belly in the tall grass.

Bobby could just barely make out the man as he walked off the ramp and over to the wrecked bike. The spaceman looked at the bike and prodded it with its foot. Then he turned and searched the area, looking for the owner of the crashed machine.

He stopped scanning the area when his eyes came to rest in the direction that Bobby was hiding. He started walking forward and when he was about thirty feet away, he pulled a silver tube off his belt and hit a button, extending it to about six feet long with a wicked-looking blade on the end.

That was all Bobby needed to see. He jumped up and began running as fast as he could, trying to put as much distance between him and the alien as he could. He was young and he was fast, so he knew he could outrun the man in the silver suit.

When he looked over his shoulder and saw the space dude was keeping up with him, actually gaining on him, he yelled, "Holy crap!"

Then he did the one thing they had schooled him to never do without good reason. Well, this seemed as good a reason as any.

Within three strides, he changed from a sixteen-year-old boy to a large, hairy werewolf and put on an even bigger burst of speed.

Coming to Lyle Creek, he leaped across with no trouble at all and kept running. As he glanced back, he saw the alien clear the ditch easily and was keeping pace with him now.

Geezus, what is this guy?

Realizing he was going to need help to get out of this, he angled his course and jumped a barbed wire fence and plowed through the field of tall grass on the other side. He was aiming for a large, silver warehouse looking building, knowing it was his best hope.

Seeing a man standing outside the building, he yelped.

"Uncle Bill!"

The man looked up and saw a werewolf coming straight at him, followed closely by a man in a silver suit and helmet, carrying a long, bladed weapon.

"Buster! Bosley! Save Bobby!"

Two dog heads popped up out of the grass, took one look at the situation and hauled ass toward the incoming werewolf and spaceman.

Bosley got there first, launching himself just as Bobby ran past him, meeting the space guy head-on and knocking him to the ground. When the man in the silver suit tried to bring his bladed weapon to bear on the hell hound, a large, black demon dog took his arm off at the elbow.

"Hey, you can stop running, you numbskull!" Bill yelled at Bobby.

Bobby skidded to a stop and loped back to his uncle's side. Together they walked back to where Buster and Bosley had their quarry down and subdued.

The spaceman made a feeble attempt to reach up to his helmet, but Bosley didn't think that was such a good idea and chomped down on his hand.

"Well, what do we have here?" said Bill as

he stood looking down at the man.

By now, Bobby had changed back, in full view of the alien.

"I think this is one of those alien hunters that's got the town in an uproar," he said to his uncle.

"Oh, ya think?" said Bill as he pulled his phone out of his pocket. Hitting a two-button speed dial, he held the phone to his ear.

"Hey, Debbie. Guess what I got for you?"

Ten minutes later, the spaceman found himself looking up at four new arrivals, three of which were dressed in some sort of uniforms.

One of them, a female from the shape of her, leaned down and fastened a plastic strip to the end of his arm and stopped the bleeding.

The one that wasn't in uniform leaned down and pulled his helmet off. Then he stood up and smiled.

"Karg, it's so good to see you again."

"You know him?"

"Yeah, dad. I do. He's definitely one of the hunters that wants to kill mom. He's one of the king's lapdogs."

Bill looked at John and said, "Dad?"

The sheriff looked at him and said, "It's a long story and we can talk about it later. Just don't ask Debbie about it. She'll give you some b.s. story about the birds and bees."

"Hey!" yelled Debbie.

"So, Bobby, tell us what happened," said the sheriff.

After he finished relating the entire story, Debbie looked down and asked, "I wonder if he's the one that did it?"

"Did what?" asked Bill.

Neither Debbie nor the sheriff wanted to say it. It ended up being Cal.

"Mabel was attacked yesterday in the department. We're pretty sure it was one of these hunters that did it."

Bill's eyes went deep red and he started to get real furry. His body started expanding before Debbie gave him the look.

"Back off, big guy," she said. "Besides, I believe Randy and Jake have first dibs on this guy."

Bobby looked away and then walked a few feet into the grass. Bending down, he picked up a silver tube, about a foot long and began looking it over.

"Stop!" yelled Jaxon as he ran over and yanked the tube out of Bobby's hand.

"Hey! I was just looking at it!"

"Are you the kind of guy that will look down the barrel of a loaded gun?"

They heard Bill mutter, "With this boy, yeah, pretty much."

Jaxon held the tube out in front of him and pressed an invisible button. The tube shot out to six feet long with a blade on one end.

"I present to you, a Rocun blade," he said to the others.

"Damn!" said Bobby. "That's cool."

"It also should be highly illegal and you just about took your own head off with it."

He swished the blade through the air and they could all hear its energy cutting through the air. He stopped and looked a little closer at the blade and saw some black goo in the groove where the blade met the shaft.

He walked over and held the blade out so his dad could see.

"I'd be willing to bet this is Mabel's blood."

"Might even be one or both of the Godwins," said Debbie.

"He killed Lowell and Hazel, too?" yelled Bill.

"Yes, he did. Well, we think he did," said the sheriff. "We'll know after I let the Johnson boys interrogate him."

"Why let them have all the fun?" asked Bill. "I can get the story out of him right here, right now."

Debbie looked at him and shook her head.

"I kind of promised Jake he could kill him."

"Just make sure he does it outdoors," said Bill. "You know it'll be messy."

They all looked down at Karg and it was easy to see he understood everything he was hearing and they could read the fear in his eyes.

"Cal, you want to run this guy to the

hospital and get them to patch him up? Then stick him into one of their holding cells."

"Sure thing, sheriff."

Cal and Debbie went to pick Karg up off the ground, but Bosley was reluctant to let go of his prize.

"Let go, you silly hell hound!" said Cal.

Bosley shook his head and didn't let go. Until Buster leaned in and growled at him.

When they got him to his feet, Debbie turned and rubbed Buster's cheeks.

"You did good, big boy."

Woof!

When Bosley whined about getting some love himself, she reached up and rubbed his head and kissed him on his big, black nose.

"You, too, Boz."

As the two deputies walked Karg across the field toward their trucks, the sheriff looked at Bobby.

"Think you can show us where his spaceship is?'

"No problem, sheriff."

The four of them took off, walking toward the treeline, followed by two large mutts.

Chapter 12 – A Bit Of Air Sickness

"It's right over there," said Bobby, as they walked into the clearing.

"I don't see anything," said Bill.

Jaxon said, "Oh, I can feel it. I can feel the energy signature it's putting out."

"I felt that, too," said Bobby, "but only after I put my hand on it."

They walked over to Bobby's crumpled bike and he said, "I saw a ramp come down over there, but it's not here now."

"See the depression, dad?"

Jaxon was pointing to a depression on the ground, right in front of Bobby's bike.

"Looks just like the ones in the Godwin's field."

"I'd guess this is the same ship that made those marks."

Jaxon started walking around slowly, looking for the other two depressions. When he found them, he went to the one closest to the ramp and knelt down. He started working on something, but because it was invisible, it looked like he was waggling his finger in the air.

Suddenly, the ship appeared and the ramp started coming down. Jaxon had been working on some buttons inside a hidden panel.

"That's the ramp I saw. Karg, was it? He came down the ramp and saw me and chased me to Uncle Bill's place."

"Shall we take a look?" asked the sheriff.

He went to step onto the ramp and then got yanked back. Strenuously. Turning around, he saw Buster looking him in the eyes. Then the demon dog head butted him out of the way and proceeded up the ramp first.

It amazed everyone to see the spaceship sink a couple of inches into the ground when the big, black dog stepped on the ramp.

Bill stepped up next to John and said, "See, I told you he likes you."

Bill looked at Bosley and asked, "Aren't you going up there with him?"

Bosley laid down on the grass and lowered his head to the ground.

John looked at him and said, "Maybe he's the only one with a lick of sense."

Then he turned and headed up the ramp behind Buster, followed by Bill and Jaxon. Bobby elected to stay down and keep Bosley company. At least, that's what he told everyone.

Buster reached the top of the ramp and slowly raised his head to where he could see what was inside the ship. After a few seconds, he climbed in and opened the way for everyone else to come in.

"Knock knock," said the sheriff when he poked his head up. "Anybody home?"

When the other two made it up the ramp, Jaxon went straight to what looked like the control station. There were four seats, two at the control panel and the other two along the two side walls. One of those seats had all kinds of buttons and extensions on it. Jaxon explained it was a med chair that could take care of just about any injury.

Other than the four seats and the control station, the space was kind of sparse. There was a large view screen on the wall directly in front of the control station, but it was black at the moment.

Another thing that caught their eyes was the blue stain in the middle of the floor.

"Can I assume that's hunter blood?" asked the sheriff.

"That would be my first guess," said Jaxon. "And from the looks of it, the hunter that left the puddle there wasn't having a good day. Probably the one that introduced himself to Mr. Godwin."

"Kind of a small ship for traipsing around the galaxy," said Bill as he looked around.

"It's just a shuttle," said Jaxon. "It could go about as far as your outer planets and back, but that's about it."

"So, I guess what you're going to say next is there is a much larger ship in orbit, somewhere around this planet," said his dad.

"Uhhh … yes. A ship about a hundred times bigger than this one."

Jaxon went back to looking at some

information on the control screens.

"Greaaaaat," said John.

"Don't you just love it when the odds are stacked against us? Reminds me of the good ol' days, fighting the Boogerman," said Bill.

"Bill, the Boogerman was only a few weeks ago! And the most excitement I want is to capture a couple of monster hunter lookie-loos on your property."

"I can give you some good news and bad news," said Jaxon.

"I'm not sure I'm in the mood for bad news right now," said John.

"You already heard it. The mother ship is about a hundred times bigger than this one. The good news is they only have a crew of about a dozen hunters and a couple of pilots."

"Is the pay and benefit package not very alluring to the hunters?" asked Bill.

"Oh, they get great pay when they succeed in their missions. But," he said as he turned a monitor toward them, "when they fail, this little sweetheart usually rips their heads off."

John leaned in and looked at the face of a blue alien woman. She looked suspiciously like Celia.

"Allow me to introduce to you the leader of this little expedition. Ursula, or Cousin Ursula as I like to call her."

"Cousin?" asked John and Bill at the same time.

"Yes, this little tyrant is mom's cousin, or should I say, the daughter of the man that killed mom's parents. They have given her only one task and that's finding mom and kill her."

"I guess family ties don't mean a whole lot on her planet," said the sheriff.

"I believe it has something to do with you, dad."

"Me?"

"Yes sir. Her marrying a human was about as low as she could have gone, according to Uncle Andrakus. She could have married Buster here and found forgiveness easier."

Buster perked up at the sound of his name.

"See that, John," said Bill as he clapped him on the shoulder. "You put a target on Celia's back."

John looked at him with no humor in his eyes.

"What are you thinking, big John?" asked Bill.

"That your face looks like a big target and I haven't been to the range in weeks."

"Oh, come on. I'm only kidding."

"Bill, they already got Hazel and Lowell and ... Mabel."

Bill stopped for a second and thought about those three. He could feel the rage building again and had to fight it back down.

"You're right. Back to the task at hand."

"Another thing," said Jaxon, "this ship had a

hunter crew of two when it landed. We're already pretty sure Mr. Godwin took out one hunter."

"So, I guess we can assume that, eventually, someone is going to come looking for this shuttle and its crew," said the sheriff. "I wonder what happened to the hunter we think was killed?"

"The hunters don't stand on ceremony too much with their dead. Most likely, his body was dumped into the incinerator over there and is being burned to ash."

John walked over to a hatch on the wall and reached for the handle.

"Careful, dad. Looking in there for more than a few seconds will burn your face off."

John nodded and pulled the hatch open. Then he looked over the lip for a couple of seconds and slammed the hatch closed. His face was already red from the heat.

"Yep, he's in there."

"It usually takes a couple of days for a body to burn completely away. That incinerator is tied directly to the engine exhaust, so it's the easiest way to dispose of waste."

"Okay, we need to get away from this ship. We don't want to be here when the others come looking for it," said John.

"According to the logs, there is another shuttle coming down in about two hours. Apparently Ursula is a little less than pleased with the two-man crew that was on this shuttle and is sending someone to *help* them. Probably gave orders to help Karg into the incinerator."

"It would be a shame to let them have their shuttle back," said Bill.

"Do we have someplace we can hide it?" asked Jaxon.

"Oh yeah, we have just such a place," said the sheriff.

He pulled out his phone and dialed a number.

"Hey Earl, still have room in that hanger out back? Yeah, something not quite that size, but close. Great, open the doors. We're coming in."

He looked at Jaxon and said, "I'm assuming you can fly this thing."

"Better than Debbie can drive her truck."

"Well, that's not saying much."

"What? I think my sister's a great driver."

Bill mumbled, "She scares the crap outta him every time he rides with her."

While John called Debbie and asked for a pickup at Earl's place, Jaxon dropped under the console and began working on something. When he stood up, he had some electronic gadget in his hands.

"This is the tracking unit for this ship. We need to separate the two so those that are coming down can't find the ship."

Bill held out his hand and said, "I'll take care of that."

"It just needs to keep them busy for a little while, trying to find it," said Jaxon.

"Oh, they'll be busy. I think I'll hide it deep inside the old gold mine off 217."

Taking the tracking device, he turned and said, "Come on, Buster! Let's get out of here."

He looked at John and said, "Fly safe."

As they walked down the ramp, Jaxon sat down and pointed to the other seat.

"You might want to sit down."

"Is the flight going to be that rough?"

"No, it's just that our ships operate on a couple of different principles, one of which involves heavy magnetism. If you're not used to it, you're going to get dizzy and probably sick to your stomach."

"Great," said John as he walked over to the seat and got comfortable.

Jaxon touched a couple of buttons on the console and the ramp closed and a view screen came on. They could see Bill, Bobby and the two dogs moving away from the shuttle. Then he turned a dial and the shuttle lifted off the ground, swinging slightly side-to-side.

"Oh," groaned the sheriff as the effects of the ship's propulsion hit him.

"Hang on, dad. We shouldn't be airborne more than a couple of minutes. Where are we going?"

"Head straight over that hill in front of us. When we get close to the edge of town, I'll show you the building we're heading for."

Jaxon moved the shuttle toward the hill and passed over it with a couple of feet to spare. John was quite sure they were going to scrape the bottom of the ship on the treetops.

When they got within sight of the town, John pointed to a large steel building.

"I see it," said Jaxon. "There's some guy opening the wide doors."

"That would be Earl. You know, son, it might not be smart if people can see this shuttle flying through the sky."

"Relax, we're still cloaked. That's probably making you sick more than anything."

John knew something was making him sick, because he was about ready to ralf all over the floor.

Earl couldn't wait to see what the sheriff was bringing him this time. He always brought some of the coolest stuff.

So, he waited. And waited.

Then had to shield his eyes because something was kicking up a hell of a lot of dirt. He could tell something moved past him and into the old hanger, but danged if he could see it.

After all the dirt and papers stopped swirling around, he looked into the seemingly empty hanger and jumped back when a ramp appeared that looked like it went up into a well-lit spaceship.

A young man came walking down the ramp, followed quickly by the sheriff, who immediately went to a garbage can and threw up.

Earl held out his hand and said, "Yeah, he never did like flying in these things. His wife used to take him around and he always got sick."

"His wife? You mean my mom used to fly him around?"

"Your mom? You mean ...?"

"Yes, sir. Hi, I'm Jaxon and the sheriff is my dad."

Earl laughed and shook his hand and then yelled, "John, you old dog! I didn't know you had it in ya."

The sheriff finally straightened up from the garbage can and wiped his mouth with a shop towel. He still looked like he could puke at any moment.

"I hate these damn things," he muttered.

"So, can I go up and take a look?" asked Earl.

"Sorry, sir. There are some bad guys coming and they are going to be looking for it. We need to hide it as best we can. I promise, after all this is over, you can look at it and even go for a ride if you like."

"Not a problem," said Earl as he ushered them out of the building. He walked over to a control panel and pressed a couple of buttons and the doors slid closed.

"This button here," he said as he pressed it, "throws up a cloak around the building, making it pretty much invisible from the sky."

"Guess you've dealt with this kind of thing before," said Jaxon.

"Your mama's ship used to be hidden in here while I worked on it. No one ever found it."

Just then, they were interrupted by Debbie's truck sliding to a stop.

She lowered the window on the passenger door and said, "Daddy, you look like crap."

As soon as she said that, John bolted for the corner of the building and puked again.

"Did you take him flying, Jaxon?"

He just nodded and grinned.

After he was finished, John stumbled to her truck and climbed in and laid his head back against the headrest.

"Stay safe, sir," said Jaxon as he shook Earl's hand again.

"Please, just call me Earl."

Jaxon climbed into the back seat and they took off at a slightly lower than usual velocity for Debbie. She knew her daddy couldn't take much more speed for the day.

After getting him back to his truck and telling him to go home and rest, Debbie and Jaxon headed back to the department and then to make a couple of rounds.

Chapter 13 – Having A Blast

Driving through the back streets of the town, Jaxon watched the houses and small farms slip by. He couldn't help but think about the Godwins and what he had brought down on them.

"What's on your mind, bro?"

He looked at Debbie and just shrugged his shoulders.

"I'm thinking about that shuttle and how the hunters won't give up searching for it when they find the tracking device."

"Where is the tracking device?"

"Bill said something about taking it deep into some old gold mine."

"The one out off 217?"

"Yeah, I think that's what he said."

"I know that place," she said.

For a moment, they said nothing to each other.

"I have an idea," she blurted.

"Okay. I'm open for ideas at this point."

"What if we could take care of some hunters when they go looking in the mine?"

Jaxon smiled and said, "I like the way you think. What did you have in mind?"

"A little surprise," she said as she cranked the wheel and turned the truck around.

"Don't you think this is a bit of overkill?" asked Jaxon.

"Are you kidding? Nothing is too good for these guys when mom is concerned. Now be careful with that box. Dynamite is a rather touchy thing."

The two of them lifted two large boxes labeled DYNAMITE from the back of her truck and a small box with some electronics in it. After she kicked the door shut, he followed her into the mine with the boxes.

About twenty minutes later, they came back out of the mine and got back in her truck.

"I wish we could sit here and watch what happens," said Debbie.

"That would be fun, but they will be scanning for any life forms in the area. If they see any, they either won't land or blast us before they land."

She jumped out of the truck and opened the back again. Pulling out a small camera, she took it and attached it to a tree branch and aimed it at the mine.

"That's the great thing about the internet," she said. "We can be halfway around the world and watch a video from the woods outside of Prattville. We can also send the command to detonate the dynamite."

"Sounds like a real blast," said Jaxon.

"Oh, I see what you did there," said Debbie with a laugh.

Starting her truck, they hightailed it out of the woods and back to the department.

The shuttle hovered over the clearing, seeing nothing but the wreckage of a dirt bike laying in the grass. The four-man crew on the craft could see the depressions from the landing pads of the first shuttle, but there was a distinct lack of shuttle.

"What does the tracking module show?" asked the officer in charge of the shuttle.

One of the junior hunters looked at a screen and said, "It's showing a short distance away. The signal is weak, as if it were being hidden under a lot of rock."

"Take us there."

As the pilot began moving away from the field, the officer looked at another hunter who was lounging on one of the seats. He looked like he didn't have a care in the world.

"Do you intend to help in any way, Durz?"

The hunter looked up and smiled.

"If and when you find the traitor, Celia, I will be glad to help, Jorgen. Until then, don't bother me."

The captain really wanted to pull his Rocun blade and kill Durz but he knew he would be way over matched in a blade fight with the merc. That and the fact Durz was another one of Ursula's cousins.

He looked at a fourth hunter, standing near

the other wall, near the incinerator hatch. That hunter just shrugged, like, "What are you going to do?"

"I found it, captain. It looks like they took shelter inside that tunnel in the mountain. I'm not sure why they would need to do that with their cloaking device."

"We saw the wreckage of that conveyance back in the field. Apparently, someone discovered them. It is my hope they were dealt with harshly."

He looked at the screen and the scans.

"Anyone near here we should be worried about?"

"No, sir. There are no living beings anywhere."

"Set us down right near the tunnel entrance."

After the shuttle settled to the ground, the captain looked at the others.

"Okay, you two are with me. Durz, why don't you stay here and guard the ship? You should be quite comfortable with that."

Durz gave him a half salute and said, "Aye aye, captain." Then closed his eyes like he was going to take a nap.

"I think we got something."

Debbie walked across the room and looked over Jaxon's shoulders. She could see the ramp was down and three hunters came down and gathered near the entrance to the mine.

The video showed the ramp going back up and then the hunters moving into the tunnel.

Debbie reached forward and moved the mouse and clicked on another button. The video shifted to a low-light camera that showed a dim view from inside the mine. About twenty yards away, they could see the blinking red light of the tracking device.

About a minute later, they saw the three hunters move past the camera, toward the tracking device. Debbie pulled out her phone and dialed a number. Before hitting SEND, she held the phone out to Jaxon.

"Care to do the honors?" she asked. "Just press that green button."

"Oh yeah," said Jaxon as he took the phone. Looking at the screen and seeing the three hunters gathered around the tracking device, he pressed the button.

The screen went black.

Durz was just about to fall asleep when the shuttle was rocked by some kind of explosion, knocking him off the seat. As he scrambled to his feet, he rushed to the console and brought up the view screen.

He almost laughed when he saw the dust and smoke roiling out of the mine entrance. Rocks and boulders blocked the entire entrance.

Oh, these humans are good.

After he took a couple of minutes to put a suitably somber look on his face, he pressed a button on the console and then turned around.

When Ursula appeared in the open space in the middle of the shuttle, he feigned sadness.

"Hey, cousin. I got some bad news for you."

After Ursula got finished throwing her temper tantrum, which included beheading the hunter who was closest to her, she screamed at Durz.

"What are you going to do about it?"

"I intend to do what I already said. I will be a small, one-man stealth force and will find our cousin, myself. Then I shall deal with her."

"Do not fail me, Durz! Or else your head will be next!"

"Oh please, Ursula. Save it. You know your threats don't work on me."

"Maybe my threats don't, but I'm sure my father's will."

"And if we have to report failure, you know as well as I do, you will stand right next to me when he kills the two of us. You, being his daughter, won't mean a thing."

"Please, Durz. Do not fail. Do I need to send some others down to help you?"

"What part of one-man stealth operation do you not understand?"

"Shut up and get to work!"

"Yes, ma'am!"

After she faded from view, he muttered,

"Bitch."

Jaxon and Debbie raced back to the mine and stopped about a half a mile away. Running quietly back to the mine entrance, they stopped on a small hill overlooking the area below.

Crouching behind a fallen tree, it shocked them to see the ramp come down and another hunter come walking down. When he reached the bottom of the ramp, the hunter walked toward the mine and stopped. He was looking at the debris in front of him when he pulled his Rocun blade out and extended it.

Swishing it through the air to make sure it was functioning properly, he made some elaborate movements with it. As he did that, Jaxon gasped.

Retracting his blade and putting it away, the hunter disappeared into the trees, heading toward town.

"What was it you saw when he was slinging that blade around?" asked Debbie.

Jaxon slumped down and sat against the log.

"There's only one hunter in the galaxy that handles the blade like that. His name is Durz and he is one of the most feared hunters anywhere. If they've brought him in, we're in serious trouble."

"No, Jaxon, it just shows they are getting desperate."

"Desperate or not, Durz being here does not

look good for us."

"Okay, we need to take some wind out of his sails, then."

"How?"

"First off, we need to remove his way to get off the planet."

"We're gonna steal his shuttle?"

"Steal is such an ugly word," said Debbie. "I prefer appropriate."

"That won't keep him on the planet. He'll just call up and have them pick him up."

"From all you've told me about Ursula, do you think he's going to be in a hurry to call her and say he had his ride stolen?"

Jaxon laughed and said, "Let's get to appropriating."

"That's my brother," said Debbie with a laugh.

"You're becoming a bad influence on me. Dressing me in blue jeans, blowing up hunters and now stealing spaceships."

"Hey, what are big sisters for?"

Jumping up from behind the log, they jogged down the hill to where the ship was sitting. Jaxon went to work on the invisible panel and within a minute, had the ramp down. He ran up the incline and Debbie followed him.

"Not much to look at in here," she said as she looked around.

"Remember, this is just a shuttle. The mother ship is much nicer."

"Right. So, what's the plan?"

"Plan?"

He dropped to his knees and began removing the tracking device.

"Yeah, sis. This is your idea."

"Well, Earl doesn't have room to hold another ship, so we need to just ditch this one where they won't find it."

"When dad and me flew in the first shuttle, I saw a large body of water near here."

"Yes, Deer Lake."

"Okay, there was a structure at one end blocking the water."

"Right, Deer Lake Dam."

"Meet me at the dam," he said as he stood up and handed her the piece of electronics. "And get rid of this tracking device. You don't want to be anywhere near it when they come looking for the shuttle."

"You be careful," she said as she turned and headed for the ramp.

When she got to the ground, she saw the ramp closing and could feel the shuttle taking off. Looking around, she ran over to a tree and hung the tracking device over a tree branch by its cables. Then she pulled her notepad and pen out and wrote a quick message and stuck it on the device. Standing back, she had to giggle, not knowing if he'd be able to read it, anyway.

Hi Durz
Missing something?

☺

Turning and hustling as fast as she could, she ran to her truck and jumped in. Gunning the engine, she sent rocks and dirt flying in every direction as she fishtailed the truck around and headed for the main highway.

Deer Lake Dam was a good twenty-minute drive and she didn't want to leave Jaxon standing out there alone.

The whole way there, she kept looking up at the sky and then kept having to mentally smack herself for trying to look for an invisible spaceship.

She got to the end of the two-lane road that went over the dam and skidded to a stop. It was a fairly calm day, with hardly any ripples on the surface of the lake.

Until there was an enormous splash about a half a mile off-shore.

"Jaxon!" she screamed.

She was just about to jump out of the truck, but jumped out of her skin when he knocked on the passenger side window. Fumbling with the door lock, she finally got it open.

"Aw, sis. Were you sad when you thought I went down with the ship?" he asked with a grin as he climbed in.

She punched him in the shoulder and yelled, "Don't ever do that to me again!"

"Ow! We have a little thing called autopilot on our ships. Don't you have something like that here?"

"Of course we do," she said.

She looked back out at the lake and said, "Great. Now there's an invisible spaceship bobbing around on the water, just waiting for some boater to come along and run into it."

"Oh, give me some credit. I left the ramp and vents open. By now it's at the bottom of two hundred feet of water."

She just nodded as she put the truck in gear and aimed it back at Prattville.

"So, tell me what you think of Lisa," said Debbie.

Instantly, Jaxon got a silly look on his face as he started thinking about her again.

"She's the most beautiful creature I've ever seen."

"Okay, first thing, don't call her a creature to her face. She may not like that."

"Got it."

"And second, don't rush into anything. There's a entire world full of women out there."

"More beautiful than Lisa?"

"Well, no. She is quite beautiful."

"Any other women out there more willing to not be scared by monsters and aliens and is my age?"

"Well, no again. Okay, you're right. Go for it, Jaxon. Just make sure you treat her nice."

"Hey, mom raised me to be a gentleman."

Debbie nodded and said, "Good for her."

A few minutes later, they rolled up to the department and went inside. It surprised them to see the sheriff behind his desk, with Lisa behind her's doing some paperwork.

"Daddy, I thought you were going home."

"That's sheriff to you, deputy. And someone needed to be here with Cal gone home for the day."

"And that's what Lisa is here for."

They both looked over to see Jaxon was hovering over the new girl.

"Hey!" said the sheriff. "She's on the clock, son. Leave her alone!"

"Yes, sheriff," he said as he stepped away.

Then he looked back at her and said, "Tonight, then?"

She just smiled.

"What?" asked the sheriff.

"Oh, nothing. We just have a date tonight."

The sheriff scrunched up his mouth and then looked at Debbie.

"I got some reports about an hour ago about a loud explosion just east of town. You wouldn't know anything about that, would you, deputy?"

"Oh, that's right," she said as she remembered what she and Jaxon had been doing all afternoon.

She stood at perfect attention and related the events of the afternoon. Jaxon was about to laugh because he could see she was yanking their dad's chain.

"At ease, deputy!"

The sheriff looked back and forth between the two of them, trying to figure out who to yell at first.

"So," he said, looking at Debbie, "you executed three hunters."

"Yes, we did, sheriff. Three hunters that are here to kill your wife and our mother."

"Durz."

They both looked at Jaxon when he said that.

"Oh shoot! I forgot about him. Sheriff, there is a fourth hunter that came off that shuttle. His name is Durz. And according to one Jaxon Dinkendorfer, he is reportedly one of the most feared hunters in the galaxy."

"And where is he right now? And please stop acting stupid!"

Debbie relaxed and sat down in her chair.

"He walked away from the shuttle, looking like he was heading this way."

"So, he could be here in town right now."

"I don't really know how fast he can travel on foot, but yes, he could be here right now."

The sheriff looked at Jaxon.

"He could be standing in this room as we speak, dad ... err ... I mean, sheriff."

John looked around and Lisa did the same thing.

"Relax," said Jaxon. "even though he would be invisible, I could feel the energy coming from his suit. He's not here."

John reached over and picked up his phone and dialed.

"Hey, Randy. I'm heading to the hospital to have a little chat with our alien guest. Can you meet me there?"

Hanging up the phone, he stood up and grabbed his hat.

"You two sit tight."

"You don't want me there?" asked Debbie.

"No deputy, I don't. As a matter of fact, I want you and Jaxon back on the streets keeping an eye out for this Durz character."

She got up and looked at him.

"Just remember, if Randy realizes he's the alien that attacked Mabel, even you won't be able to stop him from tearing him apart."

"Noted. You two be extra careful out there."

With that, he turned and walked out the door.

Chapter 14 – The Interrogation

Walking into the hospital, the sheriff nodded to Kelly at the nurses' station.

"Is your brother here yet?"

"Yes, sheriff. He's down by holding, waiting for you."

He walked down the long hallway and found Randy standing outside a heavy steel door.

"Before we go in there, I want to know if I can count on you to keep your cool?"

"Sure, sheriff. You know me."

"Yes, I do. Oh, and take nothing I say or do to you personally. You know I like you and your entire family."

"Got it."

Placing his hand against a glass panel, the door unlocked and swung open and John stepped through and Randy followed. The door swung closed behind them and the sound of heavy locking bolts echoed in the room. There were two cells in the room, both of which had hospital beds in them, with monitor screens on the walls just outside.

The bars of the cells were about as thick as the business end of a baseball bat and looked like they could hold back just about anything.

Karg occupied the one cell on the left. He looked rather pathetic, being a one armed alien hunter. He was wearing a set of orange jail coveralls and not his silver space suit. His arm was bandaged at the elbow and he was just sitting on the edge of the bed.

"Hello, I am Sheriff John of the Prattville Sheriff's Department and I'm here to ask you a few questions."

"You'll get no answers from me," growled Karg.

"Oh, I wouldn't be too sure about that."

He reached over and tapped Randy on the shoulder, causing the big man to become an even bigger ogre.

"Should have brought my club," mumbled Randy.

"No, no, no," said the sheriff. "Not just yet."

Randy's transformation had the desired effect. Karg's eyes went wide with fear and he jumped off the bed and cowered near the back wall of the cell. He wanted to get as far away from Randy as he could.

"What is this place?" he moaned.

"As I said, this is Prattville and I'm the law here. Randy, well … sometimes a job needs a hammer and he's one of the biggest hammers in the toolbox."

Karg just cowered in the corner, wondering what nightmare he'd wandered into.

"Now Randy has a twin brother, who has a shorter fuse than him and I can bring him in here if I don't get the answers I want. And if that fails, they have a little sister that scares the crap out of both of them."

"Uh huh," growled Randy.

"Why are you here on Earth?"

"You should know that as well as anyone. We hunt the traitorous fugitive, Celia, for her crimes."

"And what crimes would those be?"

Karg didn't answer.

"Because the only crime I've heard that she committed was being born in a world ruled by some jerk named Andrakus. A Loirian who killed her mother and father so he could seize control of the planet. He wants her dead because she is the rightful heir to the throne."

"That is the way of our people," sneered Karg.

"That's a pretty screwed up way of life, if you ask me."

"If you lived on Loiria, you would think differently."

"I doubt that. Next question, what would it take to get you and your hunter buddies to leave this planet and never come back?"

"Turn the fugitive over to us and let us take her back to face justice."

"Well, I mean besides that."

"There is nothing you can do to stop us. There are hundreds of us on a ship in orbit and we'll burn this settlement to the ground to find her."

"Hundreds, huh? Actually, I think you meant to say there are about twelve of you on the mother ship and Ursula, your leader."

Karg appeared shaken by the information this law man seemed to have at his fingertips.

"Oh, actually I should say, you now have about nine hunters on that ship. My deputy took matters into her own hands today and blasted three of them with explosives when they went looking for your ship. Kind of a shame, really, being as how your ship wasn't exactly where they thought it was."

"You are barbarians!" yelled Karg.

"We're barbarians? Did you or did you not kill an old man and woman at a farmhouse a couple of days ago, simply because they saw your ship in their back field?"

"It was necessary to maintain secrecy."

"How's that working out for you?"

Karg went silent.

"So, you were the one that killed them. That answers that question."

The sheriff could feel Randy becoming restless standing behind him.

"Just one more question. Did you attack the old lady in the sheriff's department that same morning?"

"She was a warrior. She died a valiant death."

Just then, Randy exploded past the sheriff, knocking him out of the way and went straight to the bars. The sheriff tried to stop from slamming into the wall.

Randy grabbed the bars, intending to rip them off the wall and then tearing the alien to pieces.

Karg slid down the wall and cowered in the corner, knowing he was about to die.

The voltage coursing through the bars caused Randy to freeze and tremble for a second before he released them.

"Let me have him!" roared Randy as he glared at the sheriff.

"Not yet," said John, as he pushed himself away from the wall. "I promise when it comes time, you and Jake will get to play tug-o-war with his body."

He patted Randy on the arm and motioned him to back away from the bars. The ogre looked at Karg one last time, slammed his hand against the bars and then moved away. John was a little scared when he saw the bar Randy hit was bent inward a couple of inches.

"If I were to turn off the electricity to these bars, my friend here could rip them apart and then rip you apart and there would be nothing I could do to stop him."

Karg brought his hands down from in front of his face.

"I'm only following orders," he moaned.

"And you think that makes what you've done okay? I can assure you it doesn't."

He motioned Randy to head out the door.

"Let me leave you with one last bit of information. After my deputy killed your three hunter buddies, she saw another one come out of the shuttle and walk into the woods, heading this way. She found out his name is Durz. I have it on good authority that if he finds you, he will kill you on the spot for your failures."

"Keep him away from me!"

"Who? Randy?"

"Durz!"

"So, he is the badass we've been told about. We'll have to keep that in mind."

The sheriff turned and walked out the door, locking it securely behind him. He turned and looked at Randy, who was still in ogre form.

"Sorry about the electricity, buddy, but I knew you'd try to kill him on the spot. And don't think for one second I don't want to pull my gun and shoot him right between the eyes, because I most certainly do."

Randy reached out and grabbed him by the arm.

"You promise me, when time comes, Jake and I kill him."

John reached up and patted his massive hand.

"Hey buddy, a promise is a promise."

Randy released his arm and John turned him and pointed him away from the holding room. As they walked down the hall, John glanced at an unnumbered door. A burning rage rose in his chest.

A promise is a promise.

Chapter 15 – Getting To Know Brother

About three in the morning, Debbie rolled over and stared at the ceiling. She couldn't get the image of Mabel out of her head. Not the Mabel she found on the floor of the department.

The Mabel she was thinking about was the one that would go toe-to-toe with her dad and take no prisoners. The Mabel that always looked like she was no nonsense and humorless, but had a heart of gold.

Knowing she would not get back to sleep, she sat up and grabbed her sweatpants and shirt. Lacing up her sneakers, she crept out of the room quietly so as not to wake Jaxon.

That didn't work nearly as well as she hoped.

His door was slightly ajar and when she glanced in, she saw his bed was made and he was not anywhere to be seen. Heading downstairs, she expected to find him sitting on the porch, but he wasn't there either.

Surely he can't be spending the nights with Lisa already.

Walking down off the porch, she saw a set of tracks through the morning dew. They were heading around the side of the house and when she followed them, she saw they headed toward the woods behind her property.

Taking off at a quick jog, she followed the

tracks until she came to the path through the woods. She didn't know why, but she went left and started putting a lot of ground under her feet.

A couple of times, she came to a stop. The first time was in the small clearing where Bill and her daddy first came in contact with the Boogerman and it was where Daisy lost her life trying to fight him. She still felt a pain of sorrow about the death of the hell hound. She was a hell hound, but she was one of the sweetest hell hounds you would ever meet. Besides Bosley.

The second time she stopped was outside the dilapidated barn where they found the Boogerman and killed him, stopping a reign of terror he had dropped over the town. She felt not one bit of sorrow for helping to end his life.

Continuing along the path, it took her another half hour before she burst out of the trees and onto a small hilltop covered with large boulders.

"Hey sis."

"Jaxon, if you're going to leave like that, please leave a note so I know where to look for your body."

"Sorry about that. I couldn't sleep and needed to get out for a little while. And hey, you found me."

"Yeah, I'm not sure how, but I did."

"It's your Loirian half that did it. We have a sense in our bodies that brings us together. It's really strong with mom. Didn't you ever try to hide from her when you were little?"

"Yeah and she could always find me."

"Bingo!"

"I never knew that was why. So, basically she was cheating when we played hide-n-seek."

Jaxon laughed and said, "Yeah, you could say that."

Just then, a wild animal came crashing through the trees and launched itself right at them. It landed about twenty feet away and crouched and growled.

Jaxon was ready to put himself between the beast and Debbie, but she beat him to it. Then, to his surprise, she squared off with the big, hairy beast and put her hands on her hips.

"Billy Ray! Knock it off!"

The werewolf stood up and the fur fell off his body, while he changed back to human. Within seconds, he was completely human, standing in front of them.

A completely naked human.

"Oh geez, Billy Ray," Debbie said as she turned her head. "Why can't you invest in some Spandex shorts like the other werewolves do?"

"I like to run free, little lady."

Jaxon stood up and placed himself between him and Debbie, trying to make it easier for Debbie to not look at the man.

"I was hoping to scare this boy," said Billy Ray. "I didn't realize you were here."

As she stood behind Jaxon, trying to ignore his nakedness, she said, "Billy Ray, this is my brother, Jaxon. And he is stronger than me and could rip your head off, so I'd be careful if I were you."

"Pleased to meet you," said Billy Ray and he held out his hand. Jaxon showed no qualms about shaking hands with a naked man.

"Jaxon, this is Billy Ray Hanson, werewolf and wannabe town ne'er-do-well."

"Aw, that's not nice, deputy. I AM the town ne'er-do-well."

He turned and looked up at the moon and howled.

"Well, back to my hunting," he said as he turned and began running toward the treeline, changing back into a werewolf as he ran.

"Stay away from Farmer Taylor's hogs! If he shoots you again, I ain't coming to save your ass!"

Raaooooww!

"Interesting town we have here," said Jaxon as he sat back down on the rock.

Debbie sat down next to him and leaned up against him.

"So, you're considering this your town now?"

"Absolutely. Seems like a great place to live."

"You know, there is a whole, wide world out there to explore."

"You're not trying to get rid of me, are you?

Maybe to keep me away from Lisa?"

She sat up with mock surprise and gasped.

"Moi? I would never. Though, I think Lisa could do a lot better, but hey, you seem to be a pretty okay guy."

"Well, thanks sis ... I think."

She leaned back against him and he put an arm around her.

"Even though you've only been in my life for a few days," she said, "I love you and I love mom and the fact that she's back. I love having a brand new baby brother."

"Who's twenty years old."

"Well, at least I didn't have to go through the whole diaper changing period with you. Or the babysitting."

"I love you and dad, too. Dad ... he's everything mom said about him."

"She talked about him while you were flying around the universe?"

"Almost constantly. She made him out to be this big, mythical man. I can see now she wasn't making it up."

"Jaxon," she said as she sat up and looked at him, "you pay attention and learn from him. If you turned out to be like him, that would be a great thing. He's as good a man as there is."

After a few seconds, she added, "Just don't tell him I said that. Wouldn't want him to get a big head."

"Absolutely," said Jaxon with a laugh.

They sat in silence for a little while before Debbie asked if he wanted to leave and go see if mom and dad wanted to have breakfast together.

"Sure. Could we call Lisa and see if she wants to join us?"

"Good lord! You're just completely smitten with her, aren't you?"

Jaxon could only grin at that.

Chapter 16 – Don't Mess With Goblins

"Can I refresh that coffee for you?"

"Absolutely," said Bill as he looked up from his newspaper

Carrie was making the rounds through the diner, checking on her customers on this slow morning. Something was going through the town and humans and monsters alike were staying indoors. She remembered back a few weeks ago to when the Boogerman was terrorizing the town. It was pretty much the same then.

As she refilled Bill's cup, she glanced out the window and stopped paying attention.

"Carrie!"

She looked down to see coffee spilling out of the cup and onto the table.

"Oh! Sorry, Bill!" she said as she started cleaning up the mess. "I'll get you a fresh cup."

She picked the overfilled cup and took it to the sink behind the counter and dumped it. Picking up a new cup and saucer, she walked back to the table and set it down. When she went to pour again, she still had her eyes on the sidewalk outside the diner.

"Here, let me do that," said Bill as he took the coffeepot from her.

After he poured the cup, he looked up at her and saw she was staring at something outside.

"What is it, honey?"

She snapped out of it and looked at him.

"I don't know, Bill. It's like something is out there. I can't see it, but I can feel it."

Bill turned and looked out the window, but saw nothing.

"You sure?"

"Right now, I'm not sure of anything," she said as if in a daze.

He looked back out the window, not realizing he was looking right at what she was feeling.

Durz trudged along the sidewalk in the small town, being careful to avoid anyone he might bump into. He didn't want to kill anyone just yet.

Coming to a stop outside what looked like a place to feed one's self, he looked through the glass. There was a large man sitting just on the other side of the window and a woman standing next to the table he sat at.

When she made a mistake with his drink, he could tell she was looking right at him. Though he knew she couldn't see him, he knew she was aware of his presence. The man looked through the window and Durz could tell he was completely invisible to him. But the woman wasn't so easily fooled.

Turning away from the window and walking away, he got off what appeared to be the main avenue. Turning right at the next street, he moved away from the main part of the settlement.

Carrie went to the door of the diner and stepped out onto the sidewalk. Looking toward the spot she felt had caused her apprehension, she could feel the sensation fading.

Pulling her phone from her pocket, she dialed.

"Debbie, this is Carrie at the diner. Something is going on."

As Durz walked through the quiet streets in the northern part of the town, he looked at the homes that appeared to be quiet and well kept. There were children playing out in front of a couple of them. Some of the other inhabitants were outside, tending to their green ground coverings.

Coming to a stop outside one home, he saw an old man tending to a section of ground that housed ornamental plants. He believed they were referred to as flowers.

Realizing this elderly man wouldn't be able to put up much of a fight, he decided he'd start his search by interrogating him.

"Good afternoon, sir," said Durz as he turned off his invisibility suit. "I was wondering if I could ask you a few questions?"

The old man stood up and looked at him.

"What kind of get-up is that?" the old man asked.

"Uh, it's actually my suit that I wear as I travel around."

"Around here, folks don't take too kindly to people trying to hide their faces."

"They don't?"

"No, sir, they don't."

A woman came out of the house, onto the porch.

"Who's that, Gerald?"

"Don't rightly know. Hasn't given me a name."

"I'm sorry, my name is Durz and I'm looking for an old friend."

"Durz?" said the old lady. "What in tarnation kind of name is that?"

She ambled down the stairs, moving slowly. Durz realized there were others watching this little interaction and he got a little nervous.

"It's the name they gave me on the day of my birth."

"Sounds like a commie name, if you ask me," said Gerald.

"Commie?"

"You're not one of them there commies, are you?"

"He looks a bit shifty," said the old lady. "Especially being as how we can't see his face behind that mirror mask."

"Well, I ... I ... don't know," said Durz. "I

don't even know what a commie is."

Durz looked down to see Gerald was holding a gardening implement with three prongs on it and it looked like it could do some serious damage as a weapon.

The old lady walked across the grass and stood right in front of the tall man in the silver suit. With the mirror mask. She had to look up at him, because in her hunched over state, she barely hit four feet tall and he was almost six feet.

"Yeah, I think he's a commie," she snarled.

"Look, I'm just trying to find a friend named Celia. Would you know where I can find her?"

"Whadhe say?" yelled the old lady.

"He said he was looking for Meelia, Betty."

"I don't know no Deelia," Betty yelled.

"No, no, Celia."

"What?"

"Celia!"

"Celia? Hell, there ain't been no Celia around these parts for nigh on twenty years!" she yelled.

"There's a Bedelia about two streets over," said Gerald, "but she's a hermit. Ain't got no friends."

Durz could feel his rage building and he was just about at his tipping point.

"Don't send him to see Bedelia," yelled Betty. "She's libel to eat him."

She looked back up at the man and asked,

"What was your name again?"

"Durz," growled the hunter.

"Yeah, that's a commie name," said Gerald as he stepped up behind his wife. He didn't stand much taller than her.

"That's it!" yelled Durz and he pulled a silver tube off his belt and extended it.

As soon as the staff extended, with its wicked looking blade, he took a swipe at the old lady, right about neck height. One quick swing of the blade to take her head right off. Then maybe he'd get the answers he was looking for.

Except her head wasn't where it was just a second ago.

"What the ...?"

Looking down, he saw neither of the old people standing in front of him. Then he felt a sharp pain in his lower leg and looked down.

There was a little gray creature latched onto his leg and was biting through his suit with no trouble. It was ripping the material to pieces; material that had proven capable of stopping the lead projectiles from the Earthling's weapons.

He raised his blade and was ready to stab the creature when he got hit in the back of the head and almost knocked off his feet. Then something grabbed the staff out of his hand and yanked it away.

Then that something started beating him over the head with his own weapon.

Before he knew it, there were others joining

in the fracas and he was getting pummeled. One of them punched his face plate, causing it to shatter. This was the first chance they got to see his blue face.

Somewhere nearby, he heard someone talking, but he was too busy trying to get these creatures off him to pay much attention. They numbered about a dozen now. They were biting and kicking and scratching and clawing. He wished he could just face off with an ordinary Kraynok, right about now.

"Hi, Debbie, it's Sonia. How are you today? That's good ... How's your daddy doing? ... Oh, sorry to hear that. You give him my best ... (screams in the background) ... oh, that? Yeah, the reason I called is, you might want to get over to the Smithers place ... Yeah, they got some blue spaceman in a silver suit here and if you don't hurry, there may not be much left of him ... Okay, see you when you get here. Toodles."

One creature pulled off one of his gloves and bit down hard on his hand, getting blood in its mouth.

"Eww, blue blood. And it's nasty! Don't anyone get that stuff in your mouth, it's gonna make you sick," whined the creature.

Another creature grabbed at his helmet and yanked it off and accidentally pressed the button on the inside. Instantly, the creature vanished in a flash of light. Then, a few seconds later, he reappeared and was soaking wet.

"What happened to you?" growled another creature.

"I don't know. I pressed this button and ended up somewhere that's nothing but water."

"What button?"

The two of them had hold of the helmet when he said, "This one," and pressed the button again. This time, they both disappeared.

In the distance, a siren could be heard and it was getting louder. Durz was hoping it was someone coming to rescue him from this hell. One creature was grasping at his white hair, trying to pull it out by the roots.

In a few seconds, some tires came screeching to a stop and he heard some feet running across the grass.

"Alright, alright! Back off everyone!"

Durz felt some of the creatures getting off him, but others needed to be pulled off, which hurt like hell because they had their teeth deep in his body.

Then he felt a heavy weight pressed down on the middle of his back as his hands were pulled back and secured.

"So, what happened?" asked the female in a tan uniform.

"Says his name is Durz," growled Gerald, now back to his human form. "That's a commie name if I ever heard one. Tried to stab Betty with his little pig sticker over there."

As he laid there on the ground, Durz saw a

young, human male walk over and pick up his blade and then shrink it back to its small size. Like he knew exactly what he was doing.

"You okay, Betty?" asked the female.

The old lady was just dancing back and forth on her feet, looking like she was ready to go another round.

"I'm fine, deputy. I haven't been in a fight like that in years!"

"Okay, well, the fight's over so you can calm down."

Gerald reached out and put a hand on her shoulder. When she looked at him, she just smiled.

"I did good, didn't I?"

"You most certainly did, sweetheart," said Gerald as he put an arm around his beloved's shoulders.

The deputy reached down and pulled Durz to his feet like he was made of feathers. Looking around, he saw a dozen little gray monsters with enormous eyes and even bigger teeth. Some of those teeth still had bits and pieces of his suit in them. Some teeth had a blue shade to them. He watched in horror as the creatures began changing into short human forms, some of them being the children he saw earlier.

Just then, there was a flash of light and a small creature was standing there holding the helmet and dripping water. He looked around for a second.

"Oops," he said as he pressed the button again.

A few seconds later he flashed back, this time with his buddy, who was coughing up water. The young human male reached down and took the helmet away from the creatures.

"Give me that before you hurt yourselves."

The creature growled at him and bared his teeth, to which the young man just pointed at him and said, "No!"

The woman looked at the creature and said, "Settle down, Henry. That helmet is evidence."

Henry changed back into his human self and had a pout on his face.

"Hello, Durz. My name is Deputy Debbie Dinkendorfer and I will be your arresting officer today."

"Just get me away from these things!"

She turned him around and marched him down to her truck, while the male ran to open one of the back doors. After stuffing him in the back seat, she walked back to the crowd.

"Thank you, each and every one of you. You helped capture a very dangerous person."

"Always here to help, deputy," said Gerald.

She nodded and went back to the truck. As she was fastening her seat belt, she looked over her shoulder at the spaceman.

"For future reference, Durz, you might want to add a section in your *Invading Earth For Dummies* manual about not trying your crap in a neighborhood full of goblins. You're lucky they didn't tear you to pieces."

The young male looked at the deputy asked, "Would they really tear him apart?"

She laughed and said, "I'm surprised we didn't show up just to find pieces of him scattered all over."

As they pulled away, Durz looked out the window at the gathered crowd of goblins and humans. He saw Gerald say something as they pulled away and he didn't need a translator to know what he said.

"Commie!"

Durz spent about an hour having some big, ugly creature named Kelly manhandle him for a few minutes while the doctor bandaged his cuts and bite marks. Then he got stuffed into an orange jumpsuit and hauled down to some cells and tossed in opposite another occupied cell.

Then the jailers turned and went out, locking the heavy steel door behind them.

"Hey Durz. What's up?"

"Karg, been wondering what happened to you."

"Well, now you know."

"What the hell kind of world is this?"

"I don't know, but to tell you the truth, I think we're safer locked up in here."

Chapter 17 – Hell Hath No Fury

"So, sheriff, what are we going to do with the two in lock up at the hospital?"

John looked at his daughter and scratched his chin.

"I really don't know. I mean, we promised Randy and Jake they could kill that first one, on account of what he did to Mabel. But, you know as well as I do, we really can't allow that."

"Can't we just allow them to take little bits and pieces of him, but not kill him?" asked Debbie.

"You know, once they get started, they won't stop until he's just a blue stain on the floor."

"Yeah. Probably against some kind of code we're supposed to uphold."

"Don't get me wrong, deputy. I'd like to kill him with my own bare hands, but then wouldn't that make us just like them?"

Lisa spoke up and asked, "Didn't you say you killed this Boogerman a few weeks ago?"

"Well, technically," said Debbie, "It was Buster and Bosley that killed him, with the help of a tiger named Buttercup."

"I'm just saying, it seems like now and then you get something that comes into town that has no problem killing monsters and humans and they have to be dealt with harshly."

"We'll figure something out, Lisa," said the

sheriff. "Rest assured, they will not be walking away from this."

Just then, Debbie's phone rang and she saw it was Randy Johnson calling. She put it on speaker and set it on the desk.

"Yeah, Randy. What's up?"

"Hey, you better get over here and I mean now!"

Before she could even say they were on their way, John was halfway to the door. She had to run to catch up. By the time she climbed into her truck, he had already disappeared around the corner.

It took less than one minute for the two of them to screech to a halt in front of the house and jump out of their trucks. Randy was standing in the front yard and cringed when there was a loud crash inside the house.

They could hear Celia inside, screaming and cussing up a blue streak. Then there was another crash. It sounded a lot like a dinner plate being thrown against the wall. It was followed closely by Jake stumbling out the door and down the steps.

"She's gone plumb loco, sheriff!"

"I think I'll stay out here and keep the boys company," said Debbie.

"Chicken," said John as he ascended the steps.

As he disappeared into the house, she looked up at the big ogres.

"What happened?"

"We thought she knew about the Godwins," said Randy.

"Oh good lord," said Debbie as she looked at the house. And cringed when another plate hit the wall.

They could hear John yelling, "Honey, put that plate down!"

Crash!

"That's an assault on a law enforcement officer!"

"Incoming, dad!"

Crash!

About that time, Jaxon came running out of the house and fell down the steps. Debbie rushed over and helped him up.

"Mom's gone completely crazy," said Jaxon. "I haven't seen her this mad since I stole that curlinogh when we were leaving Rignus 7."

"What's a curlinogh?" asked Randy.

"It's a ... well, it's kind of like a ... never mind! Let's just say she was furious, especially when the Rignus security forces sent a fleet of battle cruisers after us. Once they recovered the curlinogh, they forbid us to ever come back."

"Is Rignus a nice planet?" asked Jake.

"Picture an entire island planet that looks like your Hawaiian islands."

"Whoa," Debbie said. "I'd like to take a vacation there."

"Well, thanks to me, we're not welcome

there anymore. Mom's still peeved about that."

Debbie slugged him in the shoulder.

"Ow!"

They all stopped talking and listened.

"Sounds like it might be over," said Jake.

Crash!

"Nope, not yet," said Randy.

"Yeah, mom can really hang onto this kind of thing," said Jaxon.

"So, who let the cat out of the bag?" asked Debbie.

Jake looked at Jaxon.

"Oh, thanks for selling me out, bud."

"Sorry, dude."

"Jaxon!" Debbie yelled. "You knew she shouldn't know about that. It was hard enough for her to find out about Mabel. Now she will not stop until she finds a way off this planet."

"I know, I'm sorry. She asked where I went with you the other day and I let it slip out that I was helping with a murder case. Before I knew what was happening, she got the entire story out of me."

After a few minutes of relative calm, Debbie decided it was safe to climb the steps and look in the door. Her dad was standing in front of her mom. She wasn't blue anymore. She was full-on purple now, what with being so mad she could spit fire at that point.

"I want my remote back and I want it now!" she screamed at him. "I do not want one more person to die because of me!"

"Sorry, no can do. Debbie hid it so good I'll never be able to find it. Not that I'd go looking for it, anyway."

Celia looked past John and saw Debbie peeking around the edge of the door.

"You! In here, right now!"

Debbie stepped through the door, checking to see if her mom had any plates in her hands. Mom was disarmed, so she felt it was safe to move closer to the seething volcano of alien womanhood.

"Well!"

"Well what, mom?"

"Don't play games with me, Debbie. I want that remote and I want it now!"

"Like dad said, can't do it."

Celia's hand flew up to her snow white hair and clutched at it.

"The Godwins are dead because you wouldn't let me leave!" she screamed.

"You don't know that, mom."

"I do know that! If I had left, the hunters would have followed me."

"Honey," said John. "We're actually making headway against these hunters. We have two locked up. Debbie killed three of them and we know Lowell Godwin killed one. So that's six accounted for. Jaxon says there should be only a dozen of them to start with."

"And did you kill Ursula?"

"Ursula, your cousin?" he asked.

"She will not rest until I am dead, even if she has to burn Prattville to its foundations. I can assure you she will not hesitate to do it!"

"Well no, sadly she is still alive. She seems to be quite content to hide in her ship in space."

"She won't stay there forever."

"Well, you're not running away this time," said John. "So, start helping us figure out a way to take care of the rest of the hunters."

Celia sank down into one of the easy chairs and put her face in her hands. Debbie knelt down next to her and laid a hand on her mom's knees.

"Mama, please don't ask us to let you leave. Daddy and I have lived these past twenty years wondering whether or not you were still alive. We don't want to go through that again."

"I don't want that, either."

They looked up to see Jaxon standing just inside the front door.

Celia looked at him with tears in her eyes.

"This is not how it was supposed to be," she said. "The longer I stay here, the greater the chance they find out about you."

"I'll take my chances, mom. Like dad said, let's try to find out a way to end this."

"You sound just like your father," she moaned.

"I'll take that as a compliment."

Jaxon walked past his dad and went to the

kitchen and found the broom and dustpan. He began sweeping up the shards of ceramic plates along the wall.

Jake stuck his head in the door and asked if it was safe to come in.

John stepped over to him and said, "I am entrusting her safety to you and Randy."

"Sheriff, you know we'd die protecting her."

"I don't want anyone else to die!" yelled Celia.

"Mom, calm down," said Debbie as she took her mother's hands.

"No one is going to die, Celia," said John.

"Can you promise me that? Can you guarantee no one will die at the hands of the hunters?"

When John was a little slow at answering, she said, "That's what I thought."

Ursula paced back and forth on the bridge of her ship and the others could feel the seething rage flowing off her. Everyone knew that even so much as a cough could cause an instant beheading.

"Try him again!"

"Yes, ma'am," said the junior hunter seated at the console.

"Commander Durz. Are you out there?"

The sound of static was the same as the last ten times they tried to reach Durz and his crew.

"Commander Durz, please respond."

Static.

"Sorry, ma'am. I don't think he's going to answer."

"I've had enough of these primitive apes on this planet!"

She walked over to another console, knocking the hunter manning it out of the way.

"They want to play games," she said as she looked through a scope, "I'll show them how we play!"

She made a couple of adjustments with some knobs and then pressed a red button.

"Ma'am, that is illegal according to the ..."

He stopped talking instantly when she glared at him, fingering her Rocun blade.

"I ... don't ... care!"

As John was thinking the worst was over at his house, the early evening sky flashed brightly, followed by a loud explosion.

"That came from Main Street," said Debbie.

John and Debbie rushed out of the house, followed closely by Jaxon and Celia. Randy and Jake were looking to the south, at a rising column of black smoke.

"You keep an eye on her!" yelled John as he ran for his truck. Jake and Randy just nodded.

Debbie and Jaxon piled into her truck and took off after their father.

Chapter 18 – A Message From Above

The scene on Main Street was complete chaos. The volunteer fire department was just arriving outside the burning structure when the Sheriff's vehicles skidded to a stop next to the fire truck.

Jaxon piled out of the Blazer and ran toward the building, screaming, "Lisa!"

One fireman grabbed him and pulled him back from the flames. Debbie reached out and pulled him back and the three of them could only stand there and watch as the flames consumed the Sheriff's department.

"Oh, my god!" cried Jaxon.

"Anyone see what happened?" asked the sheriff of the gathering crowd.

"Some sort of light out of the sky, John," said Mel, the guy that owned the hardware store.

"A light?"

"Yes sir. If you were to ask me, it looked a lot like a death ray from space. Hit the building dead center and blew out every window in the place."

John just stared at the building that had been the center of his life for over thirty years. One thing he couldn't help but notice was Lisa's Beetle Bug sitting in her parking space. This was one of the first things the firemen put out as they fought the blaze.

Even though he had only known her for a few days, this felt just as bad as what had happened to Mabel. Looking over to the sidewalk, he could see his son sitting on the curb with his face buried in his hands. A blind man could see he was losing it.

The sheriff walked over to his deputy and put a hand on her shoulder.

"Was there anyone in the cells downstairs?"

"No, sheriff. We were fully vacant," she said with an enormous lump in her throat.

"Cal?"

"He shouldn't have been in yet. It's too early and I don't see his Blazer."

As if he heard them talking about him, Cal came roaring around the corner and slid to a stop next to their vehicles. As he climbed out of his truck, John walked over and said he was glad to see he was safe.

"Yeah, the blast nearly knocked me out of bed. What the hell happened?"

"We're not absolutely sure, but it appears our guests in space have just sent us a message."

Debbie mumbled, "And killed Lisa in the process."

"Killed Lisa?"

"Cal, that's her car right there," said Debbie, pointing toward the smoldering Beetle.

"Yeah, but if you think she was in there then who's that over there?"

Debbie and John turned to look where he was pointing and saw Lisa walking through the crowd with a to-go bag in her hand.

"Did I leave the coffee pot on or something?' she asked.

Debbie said nothing. She just threw her arms around the younger woman and hugged the living daylights out of her. When she was done, the sheriff did the same thing.

When she could finally catch a breath, she asked what happened.

"Death ray from space and we thought you were in there," said Debbie.

"No, I stepped down to the diner to pick up some dinner."

Debbie looked around and then turned Lisa by the shoulders and pointed at Jaxon. He was still sitting on the curb, his face still buried in his hands.

Debbie whispered in her ear, "I think he's a little upset."

Lisa walked away from her, heading over to the distraught young man.

"Did you miss me, Jaxon?"

His head jerked up at the sound of her voice and for a moment, he couldn't understand what he was seeing. Then he exploded up from the curb and wrapped his arms around her, hugging her with more strength than he realized. She finally had to beat on him to breathe.

She turned around in his arms, her back against him and surveyed the situation.

"My daddy's car," she said with a whine.

"I can fix it."

She looked over to see Earl standing there.

"It won't be the same," she mumbled.

"Sweetie, when I get done with it, you won't be able to tell the difference."

"Promise me you'll let me work on it with you," she said.

"Wouldn't have it any other way. Don't you worry. We'll restore it to its faded, rusty glory."

It only took about twenty minutes for the firefighters to put the blaze out. A few minutes later, the sheriff and his people were allowed to go in and survey the damage.

As they stepped around the firefighters, who were busy making sure there were no hotspots, they could see the innards of the building were a total loss, but the bones of the building still looked solid.

Debbie walked through the rubble and made her way downstairs. She came back up a few minutes later and said the basement was intact with just a little water damage.

"Looks like we can salvage the building,"

said the sheriff. "It's just going to take some cleanup and repair work."

"That's okay, sheriff," said Mel from just outside the charred doorway. "Whatever you need, we'll get it done for you."

A murmur of agreement went through the crowd gathered outside.

Over the next twenty minutes, the firemen made sure the fire was completely out and then left the sheriff and his people to figure out what comes next.

"I guess they really don't like not getting their way," said Debbie as she kicked some charred wood with the toe of her boot.

"Nope," said Jaxon, who still hadn't let go of Lisa's hand, "and I'm surprised they waited this long."

"You don't think they're finished?" asked Lisa.

"Oh, not by a long shot. Like my mom said, Ursula won't hesitate to level this town to get what she wants."

"Okay," said the sheriff. "I am all ears for anyone that thinks they have an idea about what to do next."

"Prisoner trade," said Mel.

"What do you mean?"

"Well, you have two of theirs in the cells at the hospital."

"True," said Debbie, "but they don't have any of ours. The only thing they have to trade us is leaving and never coming back."

"Which won't happen," said Jaxon. "She'll execute those two prisoners herself for their failures. She's not about to trade them for anything."

Silence fell over the group as they realized just how hopeless their situation was. Their unseen enemy was located hundreds of miles straight over their heads, way outside their reach.

Celia stood at the window of the house, looking toward the downtown area. The smoke from whatever had happened rose into the sky, towering over the town.

She didn't need to see it to know what it was. The sound the ray of fire made as it sliced through the sky was unmistakable. It was a sound she had heard before and hoped to never hear again.

It was the same sound she had heard the day her uncle killed her parents. He sat in the safety of his ship and rained down death on her family home. It was a minor miracle she had survived the attack and was then spirited away by loyal friends.

As she watched the smoke rise over Prattville, she shook her head. The Johnson boys were standing in the front yard, staring at the same sight.

"This has to end now," she mumbled to

herself.

Turning from the window, she went to the bedroom and pulled a bag out of the closet. Digging around inside, she pulled out a small radio transceiver. Flipping it on, she checked the power source.

Then, as quietly as she could, she snuck out the back door of the house. Making her way across the backyard, she slipped through the gate and walked into a small field.

John and the others were busy hauling debris out of the shell of a building and tossing it into a large dumpster. It was crowded with all the townsfolk that turned out to help with the cleanup.

"I guess we can make a few changes when we put the building back together," said Debbie.

"Why would we want to do that?" asked the sheriff. "The building was just fine the way it was."

"I'm just saying we could modernize the entire operation."

"I like it just the way it was," he said as his phone rang.

"Yeah, Randy, what's up?"

Debbie stopped what she was doing when she saw her dad go white in the face.

"What do you mean she isn't there?"

"Get it over with, Ursula."

The leader of the hunters sneered in Celia's face. The fugitive was standing in the center of the bridge of the ship, her hands bound behind her back.

As Ursula circled around her prey, gloating over the fact that, after twenty years, she finally had her.

"Oh, I will not kill you here. I'm taking you back to Loiria and presenting you to my father, that he may have the honor of taking your head."

"Honor? You dad wouldn't know the first thing about honor."

Celia fell to her knees when Ursula cracked her across the back of the head with her closed Rocun blade.

"You will show respect for my father! And for me!"

Celia shook her head to clear the cobwebs and said, "Take these bindings off and give me a blade and I'll show you how much respect I have for you."

She heard Ursula extend her blade behind her and saw the fear on the face of one hunter, a small female.

Finally, she is going to end this.

The blade came around slowly from behind and came up under her chin. Ursula pressed it slightly against the skin of her throat and Celia could feel it draw blood. The small cut was enough to feel her life force trickle through the wound and into the blade.

Ursula bent down and growled in her ear, "We are going to take the long way home so that I can drain you of your energy slowly. Each day you will add to my energy, but I will not allow you the relief of dying."

"Well, let's go," croaked Celia as the blade was withdrawn from her neck.

"Not just yet. We still have to find that whelp of a son of yours."

Celia's head jerked up, looking her cousin in the eyes.

"Oh. You didn't think we knew about your disgusting offspring? Now him, I promise, I will kill immediately. Right here in front of your eyes."

A war cry erupted from Celia's mouth as she spun on one knee and swept Ursula's ankles with the other leg. Ursula fell backwards, hard on the deck, knocking the air from her lungs.

Before anyone could react, Celia pounced on her cousin, driving her knee into her chest. A most satisfying sound of a couple of Ursula's ribs breaking was heard throughout the bridge.

"Die you disgusting Kraynok!"

The other hunters on the bridge sprang forward and hauled Celia off their leader and dragged her away.

Ursula rolled over and pushed herself up to her hands and knees, spitting blue blood onto the floor.

"Lock her up before I kill her!"

The little female hunter took Celia by the arm and dragged her off the bridge. As they were leaving, she caught sight of the other hunters helping Ursula into the med-chair. She knew within a couple of hours, the chair would repair any injury she caused and Ursula would be whole again.

They reached a small containment cell with an open door and the hunter urged Celia inside. When she was in, the hunter pressed a button on a panel and a force field glowed in the doorway.

"Why do you follow her, Nyssa?"

In a soft voice, the hunter said, "Because she's my sister."

"And I'm your cousin. My mother and father were your aunt and uncle."

Nyssa looked at her and Celia could see the conflict in her eyes.

"You know what she and your father are doing is wrong."

"And if I show any inkling that I believe that, she would kill me without a second's hesitation. I'm not nearly as strong as you or her."

Celia could see the tears forming in her younger cousin's eyes.

"Then say nothing," she said with a softness in her voice that comforted Nyssa. "I'll just have to figure a way out of this."

Nyssa reached to press another button and

then stopped.

"I hope your son runs fast and far."

Then she pressed the button and a door slid closed, locking Celia inside the cell.

"I do, too," whispered Celia.

Chapter 19 – Calling An Old Friend

If the situation wasn't so dire, Debbie would have found it funny. Watching her dad getting in the face of two large ogres and screaming his guts out at them. Both of them looked like they wanted to be somewhere else.

After the sheriff had yelled himself hoarse, Debbie walked over and grabbed him by the arm and pulled him away.

"That's enough! And screaming at them will not help this situation."

She turned him around and sent him toward the steps and into the house. After he went inside, she turned and looked at the brothers.

"So, what happened?"

"We don't know, deputy," said Randy. "We were out here, listening to the sounds of what was happening on Main Street and she was in the house. Jake checked on her and she was gone."

"I screwed up," said Jake, his eyes cast down at the ground. "I never should have been out of the house."

"Hey, big guy," she said as she tried to put a

hand on his arm. Her fingers would only go about a quarter of the way around his wrist. "Eventually she was going to slip away."

"So, what are we going to do to get her back?" asked Randy.

The deputy was at a loss for words. Jaxon derailed her train of thought when he came walking around the corner of the house.

"I found where they sent a shuttle down to pick her up. It's in the small field behind the house. And one thing bothers me."

"What's that?"

"I think she called them to come down and get her. There's no sign of a struggle and it's clear she walked right out the back door on her own."

"So, it seems she intends to end this," said Debbie.

"It appears so."

"How can we get her back?" asked Randy.

"I don't know if we can," said Jaxon. "Without knowing exactly where the mother ship is, we'd probably never find it. Not to mention they may have already left this system for home by now."

"What you're saying is we need some way to know exactly where their ship is in space."

Jaxon just nodded.

Debbie pulled her phone from her pocket and scrolled down the list of contacts. It wasn't much of a scroll when the first letter she was looking for was an A. Hitting the Call button, she waited.

Somewhere in a dark room, a phone rang. Well, it didn't so much as ring as it started playing a tune. A tune from Kenny Loggins called *Danger Zone*.

The room was full of large screens, showing satellite images of various places around the globe, but the two in the center were focused on the blackness of space, with a red circle in the middle of it.

There were half a dozen men and women in the room, monitoring the screens and computers, with one man sitting at a raised console, overseeing the entire operation.

When he heard the first couple of bass guitar notes of Danger Zone … he smiled. He only referred to one place as the Danger Zone and only three people from there had this number.

He picked up the phone and looked at the display and smiled even bigger.

"Show time, people," he said as he pressed the Answer button and put the phone on the loudspeaker.

"Deputy Debbie, I was wondering when you'd call."

"So, you were expecting my call, Agent Smith?"

"When a death ray comes down from space

and smashes into the sheriff's building in a town I like, you know I'm going to be paying attention. What can I do to help?"

"We need to find that ship that fired on us."

"Done."

"Done?"

"Deputy. you may think we're a bunch of yokels when it comes to dealing with the things you deal with every day, but I can assure you, we know what we're doing. Yes, we know exactly where that ship is."

"Is it leaving the system?"

Agent Smith looked at one tech who shook his head.

"No, it's still just sitting there. They launched a smaller craft about twenty minutes ago that came down near you and then went right back up to the mother ship a few seconds later. Since then, it hasn't moved."

"Is there any way you can keep it from leaving?"

"Nope, no can do."

"Please."

"Sorry, not possible."

"Agent Smith!"

"Of course we can stop it!"

"Without blowing it completely out of the sky?"

"Now you're asking for miracles."

"I know you're one of the best at what you do."

"Flattery will not get you anywhere, deputy. Well, maybe just this one time."

"Martin, they came down and took my mother hostage."

"Oh, now that's a horse of a different color," said Agent Smith as he sat up in his chair and motioned for the others to get started. Everyone in the room started changing the screens and going over the data coming in on their computers.

"The only reason we know they're there is because the idiots parked their mother ship just a couple hundred miles above a ring of satellites and every time one passes below them, it futzes with our instruments. They probably think those are a bunch of weather satellites, but ... well, they ain't. It didn't take long to figure out what we were dealing with and where they were."

He stopped talking when he saw two techs looking at him with scowls on their faces.

Agent Smith waved them off and said, "By the way, those satellites, well they're just like your monsters."

"They don't exist, right?"

"Right."

"Never heard of them."

The techs turned back to their screens.

"Okay, one of those non-existent satellites is going to pass right under the ship in just under an hour. We will be able to fire on them and disable their engines."

"Without blowing up the entire ship ... or my mother?"

"Give us some credit, Debbie. Of course, when we do this, we have no way of getting up there to rescue your mom."

"No most secret, none more secret spaceship of our own?"

"Nope, none at all."

"Well, we have that covered."

Just then, all the others in the room swung around in their chairs and looked at him. Their eyes were wide with surprise.

"Really? I'd like to know a little more about that."

"After this is all over, why don't you come to town and I'd be happy to show you."

"You have a date, young lady."

"Careful, my boyfriend's a police officer."

"I can make him disappear," said Agent Smith.

"You wouldn't dare!"

Agent Smith laughed and said, "Fifty-three minutes, forty-two seconds, Debbie."

"Thank you, Martin. We'll be ready."

As the line clicked silent, he looked around the room at the others and took a deep breath.

"Let's not make any mistakes, people."

Debbie screeched to a halt outside Earl's secret hangar and jumped out of the truck. Jaxon raced around from the other side as she opened the back of the truck. Then they had to stop because of the massive thumping coming through the ground.

The Johnson brothers came pounding up the road and toward the hanger, carrying their clubs over their shoulders.

"Damn, deputy, you're fast," wheezed Jake.

"That's what they tell me."

Earl came sauntering over and worked the panel on the side of the door to the hangar.

"Wish I was going with you," he said as the door slid open.

Jaxon turned and looked at him.

"No, you don't, Earl. Where we're going, humans have no business being."

Just then, a box truck pulled up and Bill jumped out. He raced around the back and pushed the door up. Buster and Bosley jumped down and ran around to find Debbie. After they got to licking her face, she pushed them away.

Finally, a large Cadillac pulled up and Lisa climbed out of the passenger side. She ran to Jaxon and hugged him. The other three doors opened and a bunch of small people piled out of the car.

"You sure you're up for this?" asked Debbie as she looked at the crowd of little people.

"Just try to stop us, deputy," said Gerald. "I'm itching to take it to those Commie bastards again."

"Let's go get your mama," yelled Betty.

Jaxon stepped forward and looked at the goblins.

"Okay, when we get there, all wiring and controls are off limits! Remember, we're going to be about a thousand miles above the Earth. You go biting into the wrong circuit and you're likely to blow us to pieces and we won't have any way home."

"How about them blue devils?" asked Betty.

"You can tear them to pieces, except for our mom."

"Wouldn't dream of it," said Gerald.

In the distance, they could hear the high-pitched whine of a dirt bike coming down the road. As it got louder, they saw the bike go into a power slide and shoot off the road and toward the hangar. The rider skidded to a stop and leaped off the bike.

"It was exactly where you said it was," said Bobby as he handed a device to Jaxon.

"What's that?" asked Bill.

"This is our ticket to getting on that ship," said Jaxon.

Debbie looked at the device and said, "Looks dead to me."

"The batteries are dead. Once I hook it back up to the ship's power, it'll come back on."

Debbie looked at her watch and said, "Okay, we have less than five minutes. It's time to get this show on the road."

She went back to her truck and opened the

secure vault in the floor and began pulling weapons out. Jaxon reached in and pulled the Rocun blade out and hung it on his belt.

"You sure you want to use that?" asked Debbie. "I mean with it being nearly illegal in most of the galaxy and all."

"Illegal or not, mom trained me in its use and I'm better with it than any of these weapons you have."

Jake leaned over and growled, "Club better."

He waved his big club around to make a point.

"Just be careful what you hit with that thing," said Jaxon.

"Rrrr … no controls."

Jaxon just nodded.

"Alright, let's get on board," said Debbie.

Lisa grabbed Jaxon and pulled him into a deep kiss. As everyone fidgeted around, they wondered if the two would ever come up for air. Finally, they did.

"You better not get yourself killed or I'm never speaking to you again," she said.

"I'll be back before you know it."

She walked over to Bosley and rubbed the side of his face.

"You watch after him."

Woof!

Followed by a big, slurping lick up the side of her face.

"Eww, gross! Hell hound spit."

Jaxon turned around and walked into the hanger, found the invisible leg of the shuttle and turned off the invisibility cloak. The crowd of goblins just went, "Ooooo."

"Okay, everyone on board," said Debbie.

As they started up the ramp, Lisa tugged on Debbie's arm.

"What do I tell the sheriff when he asks where you are?"

"Just tell him the truth. In a couple of minutes, he won't be able to stop us."

Jaxon was standing at the ramp, with a stack of five-gallon buckets he'd grabbed from the hangar. He stopped the Johnson brothers and handed them the buckets.

"You two are going to need to change back and wait until we're on the mother ship. It's going to be cramped on board this shuttle as it is."

After they changed back to their human selves, Jake asked, "What are these buckets for?"

"You'll see. Just take them onboard."

He looked at Buster and said, "You, too. Get small."

Buster looked at Bill and whined.

"Go ahead, Buster. You can change back once we get there."

Within a couple of seconds, the large, demon dog changed into a small wiener dog and the hell hound reached down and nuzzled him with his nose. Then the two of them ran up the ramp. Bill and Bobby followed them, changing into werewolves as they went.

That just left Debbie, Jaxon and Lisa at the bottom of the ramp, with Earl standing near the door.

"You remember what I said," said Lisa. Then, looking at Debbie, she said, "Please watch him."

"You bet. He's like the brother I never had ... and you're like the sister I never had."

"Well, sister-in-law maybe," said Lisa with a grin.

Debbie smiled and headed up the ramp. Jaxon gave Lisa one last kiss and turned and headed up the ramp. A few seconds later, it rose into the shuttle.

Earl reached out and took her arm and guided her out of the hangar. A few seconds later, they could feel the gust of wind wash out of the hangar as the shuttle lifted off the ground and moved forward.

After the shuttle cleared the building, it angled upward and began ascending into the sky.

This was followed closely by the sheriff's truck racing into the dirt lot in front of the hangar and the sheriff bailing out. Then he almost dropped to the ground when the front landing gear on the shuttle ripped the light bar from the roof of his truck.

"Deputy! You land that thing right now!"

No answer.

"Deputy!"

Somewhere nearby, he could hear his voice being echoed.

"Debbie!"

He heard it again and walked over to her truck to find her radio gear sitting on the front seat. He looked like he was going to throw his radio as far as he could, but he contained himself.

Looking to his left, he saw Earl and Lisa standing next to each other.

"You let them go!" he yelled at Earl.

"C'mon, John. You know there is no way I was going to be able to stop her."

"Personally," said Lisa, "with that crew they took, I feel sorry for those aliens."

John could only turn and look up, watching the light of the shuttle's engines getting dimmer and dimmer.

"Oh Debbie ... Jaxon," he moaned softly.

He felt Lisa step up beside him and wrap an arm through his. He pulled his arm out of hers and wrapped it around her shoulders.

"They'll be okay, sheriff," she whispered.

Chapter 20 – Going To Get Mom

As Jaxon brought the shuttle's engines online, he looked around at the assembled raiding party. Two werewolves, a boatload of goblins, two large twin ogre brothers barely containing their true selves and two dogs.

Ursula will never know what hit her!

As the ramp closed tight, he addressed the group.

"Okay, I doubt any of you have been in space before and certainly not in one of these shuttles. So, a word of warning. You will most likely feel sick from the heavy magnetism of the engines. That's what those buckets are for."

"You don't know nothing, you young whippersnapper," said Gerald. "You don't know sick until you've been on a US Navy destroyer in the middle of a battle and caught in twenty-foot seas."

"Uh huh … we'll see," said Jaxon as he started moving levers and turning dials.

Everyone stumbled slightly when they felt the craft lift off the ground and then move forward. Jaxon turned on the viewscreen and they could see the open door of the hangar passing out of the edges of their vision.

Debbie and Jaxon looked to the side to see Earl and Lisa watching them go by. Jaxon hated seeing the look of worry on Lisa's beautiful face.

He promised himself he'd come back and remove that look from her face.

"Uh oh," said Debbie. "Get us out of here, now!"

Jaxon looked forward to see their dad's Blazer come roaring into the lot in front of the hangar. The view screen was sharp enough for both of them to see the look of anger and fear on his face through the windshield.

Jaxon miscalculated the rise in the shuttle and the front landing strut caught the light bar on the top of the sheriff's truck and ripped it off the roof.

"Oh, shoot!" said Jaxon. "You think he'll be mad about that?"

Debbie smiled and said, "I think that will be the least of our worries when we get back."

The last thing they saw as he passed out of view was him jumping to his feet and yelling into his radio microphone.

"It's funny how I can't hear anything he's saying," said Jaxon.

"That is interesting, isn't it?" said Debbie. "I think he was wishing us luck with our mission."

"Yeah, I'm sure that's what he's doing," said Jaxon as he snickered a little.

Debbie looked at her dad's red face, almost filling the entire view screen.

Don't worry, daddy. We're coming back with mama.

Jaxon worked a couple of levers and the ship

angled upward. He could hear a few moans behind him. He looked over his shoulder and saw the stacks of buckets being pulled apart and handed out.

He looked at his sister and saw she was looking fine.

"It may not hit you because, like me, you're half Loirian."

She nodded as she heard someone ralph behind her. Looking back, she saw Gerald had his face buried in his bucket. Betty was just rubbing his back and shaking her head.

"He doesn't even like flying on airplanes," she said.

He wasn't the only one having trouble keeping his lunch down. Both the Johnson boys were looking pretty green, as were Bill and his nephew.

Most of the goblins were having a hard time with it, but some seemed to handle it okay. Debbie realized they were the young goblins. She wondered why she let a bunch of goblin kids come along on this rescue mission. Then she remembered how they had handled Durz.

The air inside the shuttle was smelling pretty bad from all the upchucking going on and she felt like that was going to make her sick instead of the space flight.

Once they reached the edge of space, Jaxon brought the shuttle to a stop and got down under the console and reattached the locator device. At the same time, he yanked out a handful of wires and circuit boards and tossed them away.

As he stood back up, Debbie said, "I'm assuming we don't need that stuff."

"Nope, that's the communications system. Without it, they will just think we've had system failures. All they will see is a blip that will be identified as Durz's shuttle."

"I've never asked you, how do you know so much about stealing spaceships and disabling trackers and comms systems?"

He smiled and said, "Mom isn't quite the angel you think she is."

"Uh huh. One more thing I can hold over her head when we get her back," said Debbie. "Will they be able to scan us and see how many life forms are on this ship?"

"You've been watching too many movies, sis."

"Hey!" she said as she punched him in the shoulder. "We're on a spaceship, heading up into space to raid a spaceship full of aliens, to rescue an alien who is our mother and you say I watch too many movies!"

Jaxon laughed and said, "You have a point there, but no, they can scan for life forms, but not in this shuttle. It's shielding messes with that. If we were on the ground, they could. How long, by the way?"

She looked at her watch and said, "Any

second now."

He flipped a couple of switches on the console and the screen added an overlay of a radar image.

"Right there," he said, pointing to a blip moving in from the side. "I bet that's the satellite your friend was talking about."

They watched as the blip moved closer to the center of the screen and Debbie kept an eye on her watch.

"Five ... four ... three ... two ... one ..."

Just then a small flash shot from the satellite, into space and impacted on something that was invisible. A couple more flashes and the mother ship lost its cloaking ability.

Jaxon reached out and magnified the view of the ship and they could see Agent Smith was good to his word. The ship was disabled and floating helplessly with a slight tumble.

"I guess we're up," said Debbie.

Jaxon began working the controls again and the ship moved toward the disabled mother ship.

"Shuttle Two, come in. Durz, is that you?"

Jaxon reached over and twisted a dial back and forth.

"That will sound like I tried to answer, but the comms are down."

"We've taken a direct hit from some kind of weapon. We can't receive your messages. Enter the shuttle dock slowly."

He twisted the dial again and rocked the shuttle back and forth. As they got closer to the mother ship, he dropped under to come up from behind where the entrance to the shuttle dock was.

"Now," he said to Debbie, "I need you to hold this course steady. Time for me to get dressed."

"Dressed?" asked Debbie.

He took her hands and put them on the controls.

"Jaxon, I don't know how to fly this thing!"

"You'll learn quickly," he said

Jaxon walked to the back of the shuttle bridge and opened a storage compartment, revealing its contents. A bright, shiny silver space suit, complete with helmet. Grabbing the suit, he moved back through the group, trying not to look down into their buckets.

"This is going to help us greatly," he said as he took off his clothes.

When he was standing there in his underwear, Debbie said, "Uh ... Jaxon."

"What?"

He looked around and saw a couple of the younger goblin girls were looking at him with smiles.

"Sorry, ladies," he said as he pulled the suit on. "I believe I'm already spoken for."

They looked rather disappointed to hear that.

He reached down and picked up the Rocun blade, Durz's Rocun blade and stuck it in the holster on his hip. He pulled on the gloves and then set the helmet on his head, leaving the face shield up for the moment.

"Okay," he said, moving back to the console. "Let's see how you're doing."

He looked at the console and then the screen and said, "Sis, you're a natural!"

She beamed as he turned the shuttle to bring it up behind the mother ship. When they were within a couple of miles of the dock, they felt something grab hold of the shuttle. He shut down the engines and everyone behind him felt much better.

"They are bringing us in," he said.

"No backing out now, I guess," said Debbie.

"Nope, a little late for that."

He looked at his group of mercenaries and said, "Hopefully you're all ready for what comes next. Once that ramp goes down, I'll exit. Follow me out about thirty seconds later and be ready for anything."

"We're with you!" growled Gerald, who was quickly recovering from his bout of space sickness.

"What should we do with these?" asked one goblin about the buckets.

"Why don't you take them off the shuttle and leave them on the big ship, you know … as a present."

As he talked, they felt the shuttle bump down inside the dock.

Jaxon reached up and touched a button on his helmet and the face plate changed to an opaque gold color. He felt something on his arm and looked down to see one of the goblin girls had marked his suit with a red marker.

"That's so we don't eat you by mistake," she said with a smile.

He gave her a thumbs up and then looked at the rest of the crew.

He nodded and said, "Show time!"

Chapter 21 – The Mission

The rescue team moved away from the ramp, doing whatever they could to be hidden when the ramp went down. Some goblins even climbed into the storage compartments and pulled the doors closed. Buster hid under the console, but Bosley was too big to do much of anything, so he just hid beside the door.

Bobby and Bill changed and stayed away from the door, but the Johnson boys knew they couldn't change until they walked off the shuttle. Which meant they'd have to drag their clubs off the ship behind them. Big boys or not, their clubs were a bit too large for them to carry on their human shoulders.

Jaxon stepped up to the control panel and looked around. Hoping there wouldn't be any kind of boarding party as soon as the ramp went down, he looked at Debbie and gave her a thumbs up.

"Let's go get mom."

Debbie just smiled and checked to make sure her weapon was charged and ready for action.

Pressing a button, the ramp levered down and Jaxon stood near the opening, waiting for it to fully deploy. When it contacted the floor of the shuttle dock, he started down, trying to walk with the confidence of the baddest hunter in the galaxy.

As he descended the ramp, another hunter came walking toward him. He wasn't wearing a helmet and Jaxon knew him as Mellock. He was easily the largest hunter in the guild, standing at least a foot taller than him.

Couldn't have sent an easier hunter to handle, it had to be Mellock?

"Durz, what happened down there?"

Jaxon said something, but it was muffled inside the helmet. He knocked on the side of the helmet a couple of times with his fist and then shrugged.

"Why are you wearing your helmet, anyway?" asked Mellock. "Take it off."

Jaxon went to step past him, but Mellock grabbed him by the arm and spun him around.

"I said, take it off."

Jaxon made a show of trying to get it off, but the latch was catching, but mostly he was stalling for time. Finally, he snapped the latch open and twisted the helmet and lifted it off.

"Surprise," he said with a smile.

Mellock went for his blade, but was interrupted by a tap on the shoulder. When he turned around, Jake smashed him in the face, knocking him clear across the shuttle dock, his body slamming against the far wall.

Jaxon looked and saw he wasn't moving. He turned back to Jake and said, "Thanks, man."

By then, the entire invading force had exited

the ship, including one little wiener dog. Buster stopped and looked up at Bill, who was already in werewolf form and yipped at him.

"Yes, Buster," Bill growled. "You can get big now."

Everyone stood back, including the two giant ogres and watched as the little dog became a big, demon dog. If gravity had any effect on the ship in space, the floor would have sagged as he got big.

"Okay," said Debbie, "we really only have one objective here and that is to grab mom and get the hell out of here."

"We really need to leave someone here to watch the ship," said Jaxon.

Debbie looked around at the group and shrugged her shoulders.

"I wouldn't even know where to begin in telling someone to stay with the ship. Besides, I don't know if I want to leave anyone alone that might get attacked by the hunters."

Jaxon looked at Gerald and Betty and said, "You've already proven you can handle these hunters when you have to. Is there any way …"

"Say no more,' said Gerald. "We will guard the ship. Just let them commie bastards try to take it."

"I know I probably shouldn't tell you this," said Debbie, "but if you decide you want to dismember any hunter that you get your hands on, I will look the other way."

Gerald got a big, toothy grin on his face and turned to the rest of the goblins.

"If any hunters get on the ship, we drag them back out before we tear them apart. Let's try to keep the ship as clean as possible."

Jaxon walked across the shuttle bay to the unconscious Mellock and took his blade away from him. He kicked his shoulder a couple of times to see if he was still out and wondered if Jake had killed him with that punch. He heard a small groan from the big hunter and walked away.

"Keep an eye on him," he said to Betty.

"Can we tear him apart?"

"Only if he gives you trouble."

He looked at his sister and she asked, "Now what?"

"Now we go get mom."

The entire group moved to the main doors leading out of the shuttle dock and Jaxon stopped at a display on the wall. He touched a couple of buttons with writing no one else had ever seen. The screen changed to a layout of the ship and showed a route to a room on the other side of the vessel.

"This is where she is being held."

"Looks like we have to pass through a lot of ship to get there," said Debbie.

"True, with Mellock down, I'm thinking there can't be over five hunters left and Ursula."

"What about crew?"

"There is no crew. The ship is fully automated, just like mom's ship. There are robots that take care of things like maintenance and such, but unless they have something to do, they stay in their charging pods."

"Uh, Jaxon, I believe getting shot by that passing satellite guarantees they have something to do."

Jaxon scrunched up his lips as he realized he had forgotten that.

"Let's hope we don't run into any of them. They will sound the alarm in a nanosecond if they detect us."

Jaxon looked at the ogres and asked, "Which one of you wants to lead the group through the door? I figure one of you to lead and the other to bring up the rear."

Jake went to raise his hand, but Randy grabbed him by the back of the neck and pushed him to the back of the group. Jake went to growl something, but thought better of it when his brother raised his club and pointed it at him.

Bill grabbed Bobby and sent him to follow at Jake's side and he moved forward, taking a position next to Randy.

That left the two hounds, with Bosley moving to a point in front of Debbie and Buster getting behind her.

"I guess we're ready," said Jaxon as he looked back at Gerald, who gave him a thumbs up.

He punched a button on the panel and the doors to the shuttle dock slid open and Randy and Bill jumped into the corridor on the other side. Both of them let out low growls as they scanned the empty corridor in both directions.

So far, everything looked clear.

As everyone moved into the corridor, it amazed Debbie at how empty the place looked. The corridor stretched into the distance in both directions and there was no one to be seen. A wave of fear washed over her when she realized she was a couple thousand miles above Earth, in an alien spaceship and there was no way to call for help if they needed it.

Jaxon moved to his left and began walking toward where their mom was being held. Jake and Bill took up positions just behind him, keeping their eyes moving left and right.

Each time they crossed a junction in the corridors, they all expected to run into someone, but the place was as quiet as a graveyard.

After a couple of minutes, Jaxon came to a stop just outside a door and signaled everyone to stop. He reached out and pressed a couple of buttons on a panel next to the door.

Nothing happened.

He pressed the buttons again, looking at the door and expecting it to open. It remained shut.

"This should work," he muttered. "She's behind this door."

Jake stepped forward and brushed him

aside. He grabbed the edge of the door and began pulling with everything he had. They could see the door giving, but it was still holding.

That's when Randy stepped in. He muscled up next to his brother and they both grabbed the door and pulled. Everyone could hear some locks snapping and gears grinding, trying to keep the door closed.

It was no match for the Johnson brothers. With one final grunt from the two of them, the door slid open and slammed into the wall.

"What in the hell are you doing here?"

Celia was glaring at the two of them. The big boys stepped aside and Jaxon stepped into the room, followed closely by Debbie.

"Oh, this just can't be happening!" she hissed at them.

"Hi, mom," said Debbie. "How ya doing?"

Celia just shook her head as she looked at the man in the silver space suit.

"I can't believe you let her talk you into this," she said. "Oh, open that mask so I can yell directly at your face, Jaxon!"

"Gee, mom," he said as the face plate slid into the helmet, "I would think you'd be a little more thankful."

"I didn't ask you to come and rescue me, nor did I want you to!"

"Well," said Debbie, "we're here so you're just going to have to live with it."

Bill stuck his werewolf head in the door and growled, "We should probably hold off on the reunion chatter until we get off this ship."

"And you brought Bill," she muttered as she stepped toward the broken door. "Who else did you drag into this?"

"We didn't drag anyone into this, mom," said Jaxon. "We asked and ended up with more help than we dreamed of."

She looked into the corridor and gasped.

"Bosley, Buster! And who the hell are you?" she asked, looking straight at Bobby.

"Uh, Bobby, ma'am. I'm Bill's nephew."

She could tell by the sound of his growl he was a young werewolf. Her head dropped and she just shook it.

"I want you to go and leave me here," she said. "Get off this ship now! Especially you, Jaxon. Ursula knows about you and who you are."

"We're not leaving without you, mom," said Debbie.

"Yes, you are!"

Before anyone could say another word, Jake stepped forward and grabbed Celia around the waist and heaved her up and over his shoulder. Fireman carry is not the most dignified way to be carried, unless it's out of a burning building by a sexy fireman. This was not the case and Celia was not happy at all.

"We didn't come here to argue," growled

Jake. "Sheriff John be mad if not bring you back."

"Put me down!" yelled Celia.

"When we get to the shuttle," said Debbie. "Let's go!"

They pushed their way out the door and started back the way they came and it looked like they were going to make it back to the shuttle unnoticed.

But it only looked that way.

As they were moving down the corridor, they came to one of those junctions and they ran right smack into one of the repair robots Jaxon had mentioned.

Randy, who was now leading the group back, bumped into the robot as it came whizzing around the corner. As they stood there looking at each other, trying to figure out what to do, the robot started bouncing up and down. It looked like a scared child that found the monster under the bed and didn't know what to do with it.

Randy knew exactly what to do with it. His club arced down and smashed into the head of the robot, splitting it down the middle. However, his reactions weren't fast enough and the robot set off the alarm before having its brains bashed out.

The lights in the corridor switched to red and an ear-piercing squeal filled the air. Bosley and Buster dropped to their bellies, trying to cover their ears with their paws.

"Move it!" yelled Jaxon as he ran to the front of the group and began leading them back to where they came from. The two hounds had to tough it out as they brought up the rear of the group.

As they ran, Debbie had to stifle a laugh as she heard her mom grunting as she was bouncing up and down on Jake's shoulder as he ran down the hallway. Or maybe it was her bouncing off the ceiling every time he took a running step.

The group rounded a corner and ran straight into another robot that was going to find out what the ruckus was. Bill and Bobby slammed straight into it, tearing its head off and leaving it in a smoking heap on the floor.

As they were about twenty yards from the shuttle bay, a bulkhead door slammed shut across the corridor, cutting off their escape. When they tried to turn around and find another way, another door closed behind them, trapping them in the small area they were in.

Put two large ogres, two large demon dogs, a couple of werewolves and some humanoid creatures in such a small space and it gets really crowded.

"And here I thought I was going to have to blast that scummy village from orbit to kill your disgusting offspring," came a female voice from a hidden speaker.

"Let them go, Ursula!" yelled Celia, still

draped over Jake's shoulder. At that point, he decided he might as well put her down.

"Now why ever would I do that?"

"Because it's me you want. Not them."

Just then the first door slid open and the group faced Ursula and a dozen hunters, all with their Rocun blades extended and ready for use.

"I guess I was off on the number of hunters on this ship," mused Jaxon.

Ursula smiled at him and motioned for her hunters to stand ready to kill anyone that moved.

"No, dear cousin. I said I wanted to get you and your offspring," she said as she stepped in front of Jaxon. "And here he's delivered himself right to us."

Jaxon stood there, staring straight into her eyes. He was trying to figure out a way to kill her right there, but with the close quarters he didn't think he had the room.

Ursula looked at him as if he was just the slimiest bug she had ever seen. Then she glanced at Debbie and her eyes squinted. Her mind was working overtime as she looked the deputy up and down.

Then she smiled.

"I don't believe it," she said, glancing at Celia. "You really were busy with the lowlifes that live on this planet. Looks like your son isn't the only disgusting spawn you squeezed out down there."

Celia stepped in front of Ursula and pushed her back.

"You will leave my children alone!" she hissed in her cousin's face.

Ursula wasn't one to be talked to in that manner and she hit Celia with a roundhouse punch that sent her flying into the wall. As she crumpled to the floor, Debbie screamed.

"Mom!"

She tried to move to her mother, but Ursula grabbed her by the arm and spun her around. What she got for her trouble was Debbie grabbing her by the throat and pushing her back against the wall and lifting her off the ground by the neck.

None of the hunters looked like they were ready to jump to the aid of their leader just yet. Probably because doing so would have required them to step past the two ogres, the two werewolves and the two large dogs that looked very hungry.

"My mom told me what a piece of work you are, auntie," growled Debbie. "Something tells me the galaxy will not shed a single tear over your death."

Ursula struggled to break free from this Earth woman's grip, but she was realizing she had the strength of a Loirian.

And the anger to match.

Jaxon crouched down to help Celia up and

when she saw what her daughter was doing, she stepped forward and told her to let Ursula down.

"Mom, I can end her right here, right now."

"Yes, you can, but that isn't who we are. That isn't who you are."

Debbie looked at her mom and then relaxed her grip on her aunt's neck, allowing her to slip out and away from her.

"Kill every one of them!" croaked Ursula.

She pushed her way through the crowd of hunters and they started advancing in small steps toward the band of rescuers. Their Rocun blades were humming with power, ready to slice into all the monsters they saw in front of themselves.

Bosley and Buster moved to the front of the group and both of them growled, looking forward to getting their teeth into some alien flesh.

One of the closest hunters jabbed at Bosley, sinking his blade into the hell hound's shoulder. Bosley squealed in pain, but only for a second. As the blade pulled his energy from his body, the hunter got a lot more than he bargained for. When he felt the power of Hell wash through his body, he released his blade and fell to the ground, shaking and convulsing from the horrible images rushing through his head.

Buster reached over and grabbed the blade with his massive jaws, pulled it out and crunched it in half. Bosley recovered in just a couple of seconds and moved a couple of steps forward, growling at the downed hunter. Drool was falling from his curled lips and the other hunters were trying to keep him back with their own blades.

Buster lunged forward and grabbed the injured hunter by one of his legs and dragged him backward and into the group of rescuers. Jake took one second to raise his club and smash the hunter in the middle of the chest, driving his life from his body in an instant.

"What are you waiting for?" screamed Ursula. "Get them!"

The remaining hunters charged forward with their blades swishing through the air, trying to stab their way into the group of invaders. With the lack of room in the corridor for nearly twenty beings, they had no room to bring their blades to bear.

None of them seemed to want to have anything to do with Bosley, anyway. They tried working their way around him, but that left them to face Buster, who was more than happy to tear into them.

Because they weren't sure if Buster was like the other dog, they were reluctant to stab him with their blades. Within seconds, two of the hunters were missing a leg or two and the two demon dogs got into a tug-of-war with one hunter, pulling him apart right in front of his comrades.

It took little motivation for most of the hunters to turn and race down the corridor, trying to get away from this terror.

"Get back here!" screamed Ursula. "I shall have your heads!"

As the remaining four hunters showed courage and advanced toward the group, the door to the shuttle bay opened. An old man and woman hobbled into the corridor and looked at the fracas in front of them.

Ursula was standing right there and she reached down and grabbed Betty by the neck and lifted her up.

"Stop your fighting or I will kill her right now!" screamed Ursula.

All the fighting stopped and everyone turned to look at her and her captive.

Debbie stepped forward and said, "Auntie, I would advise you to put her down right now."

"Or what?"

The two women were staring at each other when one hunter started trembling and pointing.

"Commander!" he stuttered.

"What?" she yelled at him.

Then she looked at the woman she had in her grip. Except it wasn't a woman anymore. It was a little gray creature with more teeth than your average Kraynok would have. What used to be a helpless little old lady was now a rabid little monster, who was growling and looking ready to rip her head off.

"What in the he … OWWW!!!" screamed Ursula.

She looked down to see another gray creature latched onto her lower leg and sinking its teeth into her.

Just then, Randy caved in the skull of another hunter and the rest began retreating. One reached down and grabbed the creature on Ursula's leg and pulled it off, along with a good chunk of alien flesh. This caused Ursula to scream in pain and drop Betty, who immediately went for Ursula's other leg.

While the hunters were trying to get their leader out of there, another dozen creatures came pouring out of the shuttle bay and jumping right into the fight.

"Remember!" yelled one of them. "They have blue blood and it's nasty. Don't swallow any!"

From that point on, it looked like a scene from Keystone Kops. The remaining hunters slashed as best they could with their blades, but found them to be ineffective against the raging horde of goblins.

Finally, they broke and ran from the invading army, leaving the rescue party alone in the corridor.

With Ursula. And she was seething with rage.

Randy walked straight up to her and growled, "We leave. Now."

She thought for a second about standing up to him, but looked at the dead hunters littering the surrounding floor. Looking back at the ogre, she slapped him across the face.

Bad move.

Randy grabbed her by the throat and said, "You come with us."

The entire group moved through the door, into the shuttle bay and they rushed up the ramp. Randy was dragging Ursula along like a child carrying a teddy bear.

Jake had a hold of Celia, not wanting to let her go, thinking she might try to stay on the ship. When she saw Ursula being dragged onto the shuttle, she stopped resisting and headed up the ramp.

As Jaxon got the engines back online, the monsters grabbed the full buckets and tossed them out onto the floor of the shuttle bay.

Ready to head out, Jaxon turned the shuttle and pointed toward the exit.

Then came to a stop.

"What are we waiting for?" asked Debbie.

"We got a problem."

She looked out the viewscreen and saw the empty space outside the mother ship. She also saw a glow from what appeared to be a force field over the opening.

"I'm guessing we can't fly right through

that."

"Nope."

Behind them, Ursula laughed. She was lying on the floor and had about a dozen goblins clinging to her, looking like they were ready to chew on her. They were just waiting for the okay to do so.

"Did you really think my hunters would allow you to just fly away with me as your captive?"

Celia walked over and looked down at her cousin.

"I don't know, Ursula. You tell me."

She nodded to the goblins and they began biting her, tearing small chunks of blue alien skin from her body. This had the effect of filling the entire shuttle with her screams of pain.

Celia crouched down and said, "They stop when you tell your hunters to lower the shield and let us go."

Ursula tried to stay courageous, but one tiny goblin latched onto her nose and began biting.

"Okay! Okay!"

Celia held up her hand and the goblins stopped biting. Jaxon flipped a couple of switches and they could hear a microphone click on.

"Nyssa," screamed Ursula. "Open the shield."

A second later, the shield deactivated and Jaxon pushed the throttle forward and the shuttle moved out of the mother ship.

The movement of the ship had one other effect. Everyone not used to the magnetic energy of the engines started getting sick again.

The dogs and werewolves were swaying back and forth, trying to keep from getting sick.

And every goblin puked.

A lot.

All over Ursula.

"Ohhh!" screamed the hunter leader.

"Sorry, cousin," said Celia. "These Earthlings aren't used to our method of space travel. We'll see about getting you cleaned up when we get you to lock up."

As they pulled away from the mother ship, Jaxon, Debbie and Celia looked at it. They could see it was still listing in space, having a hard time maintaining level. It looked like it would not be much of a threat for a while.

Celia looked back at Ursula, still sitting on the floor with goblins hanging onto her. A couple of the young female goblins were running their long, knobby fingers through her white hair and cooing about how soft it was.

"It appears they like your hair. Don't give them a reason to pull it all out of your head."

A few minutes later, the shuttle settled down in the middle of Main Street. Jaxon and Debbie knew they were in big trouble when they looked at the viewscreen and saw a very large man standing in the middle of the street with his hands on his hips.

He did not look thrilled.

"Uh oh," said Debbie. "Looks like we're going to get a spanking."

Jaxon looked at her and smiled.

"Let's go face the music together."

She snaked her arm through his and said, "Like brother and sister."

Chapter 22 – A Friend Comes To Town

"We got mom back," mumbled Jaxon.

"No! This is not where you get to talk!" yelled John.

Jaxon shut his mouth and backed up a couple of steps. The group was downstairs, under the destroyed sheriff's building. They locked Ursula up in one cell and Kelly was in there with her, bandaging her many, many wounds.

"Hey! I was the one that led this little raid," yelled Debbie. "If you want to scream at someone, you scream at me!"

"Oh, I'm sorry," said John. "Are you thinking I've forgotten all about you?"

He stalked around the room looking like a bull stuck in a china shop and wanting to destroy everything.

"If we weren't in such a bad situation right now," he yelled at her, "I'd have your badge and gun!"

"John, you need to …"

He turned and glared at Celia.

"And you! If you hadn't pulled that little stunt, they wouldn't have felt the need to go up there in the first place!"

"I'm not sure I like your tone," said Celia.

"Oh, really? Well then, you're really not going to like this."

He grabbed her by the arm and shoved her into a cell and slammed the door closed before she could escape.

Randy and Jake's eyes opened wide and they began backing up toward the stairs. They were getting ready to bolt for freedom before the sheriff remembered they were standing there. At least Bill and Bobby had the good sense not go down into the cell block, heading home with Buster and Bosley.

The goblins had scattered after coming down the ramp and seeing the sheriff was ready to shoot anything that moved. They were probably already back in their neighborhood.

"Let me out of here!" screamed Celia.

They heard Ursula giggling across the aisle, which caused Kelly to squeeze one of her wounds a little tighter than necessary.

"Watch it, you troll!" yelled Ursula.

That brought a quick slap from Kelly.

"You attacked a wonderful friend of mine," she growled in the Loirian's face. "I should tear your arms off!"

Ursula growled at her, bringing a growl from Kelly. The hunter tried to back away from the large, green ogre, but Kelly had a good hold on her.

"John, you open this door right now," said Celia. She looked at Jaxon and Debbie, expecting some support from them.

"Sorry, mom. You caused this," said Jaxon.

"Alright, everyone, back upstairs!" said John.

He looked in Ursula's cell and asked, "Kelly, you about finished with her?"

Kelly stood up and turned around.

"Not really, but I don't care if she bleeds to death in here."

"Is she going to bleed to death?"

"Regrettably, no."

John opened the door to the cell and let Kelly out and then slammed the door closed.

He looked at Ursula and then at his wife.

"You two should take this time to work out your differences."

He turned and followed Kelly up the stairs, closing the heavy steel door behind them. Then, to add insult to injury, he shut off the lights in the cell block.

Jaxon and Debbie were standing on the sidewalk outside the ruined sheriff's department. They looked like they were thinking a trip to the beaches of Miami was a good idea. Or maybe Mexico. Possibly somewhere in Europe, as long as it was a long way away from Sheriff John.

Kelly walked across the street to her two brothers, who were both back in human form.

"Hey, sis. Hope you're not mad at us," said Jake.

Without a word, she reached out and grabbed both of them by the ears and started hauling them down the street.

"Just you wait until mom and dad get a hold of you two knuckleheads," she growled.

Through this entire episode, Lisa stood on the other side of the street, next to Carrie and watched it all play out.

"I wonder if I'm the right person for this job," she mumbled to herself.

Carrie reached over and put an arm around her shoulders, giving her a squeeze.

"Honey, this town is lucky to have you. And even though he'll never admit it, Sheriff John needs you, too. You just hang in there."

Lisa felt a warmth wash over her, comforting her. She looked into Carrie's eyes, which were sparkling with light.

She smiled and asked, "What are you? I mean, when you're not human?"

Carrie smiled and let her catch a quick glimpse of her true self. For just a couple of seconds, she changed to an all-white, beautiful woman, with a nearly transparent body, stunning blue eyes and glowing white hair to her waist.

"I'm a white witch."

Lisa looked into her eyes and smiled.

"Cool!"

She looked around as Carrie faded back to being a waitress, took a deep breath and said, "I love this town."

Carrie laughed and squeezed her again.

Then the whole dynamic changed right in front of them.

A black SUV came rolling around the shuttle, sitting in the middle of the street and stopped near the sheriff and his kids. When the doors opened, three black-clad G-Men climbed out and surveyed the scene.

One man signaled the other two and they turned and headed up the ramp and into the shuttle.

"Hey, I don't think they should be up there," said Jaxon.

Debbie reached out and put a hand on his arm and said, "It's okay, bro."

The man in black walked over to them and pulled his sunglasses off and smiled.

"Agent Smith," said Debbie with a smile. "What brings you to our happy little village?"

"Well, rumor had it there was an alien spaceship here and we wanted to come and see it."

He looked at the destroyed sheriff's department and clicked his tongue.

"Tsk tsk tsk. Looks like our alien friends have been quite busy."

"Yeah, they got a little rowdy," she said.

"Anyone hurt?"

"Not in that attack."

He turned back to her and asked, "Who's been hurt?"

"We had a couple of locals killed a couple of

days ago and …"

Her eyes went misty and he cocked his head and then looked around.

"Where's Mabel?" he asked.

Debbie just closed her eyes and dropped her head.

"Son of a bitch," he said under his breath.

John walked over and held out his hand. Agent Smith shook it and said, "Sorry to hear about Mabel."

"Yeah, and thank you for hitting that mother ship like you did. I'm sure my idiot kids would have been killed up there if you hadn't done that."

Smith looked at the two and could see them bristle with anger when he said that.

"John, I'm sure they did what they felt they needed to do. And it looks to me like they survived whatever adventure they went on."

"They shouldn't have been up there to begin with," growled the sheriff.

"We went to save mom!" yelled Jaxon.

John went to say something, but Agent Smith put his hand up to stop him.

"And did you save her?"

"Yes, we did. And killed half a dozen hunters in the process."

"Good job," said the agent.

Just then, one of the other agents came running out of the shuttle and straight to Smith.

"Sir, you need to listen to this," he said as he

held up a recording device. "This message came in to the mother ship in orbit."

He pressed a button and some loud, alien voice yelled something.

"I don't know what he said, but it doesn't sound good."

"Oh shit," said Jaxon.

"What?" asked Smith.

"Andrakus."

"What about him?" asked Debbie.

Jaxon just shook his head.

"He's coming here."

"Oh, that's not good," she mumbled.

"And who is this Andrakus?" asked Smith.

"Umm, he's our mother's uncle," said Jaxon.

"Okay?"

Debbie said, "He's the ruler of Loiria and wants nothing more than the death of our mother. She is the rightful ruler of Loiria and he will stop at nothing to keep her from the throne."

John just muttered, "Great. Now we have an intergalactic incident getting ready to go down."

The other agent said, "We're ready to take it and go."

Agent Smith just nodded at him and he turned and hustled back into the shuttle. Almost immediately, the ramp retracted and Jaxon took a few steps toward the ship.

Agent Smith reached out and grabbed him by the arm to stop him. They watched as the shuttle faded from view, as it was lifting off.

"Where are they taking it?" he demanded.

"Someplace safe."

"There is no place safe on this planet!" yelled Jaxon. "When Andrakus gets here, it will be a shining beacon to him and his army."

Smith just smiled and said, "I certainly hope so. It should take some pressure off this wonderful town's highly overworked sheriff's department."

Debbie reached out and pulled Jaxon back.

"This isn't their first rodeo, Jaxon. Don't worry about them."

"Okay, if you say so. I just don't want to bring anyone else into this mess."

Smith looked him up and down and then asked, "Any chance I can have that space suit you're wearing?"

"Yeah, I guess so ... oh shoot!"

"What?" asked Debbie.

"I left those clothes you bought me on the shuttle."

Smith smiled and said, "Come with me."

They walked over to the SUV and he reached in and pulled out a garment bag and handed it to Jaxon.

"You look about the same size as me."

Debbie pointed toward the menswear store across the street and said, "I think Clarice will let you borrow her fitting room for a moment."

A little old lady smiled at him, waved him

over and guided him into the store.

"Now," said Smith, "we need to figure out what to do when this Andrakus fellow shows up."

Then he stopped and cocked his head.

"What in the world is that screaming? It sounds like a couple of women having a real knock-down, drag-out fight."

"Oh, that's just my mom and her cousin. We have them locked up in the basement cells."

Smith just chuckled and looked at John, who was just stalking around, cussing and grumbling under his breath.

"John, what are you getting so worked up about?"

John straightened up and looked at him.

"This fiasco is going to get Prattville wiped right off the map! How in the hell am I supposed to protect us from an attack from space? They can just rain down nukes on us from orbit and we won't even have time to fire a shot!"

"Hey, Sheriff John," said Smith with a smile, "you have the full weight and help from the U.S. government standing behind you."

"And you're well versed in intergalactic warfare?" shouted John.

"Well, I don't like to brag," said Smith, "and I can't really go into details."

"Why am I not surprised?" muttered John.

The door to the menswear store opened and

Jaxon came back out, dressed in a black suit, white shirt and black tie, which he obviously did not know how to tie.

Lisa giggled and walked over and began retying his tie while she said, "You look like a real G-Man now."

"Is that good?" he asked, while he reveled in being so close to her.

"It's only as good as the man. I think you'll be a good man."

When she finished, he walked over to Agent Smith and handed him a bag. It contained the space suit and the helmet.

"Thanks," Smith said. "This will go a long way in helping us to develop better suits for space travel."

He walked over and put the bag in the back of his SUV.

John looked at Jaxon and asked, "If Andrakus has just sent back a message saying he's coming, how long before he gets here?"

"I should think it wouldn't take him more than a day."

"That fast, huh?" asked Smith.

"Yes, sir. His ship will travel many multiples of light speed."

"I'd love to get my hands on that ship."

"It can't land, so it's doubtful you'll even get to see it."

"What kind of weapons are we looking at?"

"Pretty much anything that can destroy a

planet."

"Would Andrakus use them?"

"Without batting an eye," said Jaxon. "It's interesting, though."

"What's that?" asked Debbie.

"Well, if his intention is to destroy the planet, he would just give orders to the ship's commander. He wouldn't come all the way here, himself."

"Maybe he wants to get Ursula back."

"Doubtful. The hunters all think Ursula is brutal with failure. Andrakus is much worse. He wouldn't care if she was standing at ground-zero when the blast hit."

"Which she might very well be," said John, obviously still peeved about what Jaxon and Debbie did.

"Alright," said Smith, "I guess we need to think about getting people to safety before he gets here."

"Safety? Were you not listening?" asked Jaxon. "He will turn this planet into a dust cloud. There will be no place safe."

"Which makes no sense," said Debbie. "If he could just order our destruction from Loiria, why would he be com … Oh!"

"What?" asked Jaxon.

"Remember how you told me Loiria is a real hell hole? So hot on the surface, everyone has to live underground?"

"Yes."

"What if he's coming here to scout out a new planet for the Loirians?"

"He wouldn't be doing that, would he?" asked John.

"Like Jaxon said, he can have us blown to smithereens from billions of light years away. I'm guessing the reports he's getting from here are telling him how much of a paradise Earth is."

"Well, he can't have Earth," said Agent Smith. "We're already here and not going anywhere. And if that's his plan, I don't see him blasting us into nothingness. It would kind of defeat the purpose of taking the planet."

John was standing next to Debbie and she heard his stomach grumble. She smiled up at him.

"I totally agree. I'm hungry, too."

John turned and looked at Carrie.

"You got room for about a dozen for dinner?"

She smiled and said, "Absolutely. I'll head on back and tell them to get ready."

She turned and headed toward the diner, as Lisa walked over and put an arm around Jaxon's waist.

"I didn't realize it was going to be this exciting to know you, space boy," she said with a grin.

He laughed and said, "Let's hope we live through it so we can get to know each other better."

The group moved down the street to the diner, while two women continued their screaming match in the cell block below the destroyed sheriff's department.

Chapter 23 – Feeding The Prisoners

Later, after dinner, Debbie put together a couple of plates and some drinks and headed to the bombed out building. The prisoners needed to be fed and she drew the short straw.

As she opened the door leading into the cell block, she noticed how quiet it was. Looking in cell three on each side of the aisle, she saw the two women. They were each lying on their bunks, apparently having reached the point of not talking to each other.

"Got some dinner for you two," said Debbie as she set the bag on a small counter. Reaching into the bag, she pulled out a covered plate and slid it onto the shelf in the door of her mother's cell.

Celia sat up and looked at her daughter. Debbie couldn't tell if the look was disgust, anger or just plain rage.

"Brought you a can of iced tea because I know you like it."

She turned and looked at Ursula, who was now standing in her cell and her look was easy to read. Opening the door would lead to the hunter doing everything to kill her.

She slid a wrapped sandwich onto the shelf and placed a can of cola next to it.

"What is this?" sneered Ursula.

"It's dinner. That's a roast beef sandwich

and a soft drink. I think you'll like it."

"Is this how you poison your prisoners?"

"Poison? Why on Earth would we do that?"

"You mean you actually feed your prisoners?"

Debbie stepped back and looked at her.

"Are you kidding? Yes, we feed our prisoners."

She heard Celia behind her softly say, "On Loiria they let their prisoners starve to death."

She turned and looked at her mom.

"That's how they do it there? That's barbaric."

Celia stood up and walked to the door and picked up her plate and can of tea. She sat back down and balanced the plate on her knees.

"It didn't use to be that way," she said as she ate the chicken fried steak. "When my mother and father ruled Loiria, they were compassionate. They loved their people and their people loved them."

"They were weak," said Ursula as she picked up the sandwich and cola and sat back down on her bed. "Prisoners deserve to die and not be a burden on their community."

"Were you always this mean?" asked Debbie.

"No, she wasn't," said Celia. "When we were little girls, she and I were best friends. She wouldn't hurt a bug back then."

"And what happened?" asked Debbie.

"Her father happened. He started trying to take the throne and he forbid her from ever seeing me again. Over the years, he taught her to be the woman you see before you now."

"My father is a great Loirian."

"Your father is a murderous tyrant," scoffed Celia.

"You know nothing of what you speak!" yelled Ursula.

"Hey!" yelled Debbie, "Knock it off. You two were being quiet when I got here. Let's try to keep it that way."

"Our heads hurt from screaming so much," said Celia as she finished up her dinner.

Popping the top on her can, she washed dinner down with the cold ice tea. After she took a couple of swallows, she rubbed the cold can across her forehead and let out a sigh.

"Do you need an aspirin or something?"

"No, sweetie, I'll be fine."

Debbie turned and looked back at her aunt, who was still trying to decide whether or not she liked roast beef.

"Tell me something, auntie. If your father walked up to you right now, what would he do? Throw his arms around your shoulders and hug you, grateful to see you alive and well?"

"No, he would not. I'm sure because of my failures, he will take my head."

"Well then, you're in luck. Apparently, he's on his way here. Should be here sometime tomorrow."

"What? What are you saying?"

"We intercepted a message from your ship in space and apparently Andrakus is on his way here."

She looked at Celia and said, "At least that's what Jaxon said when he heard the message."

Celia looked up with sadness in her eyes.

"This will not end well for us."

"I don't know. We have a friend upstairs that doesn't seem to be too worried about it. As a matter of fact, if I had to guess, I think he's rather looking forward to the ruler of Loiria showing up. Sometimes I think he's an idiot, but he seems to get the job done."

"When my father gets here, he will lay waste to this village," said Ursula with a sneer.

"I guess we'll see. We have some tricks up our sleeves. Kind of like how we disabled your ship earlier today."

"I'm sure you think keeping me here in your prison will keep him from destroying this town. I can assure you, it will not."

"Well, let's hope he doesn't decide to incinerate you with the rest of the town. I have to get back out there. Lots of prep to take care of before the big day."

She took her mom's plate from the shelf and Celia reached out and took her hand and held it.

"Please be careful," she said with a tear in her eye.

"It's going to be okay, mom."

"Maybe, if you have a chance, ask your father about letting me out of here. I promise I won't be any trouble."

"I'll try, but as you could tell earlier, I'm on his shit list, too. I'm surprised Jaxon and me aren't sitting in the cells on each side of you."

She squeezed her mom's hand and said, "But I'll see what I can do. Get some rest."

She turned around and looked at Ursula.

"And you try to remember what you were like when you were a good person."

Before Ursula could reply, Debbie headed for the door, flipped the light switch to just night light levels and left the cell block.

As she locked the door, she leaned back against the wall and fought the urge to cry. She couldn't believe these secret basement cells were being used to lock up her own mother.

Hopefully dad's mood was getting better.

As she walked out of the ruined building, she found Jaxon leaning on the front of her Blazer.

"How's mom?"

"She's doing okay. I wish I could just open the door and let her out, but dad's still mighty upset with her."

"And with us. You don't think we made a mistake, do you?"

"No! We had to go get her. Now we just have

to weather the storm that is dad's temper."

He just nodded.

"You should go downstairs and see mom," said Debbie. "I'm sure she'd like to see you."

"Not a good idea. If I go down there, I might try to kill Ursula."

"Can't you control yourself, even for just a few minutes?"

"Sis, that woman chased mom and me all over the galaxy for the last twenty years. She was trying to kill mom every day I've been alive. And every day I got more and more angry about it. Yes, I could probably control myself, but I don't want to test that."

"Okay. Don't worry about it. I'm sure in a couple of days dad will let her out and you can see her then."

"By the way, dad said he was setting up the sheriff's department in, I think he called it a community center. Wanted me to tell you."

"Okay, get in. Let's head over there and see if he's cooling down at all."

As they pulled up in front of the center, Debbie almost busted out laughing. There were at least a dozen black SUVs in the parking lot, along with her dad's and Cal's vehicles. At the end of the street, they could see a couple of Army Humvees blocking the road, with armed soldiers standing near them.

"Agent Smith doesn't know how to do things quietly."

Jaxon laughed as they got out of the truck and headed inside. They found Lisa manning a computer and the phones and when she saw them come in, she smiled at Jaxon in his black G-Man suit.

He leaned over and whispered to Debbie, "Do I stand out dressed in this outfit?"

She laughed and said, "Not in this room, you don't."

He looked around and saw about twenty agents, men and women, all dressed like him. There were military personnel in their green fatigue uniforms, setting up large computer monitors and some working at big communications consoles.

Debbie looked around the open room and saw lots of black-clad people, but one stood out. He looked like he belonged, but at the same time, like he didn't. She couldn't put her finger on it, though. He was talking to a couple of agents and they were giving him their rapt attention.

He stood just over six feet tall, had pale skin and looked like he was made of solid muscle. Dressed all in black, his suit didn't look like the standard suit the government types would be wearing. It looked like the finest tailor in the world made it.

Turning his head, he looked at her. He smiled and nodded. She glanced away for a second and when she looked back; he wasn't there.

Jaxon walked over to where the large screens were set up and studied them. He could tell immediately they were star charts and had red lines and Xs marked on them.

Lisa sidled up to his side and put an arm around his waist and hugged him.

"See anything interesting?" she asked.

"Well, yes. It's almost correct, but there are a couple of things wrong on here."

A lady colonel looked up from her desk nearby and said, "I think we know what we're doing. Those images are the best we have."

Jaxon looked at her and said, "I'm not questioning whether these are the best you have. I'm only saying there are a couple of things out of place."

The colonel shook her head, stood up and walked over.

"And just exactly what makes you think these are wrong?"

"Colonel Peters."

She turned and saw Agent Smith walking over.

"Yes, sir."

"If he says there's something wrong with the charts, you might want to listen to him."

"Sir, he's just a …"

Then she looked at Jaxon again.

"Oh, you're him, aren't you?"

"If, by *him*, you mean the space boy, as my

new girlfriend likes to call me, yes."

He felt Lisa give him a squeeze.

"Okay," said Peters, a little more subdued this time, "what's wrong with the charts?"

"These markings you have right here, next to where you think Andrakus is going to come from, are out of place."

"That's a very thick asteroid field and he would be crazy to fly through it. It's at least one light year across."

"Leaving aside the fact that Andrakus is crazy, everything you said is true. The asteroid field is too thick to navigate through, but it's over here, not there. Mom and me just flew around it a few days ago."

He pointed to a spot that would put the asteroid field right in the direct path that Andrakus was likely to take.

"See if you can get your Hubble telescope to take a look, but I think you'll find I'm right."

She stepped closer to the chart and said softly, "If the field is here, then that means he'll have to deviate away from this direct path."

"Correct," said Jaxon. "I would guess he'll shift his approach to this side. It will give him the straighter approach over any other line."

Agent Smith said, "Colonel, why don't you get on the horn with STSI and see if they can look for us?"

"Yes, sir," she said as she headed back to her desk.

Smith looked at Jaxon and said, "If he can travel at many multiples of light speed, is that little deviation really going to make much of a difference?"

"Yes, sir. He'll have to drop below light speed well outside the boundaries of your solar system. He has to do that to slow down by the time he gets to Earth. So, that deviation will cost him about seven or eight hours. If he went any other way, it could take days."

Smith smiled and said, "You know, I think we're going to enjoy having you here on Earth."

Lisa stepped in front of Jaxon and said, "Just so long as you don't dissect him."

Smith laughed and said, "Lisa, stop watching so many movies. We haven't dissected an alien since, oh hell, I guess the 40s or 50s."

He turned to walk away, then looked at Jaxon.

"You know, that suit looks good on you."

After the agent walked away, Lisa poked Jaxon in the stomach and said, "See, you've only been on Earth a few days and you might already have a job. A girl likes that in a guy."

She smiled, leaned up and kissed him. After he got over the shock and could come up for air, he found he had no words to express how he was feeling.

"Jaxon! Debbie! In here!"

He looked over and saw their dad standing in a doorway right behind Lisa's desk. He didn't look like he hadn't cooled down even one degree.

"I guess I should go get this over with," he said.

Lisa squeezed his hand and said, "Stay strong, space boy."

He and Debbie reached the door at the same time and he stepped aside and waved her through.

"Coward," she mumbled under her breath.

"Close the door and take a seat," said the sheriff.

As they sat down, Cal was sitting at another table, talking on the phone. It sounded like he was trying to line up some help. After he hung up, the sheriff looked at him.

"Dean says he and Buttercup can come down first thing tomorrow. Says he's looking forward to mixing it up with a few aliens."

"That's good to hear," said the sheriff. "Can you give us a minute here, Cal?"

"Sure," said the deputy as he stood and headed for the door. He gave Debbie a pat on the shoulder on his way out.

After the door closed, John asked, "How's your mother?"

"You mean your wife?"

"Don't play games with me, deputy."

"Sorry. She's doing fine. Says if you let her out, she'll play nice. I believe her."

John steepled his fingers in front of his chin

and thought about it.

"Do you think we should keep her locked up until after this danger from Andrakus has passed?"

"I do," said Debbie. "At least we'll know where she is and somewhat safe."

"I agree with that," said John. "As long as she's locked up below ground I think she'll be safer and that will be one less thing we have to worry about."

Jaxon sighed slightly, but also nodded.

"You don't agree?" asked John, looking directly at him.

"Oh, I agree to a point, but mom will say she has as much right to fight and defend this town as anyone. For the past twenty years, she's told me about her love for Prattville and life here. She will defend this town with her life if necessary. Something I think she already proved by turning herself over to Ursula."

"We would need to make sure she can't just go back to the mother ship and plead for them to take her and leave us alone," said John.

"We can always tag her," said Debbie.

"You want to put an ankle monitor on your own mother ... my wife?"

"If it gets her out of that cell, I'd put a leash on her. It was heartbreaking to see her down there."

John nodded and then said, "Now for the reason I called you two in here."

Debbie sat up straighter, preparing for the blast that was coming their way. It turned out to be a lot less harsh than she thought.

"If either of you ever do something like that again, I swear to God, I will slap you into those cells next to her and forget where I put the key. Do I make myself clear?"

"Absolutely," said Jaxon.

"Crystal," said Debbie.

"I'm not mad that you two planned and executed a rescue of Celia. What I'm mad about is how it made me feel to watch you take off in that shuttle. I had a gut feeling I was going to lose my entire family in one day. I never want to feel that way again."

"Sorry, dad," said Debbie. "I guess we never looked at it that way. We just wanted to get mom back."

"Understood."

He looked back and forth between them, making sure they understood his feelings on the matter.

"Now, give me an after-action report on what happened up there."

Debbie looked at Jaxon and said, "Go ahead."

"Well, sheriff. We found out there were more hunters than I previously believed. Ursula had fifteen hunters behind her when they confronted us and those were just the ones we saw."

"So, you got into a battle on their ship."

"Yes, though it wasn't much of a battle. I don't think they have any clue as to the citizens in this town. It caught them by surprise."

John looked at Debbie and she gave a half smile.

"Buster and Bosley got their pound of alien flesh and I'm pretty sure the goblins got about ten pounds between them. Bobby and Bill got hold of a couple of them and the Johnson boys reduced three to piles of goo."

"No one got injured in your rescue team?"

"No. Well, Bosley got stuck with a Rocun blade and when it started sucking his life-force from his body, I think it surprised the hunter the kind of life force he was getting. I guess the images he got from a Hell hound were a bit … overwhelming. Then Buster and Bosley tore him in half. It was rather messy."

John stifled a grin with a cough.

"Anyway, after we sent the hunters running," said Jaxon, "we were able to capture Ursula and get back on the shuttle and come home."

"Okay, you two consider yourselves grounded until this is over. I don't want either of you getting on a spaceship until we've dealt with Andrakus."

"That's fine," said Debbie. "Agent Smith's buddies took the one from Earl's garage, so now the only ship we have access to is mom's, on the far side of the moon."

"I'm assuming her remote return device is still well hidden."

"Yeah, under quite a few tons of rubble that used to be our building. I taped it to the back of the microwave in the break room."

"Well, at least we know what to look for when this is over."

He sat back and stared at the two of them for a few seconds, causing them to get a little uncomfortable.

"Alright, get out of here before I change my mind. And Jaxon, you look good in that suit."

"Funny. Agent Smith and Lisa said the same thing," he said with a smile.

"Debbie, go let your mom out, but make sure you tag her first."

"Got it, sheriff."

As they walked out of the room, Debbie squeezed her brother's arm.

"See, I told you he was a good man. Want to go with me to give mom her freedom?"

"Sure."

Within ten minutes, they walked out of the ruined department building, Celia with her brand-spanking-new ankle monitor with blinking lights.

Ursula was screaming to be let out, but they just ignored her.

Debbie dropped Celia off outside the community center and she and Jaxon made a quick trip around town. Then she introduced him to a marvelous thing called a chocolate shake.

"Might as well enjoy it now," she said. "We might be blown to smithereens by this time tomorrow."

"I don't know, sis. I'm having a good feeling about this."

Well, I'm glad someone does.

Chapter 24 – Andy Comes To Town

The new day dawned with Jaxon standing in front of the large screen, watching a red blip move slowly across the screen. It skirted the newly positioned asteroid field and then made a beeline toward Earth.

Colonel Peters stepped up beside him and looked at the screen.

"Based on his current speed, we expect he'll enter Earth orbit in about six hours."

Jaxon pointed to a spot on the screen near Earth and asked, "Have we heard anything from the mother ship?"

"Not much. Thanks for that translator, by the way. Anyway, they have maintained comms with Andrakus' ship, trying to convince him they should turn and leave this planet because of the, and I quote, horrible monsters they've been encountering here."

"Aw, that's just rude. Our monsters are kind of cute."

The colonel just laughed.

The front door opened and John and Celia walked in together, looking like they had patched up any hard feelings they had about yesterday.

As they walked over, he could see they were holding hands and it looked like his mom was quite happy to be at his side.

"What are we looking at, son?" asked John.

"We're about six hours away from the arrival of Andrakus. The hunters in orbit right now are trying to convince him to take them and leave. I can assure you that won't happen."

Then he leaned over and kissed his mom on the cheek.

"Good morning, mom. Sleep well?"

She blushed and lost her human hue again. Now she was just blue and pink in the cheeks.

"I slept fine, thank you very much."

Just then, the door opened again and a large state police officer walked in, followed closely by a huge Bengal tiger.

"Holy … what the hell is that?" stammered Jaxon.

"Hey Dean," said John as they shook hands.

Dean looked at Jaxon and then smiled.

"This is Buttercup. He's my cat."

"He's about the coolest thing I've ever seen," exclaimed Jaxon.

Buttercup walked up to him and their heads were at the same height. Jaxon just stared into his eyes for a second before he reached out and scratched him behind an ear. A Bengal tiger can rattle the windows when it purrs, which is exactly what he did.

As he stood there enjoying the scratch, Agent Smith walked up and shook hands with Dean.

"Shooting any trees lately?" asked Dean

with a laugh.

"Nope, just spaceships now."

"Oh, you G-Men get all the fun toys."

John said, "We have a few hours before the festivities begin, so we're heading down to the diner for breakfast. Who wants to join us?"

Before he could say another word, Jaxon walked over and took Lisa's hand and they headed for the door.

Buttercup wandered to the side of the large room and curled up in a ball against one wall. A few of the agents that walked by him steered very clear of him.

It was another party of about a dozen that walked into the diner and Carrie's face lit up when she saw them. She had a special smile for Agent Smith, who she seemed to have taken a liking to.

Debbie walked in a couple of minutes later, accompanied by Bill. She saw Billy Ray sitting at the counter and asked him to join them.

Last to show up were the Johnson brothers. Each one was sporting bandaged ears. Debbie giggled about it and said it looked like Kelly was a little rough on them.

"Kelly?" said Jake. "This was from our mom."

Everyone got a good laugh out of that, including Jake and Randy.

"Yeah," said Jake, "dad says he's going to keep mom at home to give the aliens a fighting chance."

After everyone ordered, John stood up and called for attention. The entire diner went quiet as all the other patrons stopped to hear what he had to say.

"Folks, I guess I don't need to tell you the next few hours are going to test this town more than it has been in the past. What we went through a few weeks ago with the Boogerman will seem like a minor inconvenience."

He saw a bunch of nods throughout the diner from those that lived through that nightmare.

"I just have to ask most you to stay off the streets and away from this coming confrontation. I don't want any of you getting hurt. Let the sheriff's department and the government and military handle this."

Gerald stood up and said, "Sheriff, this is our town, too. We don't intend to go down without a fight."

Some rumblings went through the gathered crowd, most of them saying they were with Gerald. Betty looked like she was ready to get back to it.

"Gerry," said the sheriff, "I can't tell you to stay away. I can only ask. And from what I understand, you and your goblin friends put a serious hurt on the hunters yesterday on their ship. For that, I am grateful, especially for helping bring my Celia back to me. Please don't get hurt this afternoon."

"We're with you, sheriff. Just let them commies come down here and try something."

You would have thought there was a presidential rally going on inside the diner when the place erupted into cheers. The sheriff could tell his attempts at warning the townsfolk to take shelter were going to go unheeded. In the back of his mind, he was grateful and pitied any hunter that showed his face in Prattville today.

He just smiled and nodded to the folks and sat down as Carrie and a couple of other waitresses began bringing out their breakfast. Not much was said as everyone fueled up for the coming battle.

An hour later, they all headed back to the community center to check on Andrakus' progress. It appeared he was still about five hours away from meeting up with the other ship in orbit.

Agent Smith started moving his military assets into position around the town. They had every road leading into Prattville blocked off, turning travelers away with a story of a chemical leak. Never mind the fact there wasn't a chemical plant within a hundred miles of town. With the visible soldiers in full chemical protective gear, it was an easy sell.

The sheriff and his deputies hit the streets in their vehicles, looking to coax people to stay in their homes and not come out until they gave them an all-clear. Most of the humans locked themselves in their homes, while the monsters prepared to defend their neighborhoods.

Debbie and Jaxon rolled through the northern part of town, stopping to talk to the few people they saw out and about. Jaxon was still wearing the black suit Agent Smith had given him and Debbie was thinking he liked the idea of being a G-Man.

Bill rode with the sheriff in the south and they had Bobby in the back seat. Every now and then, Bill would turn around and see his nephew had a look of fear on his face.

"You scared, boy?"

Bobby looked at him and sneered, "No!"

Bill turned back around and looked out the front window.

"If you had any brains you'd be scared."

The sheriff just nodded his agreement.

Agent Smith was riding with Cal and they drove out to the roadblock in the west. They found a platoon of soldiers out there with their Humvee mounted 50-cal machine guns and rocket launchers.

They were holding back a couple of Hobart police cars. Cal got out of his SUV and walked to the cop cars. Agent Smith stopped to talk to the troops and see how they were holding up.

"Chief Handley, how are you doing today?"

"Well, Cal, we heard there was going to be some action here today and we thought we might come by and help. These soldiers told us it was a chemical leak, but being as how you aren't geared up like them, I call that story bogus."

Cal laughed and said, "No, sir. We are expecting a bit of trouble of the intergalactic kind. Should be here in just a short time."

He looked through the chief's car to the other car sitting next to him.

"Hey, Tom."

"Cal," nodded Tom. "How's Debbie?"

"She's fine so far. You know her. She's ready to kick ass and take names."

Tom laughed because he knew her well.

"If you two want to come in, I won't keep you out," said Cal. "Just know it might get really bad in there today."

"Chief Handley?"

The chief reached over and keyed his mic.

"Yeah, Flo, what's up?"

"I don't know how to tell you this, but Chester left here a few minutes ago."

"Maybe he's just going home. He needs to take some time to grieve for his parents."

"That's what we thought, but … well, he checked out that confiscated Barrett sniper rifle and a case of rounds. Said he was going to the range to get some practice, but witnesses said he looked like he was heading to Prattville."

"The range is in the other direction."

"Yes, sir, it is."

"Thanks, Flo."

The chief hung his head.

"I guess we don't need a crystal ball to see where he's headed."

"I'll make sure the troops here keep him out," said Cal.

"Won't do any good," said the chief. "They probably won't even see him. He knows every back road in this area."

Cal keyed his mic and let the sheriff know about Chester. There was a fair bit of swearing before the sheriff cut off his mic.

"I'm heading back into town," said Cal. "If you two want to join us, you're welcome, but I wouldn't think badly if you turned around and go home."

"I'm coming in," said the chief.

"Me, too," said Tom.

"Okay," said Cal as he motioned for the troops to let the two cars through.

As he and Smith got back into his truck, the agent said, "I heard you mentioned Chester. Isn't he the CSI from Hobart?"

"Yes, sir, he is. He is also the son of Helen and Lowell Godwin, the first two people killed by the hunters just last week. Sounds like he's going to go full Rambo on these aliens."

"We need all the help we can get," said Smith.

"Yes, Martin, we do, but Chester is a geek. I love him to death, but he is not a soldier and is as likely to get himself killed as anything."

Agent Smith looked out the window at the passing fields as they headed back to town.

"Sometimes it's the geeks that can surprise the hell out of you," mumbled Smith.

Cal just bit his lips, trying to keep from agreeing with the agent.

"Agent Smith."

"Yes, colonel," said the agent into his radio.

"He's arrived and has stopped next to the other ship in orbit."

"Are they doing anything yet? Like sending down shuttles or the like?"

"No sir. They just arrived a couple of minutes ago and have done nothing yet. Oh wait. Okay, Andrakus' ship is shooting some sort of energy beam at the other ship and appears to be arresting its tumbling."

"Alright, we'll be back there in a few minutes."

"Understood."

"Looks like the show is about to begin," said Cal. "I really hope you have some tricks up your sleeve or this is going to be a brief war."

Smith smiled and said, "Oh, it's going to be short. Just not the way you think."

A few minutes later, they rolled up outside the community center and parked with the other sheriff's vehicles. Along with the two from Hobart and one state police car.

As they walked into the open room, there

was a crowd of people gathered around the large display screen.

"What's going on?" asked Cal as he stepped up next to Debbie.

"Shhh. Listen."

At first, there wasn't anything to hear, but everyone was being silent, as if this was a church.

Then an alien sounding voice came over a speaker in front of the screen. The translation device was about two seconds behind the original transmission.

"Return my daughter, Ursula and the war criminal known as Celia. You have ten of your Earth minutes to comply."

John was standing in the center of the group and holding the mic.

"I don't need ten minutes," he said into the mic. "Your daughter is under arrest for murder and will be dealt with accordingly. And the person you refer to as a war criminal has done nothing to warrant that label."

Agent Smith stepped up next to John and just listened.

"Tell him to go pound sand."

John looked at him and smiled. "I'm trying to keep from escalating this into an intergalactic incident."

"Why?" asked Celia. "He's not going to. I'm sure he's hoping you'll tell him to go to Hell. He'll use that as an excuse to start this battle."

John keyed the mic again and said, "After consulting with my advisors, I am going to have to respectfully decline your offer."

"Chicken!"

John looked over his shoulder at Debbie, who had a grin on her face a mile wide. He almost laughed. Almost.

"Hubble coming online, sir," called out Colonel Peters.

The star chart on the screen switched to a small picture in the corner and a large view came on the screen from the Hubble telescope.

"Holy crap!" exclaimed the colonel. "How big is that thing?"

"About five times the size of the smaller ship," said Jaxon. "With the capability of moving a few hundred troops."

Lisa poked him in the ribs and asked, "You sure about those numbers this time?"

He grinned and said, "Hey, Ursula must have had those hunters stacked on top of each other."

Andrakus' ship dwarfed the hunter ship, making it look like a shuttle up next to it. As they watched, a couple of shuttles left the smaller ship and headed for the battle cruiser.

"What are they doing?" asked Lisa.

Celia spoke up and said, "Moving the surviving hunters from Ursula's ship."

After a few minutes, it looked like transferring beings from one ship to the other was complete. Agent Smith looked at the colonel and said, "Fire!"

"What?"

John had a look of fright on his face.

"Just part of the plan, John. Now that we know Ursula's ship is empty, we'll put it to good use."

Colonel Peters was on the phone with someone and said, "The order is given. Fire!"

One second later, a bright flash arced across the screen and slammed into Ursula's ship, which was followed by an enormous explosion. An explosion that happened so close to Andrakus' ship it got knocked sideways.

It slammed one of the shuttles against the side of the battle cruiser and disintegrated in a small puff of an explosion.

"Oops," said Smith. "Didn't mean to kill them like that."

A few in the crowd let out a cheer when they saw the cruiser listing to one side.

"Let's not get ahead of ourselves, folks," said Smith. "I'm sure his ship can take a little more than that."

"Sir, we have a signal coming in," said the colonel.

"Another demand to give up these two women?"

"No sir, this is a video signal."

"Really? Well, let's not keep his majesty waiting. Let's do this face-to-face."

A second later, the Hubble view shrank and took the place of the star chart. The screen was then filled with the image of Andrakus, in all his blue glory. Except, like Celia, he had gone completely purple. His rage was very easy to read.

"How dare you fire on my ship!"

"We didn't fire on your ship," said Smith. "We fired on the empty shell of your daughter's ship after it was vacated. We can't have that space junk floating around up there. Sorry if we put a scratch on your ship."

"Now you shall feel the wrath of the Loirian empire!"

"Empire? We have small cities that have more people in them than your entire civilization. And if you're intending to ray gun us to death, I would advise against it."

"You advise us against it? Let me show you the power of our ship!"

"Don't do it," said Smith rather calmly.

Just then, a flash came from the battle cruiser, followed by another explosion in space, this time from the cruiser.

Andrakus was thrown off his feet and skidded across the floor of his bridge, slamming into the bulkhead.

"I told him not to do it," said Smith as he elbowed John in the arm.

"What did you do?" asked John.

"Just introduced him to some tech we've

been developing. I'd tell you what it is, but then I'd have to … well, you know."

"You're just going to make him more angry," said Jaxon.

"That's the point," said Smith with a wink.

"You want him to get angry?" asked Celia.

"Sure, if he gets mad enough, he's going to make some monumental mistakes. The one mistake I'm hoping he makes is coming down here personally so we can have a chat."

"If he comes down here," said Jaxon, "he'll be bringing about a thousand Loirian soldiers."

"You don't think this town can handle them?"

"Two hunters killed the Godwins and one took down Mabel."

"And how many hunters did your little raiding party take down yesterday?"

"Well, six, but … oh," said Jaxon as he realized what was going on.

"Would you say the hunters are more fearsome than the soldiers or the other way around?"

Jaxon just shrugged, but Celia spoke up.

"The hunters would be more so, because most of them do not operate within any kind of code. They kill just for the pleasure of killing. I can't remember the last time they brought back one of their targets alive. The soldiers, while under the command of Andrakus, are still just ordinary Loirians pressed into service."

Smith thought about that for a second and then turned to the colonel.

"Get word out to our troops that we are to avoid killing any of the Loirian soldiers if possible. Kill them only if lives are threatened."

"Yes, sir," said the colonel as she got on the radio.

They turned their attention back to the screen and Andrakus was picking himself up off the floor, but having to hold on to a console. There was a good thirty degree tilt to the ship because of the blast.

"Hey, Andy," said Smith. "How ya' doing?"

Celia giggled behind him and said, "The last Loirian that called him that lost their head."

Smith smiled at her and said, "That's good to know."

Andrakus clawed his way around the console and got his face right in the camera. There was some blood running down his face from a couple of cuts on his forehead.

"Oooo, you might want to get those wounds looked at," said Smith.

"I shall wear my scars with pride as a reminder of the day I walked across the bones of your people!"

"Can't we just shake hands and call it a day? Come on down and we'll fire up the bar-b-que and discuss this over a couple of cold ones."

"Oh," screamed Andrakus, "I'm coming down and I will personally remove your head!"

Without waiting for a reply, the ruler of Loiria turned and crawled his way off his bridge, leaving a couple of pilots looking at each other and shrugging. They were hanging onto their consoles, trying to get the ship to level out.

Smith turned and looked at the crowd behind him.

"See, mistake. He should never take it so personally that he injects himself into the conflict."

He looked at Lisa and said, "You should get on your town's alert system and let the people know what's coming."

Her eyes went wide and she looked at the sheriff.

"Do we have an alert system for the town?"

"Yes, we do," he said as he walked her over to her desk. "I keep forgetting you're not Mabel."

"I don't know if I'll ever be able to replace her," said Lisa softly.

"Hey," he said as he put a large hand on her shoulder. "We are damn lucky to have you here. Don't you forget that."

Then he got her sat down behind the computer and showed her where the town's website was and the alert page.

"I can assure you, Lisa, every citizen of Prattville is sitting in front of their computers right now, waiting for this alert. Tell them to prepare for battle or to lock themselves in their safe shelters."

"Do they have safe rooms?"

"Of course they do. In a town full of monsters, it's kind of a requirement."

He left her to craft the message any way she saw fit and went back to the screen.

Everyone started getting excited when they saw five smaller vessels come out of the rear of the cruiser and turn and head for Earth.

"Let the games begin," muttered the sheriff.

"Hey, John, it's going to be fun. Trust me."

Everyone watched as the Hubble panned to the left and followed the five shuttles as they approached Earth's atmosphere. The Hubble had to stop when the ships got close to Earth because the brightness of the planet could have fried its mirrors. They replaced its image with an image from a ground-based telescope that was located in ... well, that's top secret.

Debbie saw the strange man in black again, but still couldn't put her finger on what seemed off to her. He was standing near the back of the crowd and watching the events unfolding on the screen.

Every time she thought about going to him and introducing herself, he disappeared and she couldn't find him.

I have more important things to worry about than who this guy is.

Chapter 25 – We Have An Alien Problem

It only took a few minutes for the Loirian ships to arrive over the town of Prattville. It shocked those manning the ships to look through their view screens and see hundreds of town residents standing in the streets and waving at them.

One commander made the mistake of telling Andrakus that maybe they should just go home. The ruler of Loiria wasted no time in running him through with his blade. As the commander lay there dying, Andrakus ordered a couple of soldiers to toss him into the incinerator, even though he was still alive.

The other shuttles set down on the four streets leading to the center of town and Andrakus had his shuttle land right in the middle of town. Right in front of the largest group of townsfolk. They were just standing there waiting for him to land his ship.

He could see Agent Smith standing front and center with his arms crossed in front of him. After the shuttle settled to the ground, he saw the agent wave and smile at him.

His anger was almost to the point of causing his head to explode.

"I am going to stick his head on a pole, right in the middle of this avenue!"

When the ramp went down, the soldiers trooped off and he followed behind them, with his six royal bodyguards around him. When each shuttle emptied, there were a thousand soldiers standing in rank-and-file across each street.

As the ship's troops got lined up across the roads leading into the center of town, John looked around. He wondered if those soldiers would be as confident in the coming battle if they knew most of the people in front of them weren't people at all.

All the monsters were just waiting for something to set the conflict off and then they would change and get their game on. Gerald and Betty were standing in the middle of the Main Street crowd, along with a bunch of other little people. Betty was bouncing up and down on the balls of her feet, ready to sink her teeth into some blue flesh.

Andrakus couldn't believe how calm everyone seemed to be. He thought they should cower in fear of his mighty army.

"I will give you one chance and one chance only," said the ruler of Loiria, "to avoid having your town destroyed and all your citizens crushed under our might. Turn over the war criminal Celia, return my daughter Ursula and any prisoners you may have. Do this and we will leave this planet peacefully."

Agent Smith stepped forward and raised his hand.

"Hey, Andy," said Smith, causing the Loirian to bristle and strengthen his resolve to kill this man. "Agent Martin Smith with the United States government. I'm sorry, but we're going to have to say no can do."

"You would toy with the lives of your people?" roared Andrakus.

"Well, see, the problem is, your niece hates your guts. Her children don't think too highly of you either and would like to see you dead. Your daughter? Well, she caused the deaths of three of our beloved citizens and, well we can't let that go unanswered, so she will stand trial for those crimes."

"So, you are choosing war!"

Agent Smith turned and looked at the gathered crowd and asked, "Anyone here want to give in to Andy's demands?"

"NO!" was the thunderous response from the crowd.

He turned back to Andrakus and smiled.

"Now, you were so kind to give us the opportunity to avoid this battle, which I guess we will not take, so I'd like to extend to you the same courtesy. Take your troops, get back on your ship and leave this planet and never come back. And you get to live."

Andrakus raised his hand and barked an order and all the soldiers snapped to attention, charged their space weapons and prepared for battle. All their silver space suits shimmered as their personal force fields activated. The energy coming from the alien troops caused a bit of static electricity in the air. Everyone could feel the hairs on their bodies standing on end.

"Okay," said Smith, rather nonchalantly. "Corporal Melton!"

An army corporal came running through the crowd, carrying a small device that looked like a miniature rocket. He set it on the ground with the pointy end up, flipped a switch and then handed a small remote to the agent.

"What are you doing?" bellowed Andrakus.

"Oh, just leveling the playing field," said Smith as he held up the remote and pressed the button.

The small rocket shot off the ground and when it reached an altitude of about two hundred feet, it exploded with a blinding flash. A loud boom echoed across the sky and then ... nothing.

"Is that the best you got?" laughed Andrakus.

"Oh Andy, that's just the beginning. You should check with your troops before you give the order to attack."

The evil grin on Andrakus' face faded as he looked behind. All of his troops were pounding on their weapons, pressing buttons inside their helmets and looking genuinely afraid.

"Sir, our weapons are now inoperable," said one commander. "Our protective shields are also down."

"What have you done?" yelled Andrakus.

"Oh, it's just a little toy we call a localized EMP. It knocked out every electronic gizmo within a couple of miles of here. Which means your weapons are useless."

"That would also make your weapons useless."

"Really?"

John stepped up beside him, leaned over and said, "Yes, really."

Agent Smith just smiled at him, pulled his 9mm pistol from his shoulder holster, pointed without looking and squeezed the trigger. The bullet slammed into the kneecap of one of Andrakus' body guards sending him to the ground in agony.

"Nope," said Smith. "Seems to work just fine."

"You realize none of our electronic weapons will work either," said Debbie.

"Yes, but your regular guns will. Besides, I'm guessing most of the town's residents don't need electronics to do their thing."

Jake and Randy both growled, standing directly behind the sheriff. Both were still in human form, with their clubs dragging on the ground. Smith smiled at them.

"Would you two like to show our visitors what they have to look forward to?"

"With pleasure," said Jake as he shouldered his way past the sheriff.

Debbie reached out and grabbed Randy by the arm and said, "Try not to kill anyone yet."

"No promises, deputy."

The Johnson boys stepped to a spot about ten yards in front of Andrakus, their clubs raking along the ground behind them.

"You really should leave," growled Jake.

"I don't think we'll be going anywhere," growled Andrakus back at him. "Are you the best they have?"

"Oh, no," said Randy, "we're just the beginning of your nightmare."

Then the two brothers bumped shoulders and changed right in front of the emperor and his troops. The effect was everything they could have hoped for. Some soldiers turned and ran right back up into the shuttle, though they weren't going anywhere, with all the electronics on the ship still out of commission. Those that remained started backing up.

When Jake took a step toward Andrakus, his bodyguards moved to intercept him and it was the last mistake they would make. He swung his club with all the gusto of a major league baseball player and sent two of them flying. One landed on the roof of the shuttle while the other one skidded across the ground, ending up underneath the engine bells in the back.

Randy came around his brother and backhanded two more bodyguards, leaving just one to protect the ruler. When they took a step toward him, he cowered in fear and Andrakus shoved him forward and into their clutches.

Randy just grabbed him by the front of his suit and tossed him over his head like a sack of potatoes. He landed in a heap at the feet of Agent Smith and the sheriff. Corporal Melton jumped down and secured the alien with a zip-tie around his wrists.

As the brothers began moving toward Andrakus, he produced a Rocun blade from under his cloak and extended it. It horrified him to find out it was nothing more than a blade on a staff. The life-energy sucking capabilities were not working, like every other weapon they brought.

There was a commotion behind them and when the brothers turned to see what it was, Andrakus stabbed Randy in the shoulder. As Randy roared in pain, Jake swung around and saw his brother with a blade stuck in him and it made him madder than hell. He balled up his fist and connected with a roundhouse punch, sending the ruler of Loiria flying and slamming into one of the landing gear struts of his ship. Andrakus crumpled to the ground like a wet towel.

As they were dealing with him, some hunters, who had come down on the other shuttles, started their own minor battles with the townsfolk. Rocun blades came out and they were wading into the crowd, slashing and slicing. Though they weren't having much luck getting their blades on anyone, they still caused a bit of panic in the townsfolk.

Jaxon pulled his blade from his belt and went to

charge into the fracas, but Debbie grabbed him and held him back.

"Get back here!" she yelled at him.

"I will not let any of these people be killed by these hunters!"

She had a firm grip on the back of his collar and pulled him back, even though he struggled to get free. He was no match for his big sister, even though she was a good foot shorter than him.

"They don't need your help! Just stay back, bro. They might tear into you!"

He stopped struggling for a moment and looked to see she was right. Every monster had changed into whatever form they possessed and was having their way with the hunters.

The goblins appeared to be having the most fun. They looked like a bunch of little chainsaws going through the hunters, tearing pieces out of each one they could get their claws on.

A few of the braver soldiers waded into the fight to help the hunters, but found no success at all. Werewolves were pouncing on them and gargoyles were using them in games of tug-o-war.

Billy Ray was even taking part, glad about not having to worry about Debbie throwing him in jail again. His fangs proved to be just as deadly as any weapon the alien soldiers could bring to bear.

There was even a wendigo laughing every time a soldier stabbed him with their blade; just before he smashed him on the top of his head, trying to drive him into the ground like a nail.

A large brown, grizzly bear and Bengal tiger were rampaging through a platoon of soldiers, sending them flying in every direction. Buttercup and Billy Ray got into an argument over one soldier and ended up with each only getting half. Then they spent the next few seconds growling at each other until Dean, the bear, cuffed Buttercup upside the head and told him to knock it off.

At that moment, one hunter grabbed two small children by the backs of their jackets and held them up high.

"Cease all hostilities or I will kill these two young ones!"

The fighting stopped as everyone in the mob turned to look at the hunter. One goblin walked over to the hunter and looked up at him.

"Only a coward Commie would hide behind a face mask and use children as a shield," he growled.

The hunter looked down at the short goblin in front of him and then at the crowd. He couldn't understand why no one was begging him to spare the lives of these two little ones.

"Sissy! Tommy!" yelled the goblin. "Join the fight!"

Within seconds, the hunter found himself holding two snarling young goblins and they started sinking their teeth into his hands and arms. Before he got away from them, their mother and father joined in his dismemberment.

The last thing they heard from the hunter was a screech in pain and one goblin yelling, "This blue blood is nasty!"

Fighting resumed, but it was plain the soldiers of Loiria were thinking this was a huge mistake. Some crept back up the ramps to their shuttles, hoping no one would notice them and they could hide from the horror unfolding before their eyes.

Two commanders stopped them from hiding on the ships, forcing them back to the battle. They even executed a couple of them to get their message across.

When Chief Handley saw that, something inside him snapped and he shot one of the commanders between the eyes. When the other Loirian soldiers saw the Earth man fighting for them, they killed the other commander and then retreated into their shuttle, never to join the battle again.

For a while, it looked like the aliens were going to have a rough day and be sent home with their tails between their legs.

Sometimes appearances can be deceiving.

Chapter 26 – Chopping Down A Tree

As the fighting continued and seem to get worse, no one was paying attention to Andrakus and his bodyguards. After the guards could stand up again, they helped their leader to his feet and he fought to clear the cobwebs from his head.

Randy was tending to Jake's stab wound, along with Kelly. At the same time. John and Celia were trying to keep Debbie and Jaxon corralled and away from the action. Much to Debbie's displeasure.

"Stand down, deputy!" yelled John. "Let the townsfolk have their fun."

"But sheriff, we're part of the townsfolk," she yelled back at him.

Some movement caught her eye and she saw a soldier run down the ramp from the ship and went straight to Andrakus. The soldier pointed toward the burned out sheriff's department building and Andrakus began waving toward it.

"Uh, dad. Something's going on."

A group of six soldiers and two bodyguards started toward the building and it took John about two seconds to realize what they were doing.

"They've figured out where Ursula is," he said to Debbie.

He pulled his gun and began sprinting

toward the building, with Debbie right on his heels. As they got closer, he fired a shot over the heads of the soldiers. The two body guards stopped and faced the two incoming law enforcement officers, showing they were ready to take on the threat.

Two soldiers disappeared down the steps in the back of the burned out building and the others joined the guards. One guard pulled his blade and it snapped open just as John fired another shot.

However, firing a pistol while running is never a straightforward thing and the shot went wide, hitting one soldier behind the guard in the face mask. He dropped like a rock.

Before the sheriff could fire another shot, the guard stepped forward and stabbed at him, just barely missing a strike at his chest. But it was close enough to slice across the top of his shoulder and knock John off his feet.

Debbie fired and because of her police and military training, it was a direct hit, center mass. None of this *shoot them in the leg* nonsense. The guard fell backwards like a tree falling in the forest and his blade skittered away.

The second guard jumped forward and raised his blade to drive it into the sheriff's gut as he was down. Debbie tried to get another shot off, but got knocked to the ground herself by something big and hairy jumping past her.

A loud growl hit her ears and a squeal of

terror came from the guard as a werewolf barreled into him, taking him to the ground and ripping his throat out.

Debbie jumped up and pointed her gun at the soldiers, who just put their hands up and backed away. She wasn't sure if it was her gun that caused them to move back or the large werewolf staring them down like a bunch of steaks.

"Get him out of here," growled the werewolf over its shoulder.

As Debbie pulled her dad to his feet, she said, "Thanks, Billy Ray."

As she helped her dad back to the middle of the street, Billy Ray backed up, keeping his eyes on the soldiers, none of which were too keen on trying anything. It was probably the sight of the two dead guards on the ground in front of them that took the fight out of them. One missing his throat.

As she turned the sheriff over to Kelly and other medical personnel for treatment, Debbie turned back around and looked at the building. The two soldiers that had gone downstairs came back up with Ursula in tow and they guarded her back to the ship.

"Oh, that's not good," mumbled Debbie.

"No, it's not," said Celia, stepping up behind her daughter.

"We could have done without having both leaders able to lead their fight."

"No, sweetie, I meant it's not good for her."

Agent Smith stepped up beside them and said, "I can take her out if you like."

He was holding his 9mm pistol in the ready position, just waiting for the okay.

"That won't be necessary, agent," said Celia.

They watched as the small group reached the ship and Andrakus looked at his daughter. Then, to everyone's surprise, except for Celia, the leader of Loiria pulled his blade and stabbed his daughter right through the chest. She never cried out or begged for mercy. She died like she knew she had it coming.

"Good God!" exclaimed Smith as he fired a shot at Andrakus.

One guard jumped in front of the bullet and died thinking he was a hero for defending the ruler of Loiria. The truth was the ruler of Loiria didn't know his name and didn't care one way or another about him.

Agent Smith went to fire again, but one of the remaining guards grabbed a soldier by the back of his suit and held him in front of Andrakus, giving Smith no target.

Debbie reached up and put a hand on his wrist and said, "Don't."

As he lowered his weapon, they could see the fear on the face of the soldier and then the relief that Smith wouldn't shoot him.

"Corporal Melton!"

The corporal came running through the

crowd and straight to Agent Smith.

"Yes, sir?"

"Are the drones back up and running yet?"

"Only a couple of them. We had them shielded from the blast. We're still working on the rest, repairing circuit boards."

"I only need one," said Smith, "with about two pounds of C4 and a remote."

The corporal got on the radio and within seconds, a second corporal ran up with a radio control and handed it to Melton. He handed a small remote to the agent and then high-tailed it back to the army's holding area.

A second later, Debbie heard a buzzing over her head and looked up to see a small drone hovering over them, with a block of C4 attached to its bottom.

Agent Smith looked at the corporal and said, "Right up the ramp, corporal."

"Yes, sir," said Melton as he pushed a couple of levers forward on the control panel and the drone shot toward the alien ship.

As it flew past the alien soldiers and Andrakus, they tried to bat at it with their blades, but they all missed. The drone disappeared up into the ship, leaving Andrakus wondering what was coming next.

"You should have taken my offer, Andy," yelled Smith.

A couple of soldiers came running down the ramp as fast as they could before Smith held up the remote in his hand and pressed the button. They heard a loud explosion from inside the ship and it rocked back and forth on its landing struts. Black smoke poured out of the opening and drifted up into the afternoon sky.

The look on Andrakus' face was a mix of anger and fear. It was finally dawning on him these humans were more than up to the task of fighting back.

Now his shuttle sat destroyed in the middle of this nightmare of a town.

As he was trying to figure out his next move, they heard a loud screeching from the main part of the battle. A screeching so horrendous and ear-splitting, it stopped all fighting in the middle of town.

Everyone swung around to see what was happening and it was a sight that would live in the nightmares of all that saw it.

Especially Jaxon.

A large hunter, easily as big as the Johnson boys when they weren't ogres, was standing in the middle of the intersection with his blade held high. What was terrifying was the small goblin impaled on the blade he held over his head.

Jaxon felt the breath get knocked out of his chest when he realized it was the little goblin girl that had marked his suit to keep him from getting eaten. As she screeched in her death throes, the entire crowd backed away.

The hunter reached up and clicked a couple of latches on his helmet, lifted it off and dropped it to the ground.

"Mellock," gasped Jaxon.

"Is there no one that can stand against me?" Mellock raged at the crowd.

As the little goblin hung limp on the blade, Randy stepped forward, ready to beat this hunter into the next millennium. He had no love for the goblins himself, but for one so big to kill one so small wasn't something he was willing to stand for.

Before he could take up the challenge, Jaxon stepped forward and told him to stand back.

"I got this, bro," said Jaxon.

"You sure?" growled Randy.

"Very."

Lisa stepped forward and said, "You get yourself killed and I'll never speak to you again."

He smiled at her and took off the black suit coat he was wearing and handed it to her. Corporal Melton came running up and handed a Rocun blade to him.

"I think we got it fixed, but with it being alien … well … who knows?"

"I'm sure it will be fine," he said to the corporal.

Debbie was trying to get to him, to keep him from fighting the big hunter, but Celia had a firm hold on her arm. Celia leaned in and said, "Let him do this. He may just surprise you."

"Oh good lord, no," stammered John as he saw what was happening and struggled to his feet. Celia motioned for Kelly to keep hold of him.

Jaxon leaned over and gave Lisa a kiss on the cheek and said, "Don't worry."

Jaxon turned and stepped into the middle of the intersection and stared Mellock down. The big hunter just sneered at him, being at least a foot taller than him. He swung his blade and the goblin slid off and landed near the feet of Jaxon. A couple of other goblins ran forward and gathered up her body.

"Ah, the half-blood whelp of that disgusting Loirian female. I shall enjoy killing you."

"You'll enjoy trying," said Jaxon, as he watched the little goblin being carried away. "You never should have killed one of my friends."

"By the time I'm finished, I will lay waste to this entire village," crowed Mellock.

Jaxon took a couple of steps forward and brought his blade up and extended it. He smiled with a bit of satisfaction when the slight hum emanated from the blade and he could feel the energy prickling at his skin.

A look of concern crossed Mellock's face. Obviously, his blade was still just a blade. His face grew darker though, when he looked at Jaxon and realized he was more than a match for this small half-human, half-Loirian.

Jaxon twirled his blade in his hands, the sound of its energized edge singing through the air. His eyes never left the hunter's as they began circling each other. Jaxon's movements with the blade were elegant and precise. It was clear someone had well schooled him in the blade's use.

Mellock swished his blade back and forth and it was clear he was more of a smash and slash type of bladesman.

With a quick lunge, Mellock stabbed at Jaxon, but found his strike was batted away with no problem. Keeping the momentum of the blade moving, he brought it back up and around, straight at Jaxon's head. He found nothing but air. Jaxon had gone to his knees and rolled to the side.

Jaxon came up and slashed his blade across the back of Mellock's right knee, bringing a grunt of pain from the hunter. As Mellock hobbled backwards, Jaxon twirled the blade again, showing he was ready to continue the fight.

"I certainly hope you are not ready to surrender," said Jaxon.

"It is just a scratch," growled Mellock.

"I'm going to take you apart, one scratch at a time."

Mellock regained his composure, shutting out the pain in his leg and began moving easily again. One thing he couldn't ignore was the loss of energy he had suffered when the blade cut through his skin. Somehow, the humans had figured out how to repair the Rocun blade and that was his disadvantage.

A slight commotion occurred just outside the gathering and Jaxon spared a glance to see that some of the Loirian soldiers were getting brave and trying to come to Mellock's defense. They were thwarted when the mysterious man in black appeared in front of them. Black wings unfolded from his back and a roar issued from his mouth. It was probably the four-inch fangs that caused the soldiers to back up.

"A vampire," gasped Debbie under her breath. She didn't recognize him. With the loss of Stefan and Milly recently, he didn't match either of the two vampires she knew still lived in Prattville.

Mellock roared, "I have no need of your help! Stand down!"

The Loirian soldiers backed off to let the hunter deal with the problem on his own. Of course, if asked, none of the alien soldiers really cared for the hunters, anyway.

Mellock slashed forward and Jaxon blocked the attack, but the bigger hunter was much stronger than him. He definitely felt the power of the attack when the shafts of their blades slammed together. It almost drove him to his knees.

As he stumbled backward, Mellock went on

the offensive and drove him back on his heels. Jaxon tripped and fell back and into the arms of Carrie, who raised her hand and cast a spell that drove Mellock back a few steps.

"I can end him right here, right now," she said. "All you have to do is give the word."

Jaxon smiled at her as he gathered himself and said, "If he kills me, you can tear him apart."

"Please don't let that happen. Lisa would never recover."

Jaxon looked across the open space and saw Lisa standing there, her hands in front of her mouth, looking terrified her new boyfriend was going to be killed right in front of her. He gave her a quick smile as he stepped toward Mellock, twirling his blade in his hands.

"You really should lay your weapon down," he said to the hunter.

Mellock sneered at him and said, "You underestimate your skills, little one. It will be my pleasure to kill you in front of your friends and family."

Jaxon shrugged and said, "Okay. Just remember, I gave you a chance."

He lunged forward, his blade aimed directly at Mellock's gut, which got deflected easily. The hunter swirled his blade through the air, sending Jaxon's blade well away from him and also spinning the half-breed's body around.

In any other situation, this may have proved

fatal for Jaxon, except it was exactly what he had intended. As he spun, he dropped to one knee and his entire body twirled around that point with such speed, it caught Mellock off-guard.

As Mellock's blade swished over his head, missing by mere inches, Jaxon's blade came slashing around and sliced across the backs of both the hunter's knees. The sound of ripping fabric was accompanied with the sight of blue blood pouring out of the gash in the space suit.

With a roar of pain, Mellock stumbled backward, trying to keep his feet under him. He found his legs would not support him much longer. With one desperate move, he tried to slash at Jaxon's head, but the son of his hated enemy just sliced his hands off at the wrists.

The severed hands fell to the ground with the blade clattering across the asphalt. Jaxon bent down and picked up the blade and pressed the release and the blade collapsed to its smaller size.

Mellock's legs refused to support his large body any longer and he fell backwards, his head slamming into the pavement. As he shook his head to clear his vision, he saw Jaxon step up to him and look down.

"You can kill me, but know this ... you will always be the disgusting offspring of a traitor to her people."

Jaxon just shook his head and said, "I can live with that. But I have no intention of killing you. Killing you with this blade would cause your energy to become part of me and that's the last thing I want. Besides, that would be an honorable death for a warrior. You deserve no such death."

"Kill me!" bellowed Mellock.

Jaxon stared at him for a moment and then looked at the goblins standing nearby.

"He's all yours."

He turned and walked over to Lisa and smiled.

"Hey beautiful lady."

She threw her arms around his neck and kissed him, causing his mother to just shake her head.

Mellock didn't receive as warm a welcome.

The goblins moved slowly around him as he screamed and begged for mercy. The last thing anyone heard from him was a screech of horror as the goblins jumped on him and began tearing him apart, one piece at a time.

Even more alien soldiers lost the will to fight when they saw parts of the hunter flying through the air. They began dropping their weapons and surrendering to the soldiers of Earth, not wanting to suffer a similar fate.

The story of Mellock, the largest hunter of all time, ended in a puddle of blue goo in the middle of the intersection in a small town in Nebraska known as Monster Town. Or, as the locals would prefer, Prattville.

And the goblins still didn't care for the taste of blue blood.

Chapter 27 – A Trip To Warmer Climes

With the death of Mellock, that left two surviving hunters in the entire galaxy. Well, four if we're counting the two still locked up in the detention cells in the hospital.

Both hunters took up positions near Andrakus, trying to convince him it was time to retreat, but he screamed at them to remember their places.

While Jaxon had battled the big hunter, fighting had come to a standstill in the area. Everyone had been mesmerized by the fight between the two warriors. It would have been better if some had paid attention to what was going on around them.

The last remaining body guard had worked his way forward, with no one noticing him, until he was directly behind Celia and Debbie. Before anyone could react, he slammed his weapon down on the head of Debbie, knocking her to the ground.

Celia didn't have time to react as he grabbed her by the white hair on her head and began dragging her backwards. As she struggled to get free, a couple of werewolves tried to get at them, but the guard brought a dagger to her throat and threatened to kill her if they didn't back off.

Bill and Bobby stopped there, but didn't back off.

Celia tried to pull away, but he had her hair wrapped firmly around his hand and would not let her go. She was his prize to present to the ruler of his world.

Debbie climbed to her feet, rubbing her head and started toward her mother and the guard, but stopped when she saw the dagger.

"You!" the guard commanded, as he pointed to the nearest shuttle that was still operational. "You will follow us into that ship over there and prepare to return to Loiria and stand trial for your crimes!"

"What crime?" she yelled.

"You are an affront to all Loirians! We will put your mother to death for allowing herself to spawn you!"

Debbie could see there was no fear in her mother's eyes. Only anger blazed in her blue eyes, but she was being held in such a position she couldn't fight back or break free.

"Follow us or I will kill her," demanded the guard.

Debbie stopped, straightened up and folded her arms across her chest.

"I'm not going anywhere," she said calmly, "and neither are you."

The guard pressed the point of the dagger into Celia's neck and took a step back.

"Kill her n …," screamed Andrakus, but then stopped as his eyes went big.

"I will kill her right in front of you!" yelled

the guard.

"No … you won't."

He took one more step backwards and bumped up against something.

Something cold and wet pressed against the back of his neck and it felt quite icky. Craning his neck back and up, his eyes caught sight of the largest, blackest beast he had ever seen. Even the Kraynok back home weren't this big. Or scary.

The last thing the guard saw was the mouth of the beast opening and two rows of white teeth clamping down over his head.

The mouth of the beast chomped down hard and the body of the guard fell to the ground. Minus one head. The beast opened its mouth and the head tumbled out. Celia looked down and kicked the head away, leaving it to roll across the ground and come to a stop at the feet of Andrakus.

Debbie walked up to the beast and rubbed her hand over its drooping jowls.

"It's good to see you learned your lesson with the Boogerman, Buster."

Then she kissed him on the nose and said, "You're such a good boy."

She heard a little whimper and turned to see Bosley standing there, looking at her.

"You, too, Bosley," she said as she scratched him behind the ears.

Celia leaned over and ran her fingers

through Debbie's hair and asked, "How's your head, sweetie?"

"Proving dad right again. About being hard-headed, I mean. I'm fine."

Then both women turned and faced Andrakus as Agent Smith stepped up behind them.

"Last chance, Andy," said Smith. "Pack up your troops and go home. I will not warn you again."

Andrakus was seething with anger and the agent could tell he would never give in. He'd rather die on this foreign planet than admit defeat.

The ruler of Loiria spit on the ground at the feet of the ladies and growled, "I will blast this repugnant planet from its place in this system unless both of you walk willingly up that ramp and into the ship."

Smith stepped forward between the two women and placed himself in front of them.

"These ladies are not going anywhere with you. Not now, not ever. If you continue down this road, you will die face-down in the middle of this street."

"I'd rather die …"

Another scream cut through the air, this time a scream of pleading.

Everyone looked over to see one of the last two hunters had grabbed a young girl and was holding her off the ground by the throat. The girl, only about six years old, struggled to breathe, but the hunter didn't seem inclined to let her.

"I tire of this game," growled the hunter from behind his mask. "It ends now unless you follow the instructions of Andrakus, ruler of Loiria!"

Debbie leaned over and whispered in Agent Smith's ear.

"Martin, she is just a normal human girl. She's not a monster in any way."

Smith raised his gun and pointed it at the head of the hunter, but he kept the little girl directly in his line of fire. He had no shot and couldn't take it. It almost caused him to have an emotion as he watched the little girl struggling to breathe.

Almost, but he didn't have time to form one.

It is said that the bullet from a high-powered sniper rifle travels at more than twice the speed of sound. That means the bullet will hit its target before the sound of the shot is heard.

There really was nothing more than a *zzzziiiifff!* heard before the hunter's head exploded in a blue mist. For a second, he stood there, still clutching the little girl, but then she fell from his grasp, landing on her feet. The hunter's body toppled backwards, slamming to the ground in front of Andrakus.

When the little girl looked at all the blue goo on her arms, she wailed, "Ewwww!"

Her grandmother, a ghostly apparition, floated forward and grabbed her by the ear.

"I told you to stay home, young lady!"

"But, nana! I wanted to see the aliens!" she squealed as her grandma hauled her away from the scene.

Cal, who was standing guard over the sheriff, looked over his shoulder toward some buildings a hundred yards away and said, "I guess we know where Chester is."

The sheriff tried to push himself to stand up, but Cal pushed him back down.

"Stay down, John. Things look to be going fine without you."

Back at the point of confrontation, Andrakus was still defiant in his desire to take his niece and her kids aboard the shuttle and leave Earth. He lunged forward when Agent Smith was busy watching the child-attacking hunter.

Ramming a dagger into Smith's side, he reached out and grabbed the pistol from his hand and stepped back. Agent Smith dropped to the ground, gasping for breath, as Debbie whirled around and came face-to-face with the agent's 9mm pistol.

"Now, I will only say this one time," growled Andrakus, "you, your brother and your mother will get on that shuttle and return to Loiria with me and stand trial for your crimes! Any hesitation and I will use this primitive weapon to take your life from you!"

Celia stepped forward, placing herself in front of Debbie and looked straight down the barrel of the gun.

"My children are not going anywhere with you. You can take me, but I am the only one that will leave here."

They heard a body hit the ground and turned to see Kelly holding Agent Smith and working to stop his bleeding. His face had gone white and there was an enormous pool of blood on the surrounding ground.

"I need to get him to the hospital or he could die," said Kelly to Debbie.

"If he dies, he dies," growled Andrakus. "Makes no difference to me. No one moves until the three of you get on the shuttle. Then I'll have to decide if I should turn this disgusting planet into a dust cloud."

He stepped forward and grabbed Celia by the front of her shirt and pulled her close.

"You have been a problem for me for far too long. It is about to end."

"You're not taking my children!"

"You are not in a position to argue with me, Celia," he screamed, spit hitting her in the face.

"But I am, father."

He turned his head just in time to see the last hunter, a small female, slam her blade into his side. As the blade sliced into his body, his grip on Celia relaxed and the gun fell from his hand.

Nyssa used the blade to back him up a couple of steps as he fought for breath.

"I have wished for a very long time for you to change your ways," she said, as her face shield opened. "I have hoped you would become a more caring, loving leader of your people. But I can see now my hopes and wishes have been wasted."

Andrakus gasped for breath.

"I am your father," croaked the old, blue man, as he remained impaled on her blade.

"Something I have become increasingly ashamed of," she said with sadness in her eyes.

As Andrakus struggled to remain alive, a large brown dog moved up in front of him and stared him in the eyes. The ruler of Loiria became terrified when the dog's eyes blazed red and its fangs were bared.

"Release him, Nyssa," said Celia.

"As you wish," said the young hunter, as she pulled the blade back.

Andrakus fell to his knees, clutching at his side, trying to stop the bleeding. The dog stepped forward, growling in the face of the alien ruler.

"I shall return," gasped Andrakus, looking up at Celia.

"I don't think so," said Celia. "This is Bosley and he is a Hell hound. He is about to take you and present you to his master. I'm not sure if you've ever heard of his master, but his name is

Lucifer. He's going to love you."

Andrakus looked at Bosley and his face went from blue to white as he looked at the foot-long fangs appearing from the dog's mouth.

"Mercy," gasped Andrakus.

Celia leaned over, looked him in the face and said, "Save it for Lucifer. Bosley!"

The Hell hound lunged forward and grabbed Andrakus by one of his arms and began dragging him down the street. Buster stepped forward to chase after them, but stopped when Bosley disappeared into the darkness with his prize.

The large black dog sat down on his haunches and whimpered, looking back and forth for his buddy.

Celia stepped up beside him and rubbed the side of his face.

"He'll be back, Buster. Just give him a moment."

Buster whined and laid down in the middle of the road and laid his head down on his paws.

"Your highness."

Celia turned around to see one of the captains of the Loirian military standing there. Debbie and Jaxon stepped up next to her.

"We know you are the rightful heir to the throne of Loiria," said the captain. "We should have fought for you sooner and for our lack of courage, we can only ask for your forgiveness."

"There is no need for forgiveness, captain."

"Please return to Loiria with us and take up your rightful place as our leader."

Celia smiled at him and then looked at her two children.

"Captain, my rightful place is right here beside my children and my husband. I have been away from two of them for far too long."

"But Loiria needs a ruler. One with courage and love for the people."

"Of that, you are correct," she said. "There is another who will be much better for this position. One that I am sure will fulfill those requirements you just named."

She stepped over and put her arm around Nyssa, walking her back over and in front of the captain.

Looking at the captain, Celia said, "My first and last edict as ruler of Loiria is that you swear allegiance to Nyssa, promising to protect her and get her safely back to Loiria."

The captain straightened up and nodded toward Nyssa.

"Your highness, it will be my solemn duty and the duty of this army, to protect you and deliver you back to our home world."

Nyssa reached up and released a couple of latches on her helmet and lifted it off her head. She handed the helmet to the captain.

"Please prepare our troops for departure and ready the shuttles to leave this planet."

He bowed to her and spun on his heels and

headed for the troops, giving orders for them to retreat to the shuttles.

Nyssa turned to Celia and her eyes were growing misty.

"I don't know if I have it in me, cousin. To rule over the people of Loiria, I'm not sure what I'm supposed to do."

Celia leaned forward and kissed the younger Loirian on the forehead.

"You will know what to do, Nyssa. First thing, when you get back to Loiria, find the remaining members of the Council and learn from them. They will guide you. Second, trust your instincts. I know you. You're a good person."

Nyssa wrapped her arms around her cousin and gave her a big hug.

As she pulled away, she said, "Goodbye, Celia. I hope we meet again."

She turned and looked at Debbie and Jaxon and smiled.

"I wish I had time to get to know the two of you. I think we could have been friends."

Debbie stepped forward and put her arms around the new ruler of Loiria and hugged her.

"We already are friends," she said into her ear. "Come back and visit anytime you want."

A couple of Loirian soldiers came running over and took up positions on each side of Nyssa. Apparently, they were her new bodyguards.

"You look after her," said Debbie, eyeing each one. "Don't make me come after you."

What passed for eyebrows were raised on each soldier's face.

"Yes, ma'am," said both in unison.

Nyssa smiled at her extended family and turned to head for the shuttle. Suddenly, she found her way blocked by one of the government agents.

"I'm sorry, but I can't let you leave. Being the new ruler of Loiria, you will need to answer for the crimes that occurred here."

Debbie stepped in front of the agent as Agent Smith croaked, "Agent Taylor, stand down!"

"I will not, sir! This has gotten too far out of hand and it seems you are incapable of doing what needs to be done."

"I would advise you to back off, agent," said Smith from the gurney they had placed him on.

"You should listen to him," said Debbie, who stood a full head shorter than Taylor.

She glanced over and saw Billy Ray standing there, wearing a bright pair of red Spandex shorts, looking like he wished he had a bucket of popcorn for the coming show.

She looked back at Taylor and said, "Back off!"

Taylor poked a finger into her shoulder and said, "Look, little lady. I don't take orders from you and you'll be lucky if I don't round up this entire town."

Then, his face went white as a sheet as she grabbed his finger and bent it backwards. If that had been the extent of it, he might have gotten away with nothing more than a missing finger.

She grabbed a handful of G-Man shirt with her other hand, lifted him off the ground and body slammed him face-down into the pavement.

If that hadn't been enough to drive the breath from his lungs, her knee coming down in the middle of his back certainly was. She grabbed one arm and slapped handcuffs around the wrist and then grabbed the other arm and finished the job.

She stood up and looked at Agent Smith who just gave her a wry grin.

"He's new. He'll learn."

"Yeah, if he lives long enough."

"Deputy," groaned the sheriff, "if you're finished playing with the agent, could you and Cal look after the rest of the townsfolk?"

"Sure, daddy ... I mean, sheriff."

Nyssa looked at Debbie and said, "You still have two of ours locked up?"

"Uh, yes we do."

"They are the last two hunters in the entire galaxy. I shall have no need of their services anymore," said Nyssa. Then she nodded toward Agent Taylor and said, "When you allow him up, you can turn those two over to him."

Debbie smiled and thanked her. The two soldiers then guided her away and toward one of the shuttles.

Debbie and Jaxon walked away with Cal to check on the others, while Celia walked over to her husband's side. He was lying on a gurney next to Agent Smith. She reached down and ran a hand over the side of his face and kissed him on the lips.

"Mind if I stick around for a while?" she asked.

He smiled and said, "I was kind of hoping you might."

Kelly stepped up and said, "Okay, I gotta get these two knuckleheads to the hospital."

"Knuckleheads?" said Smith.

"You got yourselves stabbed!" she said in exasperation.

"If memory serves me correctly," said John, "so did your brother."

"Oh, I haven't forgotten," said Kelly as she morphed into a large ogre. "And I will be the nurse to the three of you!"

"Oh gawd," whimpered John.

"Help!"

They all turned and saw Taylor still laying on the ground with his arms handcuffed behind his back. A little wiener dog was peeing on him.

"Buster!" yelled Bill as he charged over. "That is not funny!"

Buster just looked up at him and yipped one

time.

"Okay, it was a little funny. Now stop it!"

Just then, there was a flash of light and a crack of thunder that caused everyone to jump. Bosley came bounding out of the portal, his fur smoking as if he had been some place extremely hot. Buster ran over to him, yipping that he was glad to see he was back. The two of them bounced around each other like a couple of kids.

Colonel Peters came around the ambulance as Agent Smith was being loaded.

"Sir, the alien crew is saying their shuttles may not fly after that EMP. They are asking for our help."

"Colonel," said Smith, "I leave that in your capable hands. Give them all the help they need to fix their ships and head home."

"Yes, sir," she said as she hustled away.

As John and Agent Smith were loaded into the ambulance and driven away, the town's residents began clearing away debris. Some began drifting back to their homes. Cal, Jaxon and Lisa moved through the people, checking to see if anyone needed any help.

Debbie needed to see someone else. She walked across one corner and straight up to the tall vampire.

"Hi, my name is Deputy Debbie," she said, holding out her hand. "I know of the other two vampires here in town, but I don't believe we've met."

He looked down at her and smiled.

"My name is Voltar," he said as he took her hand, raised it to his lips and kissed it. "I believe you knew my brother, Stefan."

When she heard that, she gasped, felt her knees go weak and then she lunged at Voltar and wrapped her arms around him. And started crying. Not knowing how to handle this, he just held her close.

"I was so sorry to hear about Stefan. He wasn't just a good vampire, he was a good man and a good friend."

"That he was," said Voltar, with a hint of sadness in his voice. "but don't cry for him. He has been reunited with his love. Your friend, Julie, also couldn't stop crying over losing him."

"You've seen Julie? How is she?" she asked, her voice muffled against his chest.

"Last I saw, she was being rushed out of Romania, having received some bad news from home. What news, I can't say."

She pulled back and looked up at him. "I'll have to go over there and find out what's happening."

"Hey deputy. New friend?"

She turned to see Tom walking up, followed closely by Chester, carrying a huge rifle and smeared with camouflage paint. She wiped her eyes and stepped back and introduced them to Voltar.

Then she looked at Chester and said, "Nice

shootin', Tex."

He just smiled and shrugged.

So ended the great, intergalactic battle in the streets of Monster Town. It was funny that no one outside of Prattville heard a thing about it, though there were rumors all over the internet about something having happened there. Very few of the conspiracy theory-loving people out there believed the story about a chemical leak for one second.

Chapter 28 – The After Action Report

It didn't take long for Prattville to return to normal. Within a week, they cleared all evidence of the alien invasion and local businesses were open and welcoming to all.

Debbie jumped in her Blazer the next day and pointed herself east, heading for the big city and answers to what was happening with Julie. If she expected to find answers, she was going to be disappointed. Father Dooley told her nothing other than Julie was on a mission for the church. But one thing he couldn't hide was the fear in his voice and eyes.

She ended up returning to Prattville with a large ache in her soul, knowing Julie was in trouble and there was nothing she could do about it.

A battalion of army engineers descended on the town and began reconstructing the sheriff's department, promising to have it finished within four weeks. It was going to be nicer and more modern, much to the displeasure of one certain sheriff.

"I liked things just the way they were," he pouted, sitting in his chair behind his desk at the community center.

"Oh, daddy," said Debbie as she put her arms around him from behind, "it will do you good to step into the 21st century."

"Doesn't mean I have to like it."

They heard the door to the center open and the sound of women's shoes walking across the floor. They could see Lisa jump up from her seat behind her desk.

"Good afternoon, young lady!"

Lisa said, "It's good to see you back and on your feet."

"Did they release that old bat today?" said John loud enough for anyone within a mile to hear.

The old bat stepped in the office's door and said, "Watch it, young man or I'll pull your arms off!"

"I thought you were dead, you mean old woman!"

"You wish!" said Mabel.

Debbie laughed, walked over and put her arms around Mabel and gave her a hug.

"It's good to see you up and around."

"It's good to be out of that hellhole of a hospital," she said. "That Kelly is a right pain in the ass when you're under her care."

"Tell me about it," muttered John.

"How are you feeling, sheriff?"

"A little sore," said John, as he rolled his shoulder around. "I didn't get hurt nearly as bad as you."

"You didn't come to visit me in the hospital."

"They wouldn't let me in! Said I'd probably catch something from you."

Debbie giggled and said, "I think it was the other way around, dad."

She leaned over and kissed Mabel on the cheek and said, "He tried to get in to see you, but Kelly went full ogre on him and almost threw him out."

Lisa stepped to the door and leaned against the frame.

"So, I guess you'll be ..."

"No, I won't," said Mabel. "The job is yours now, sweetie. From what Kelly has told me, you fit right in here."

"You're not coming back to work?" asked Debbie.

"No, darlin'," she said. Then, looking at the sheriff, she said, "Consider this my resignation."

"What are you going to do with yourself if you can't terrorize me?" asked John.

"Well, first, I'm going on vacation. I'm heading down to Cabo to spend some time on the beach and get some sun. I'll have cute brown boys bring me drinks with little umbrellas in them. After that, I don't have a clue."

"Just don't eat any of those boys," said the sheriff out the side of his mouth.

"Daddy! She hasn't eaten anyone in what? Twenty years?"

Mabel poked her in the ribs and said, "You're getting to be too much like your dad."

"I'll take that as a compliment. Hey, Thanksgiving dinner tomorrow night at mom and dad's house. You going to be there?"

"Wouldn't miss it."

Thanksgiving night came and it was a full house. A lot more people crammed under one roof than they designed it for. And a couple of dogs, one of which was under orders to maintain his small size, lest he bring the aforementioned roof down on their heads.

The hell hound was curled up near the fireplace, snoring loudly and enjoying a moment of peace. Bill was sitting on the couch with the wiener dog laying across his lap.

John and Bill spent a considerable amount of time trying to explain the intricacies of American football to Jaxon. Most of it flew right over the young half-Loirian's head, causing the sheriff to whine to his wife about not teaching their son about the important things in life.

Most of it was lost on Jaxon, not because he wasn't interested, but because he had most of his attention focused on the beautiful young lady helping Celia in the kitchen.

"So, mom, have you heard anything from Nyssa?" asked Debbie.

"Heard from her this afternoon. Thanks for giving me back the remote to my ship, by the way. The radio allows me to keep in contact with Loiria."

"You're welcome. What did she say?"

"Said things are changing back home and for the better. Though it's still not a very hospitable place to live, she says the people are becoming more relaxed since her father is now out of the way."

Lisa spoke up and said, "I wonder how Andrakus is doing? It can't be too much fun where he is now."

"Lisa," said Celia, "he was my uncle and I am not losing any sleep worrying about how he's doing. You shouldn't worry about it either."

Lisa just bit her lips and nodded.

"Well, I have some news," said Debbie. "I've been talking with Agent Smith and he says there may be a way to offer the people of Loiria a home here. He's looking into finding a place where we can stick a couple million Loirians where they could have their own society and get off that planet."

Jaxon wandered into the kitchen and reached past Lisa to grab a handful of chips.

"They wouldn't even need to find a place here," he said, popping a chip into his mouth.

"What do you mean?" asked Debbie.

"The Loirians would be good at colonizing just about anywhere. They could set up a small city on the far side of the moon. Even Mars would be a good choice."

"So, why haven't they done it before now?" asked Lisa. "I mean, it's obvious they can travel the galaxy. Why stay there?"

"Andrakus, my beautiful sweetheart," he said as he kissed her cheek. "He knew if they left Loiria and life became easier for the people, they might rise up against him. Keeping them living in fear and under such horrid conditions allowed him to keep control."

"That is just so wrong," mused Lisa.

"I'll talk to Martin tomorrow," said Debbie. "Though it would be awkward to put them on Mars when we have billionaires setting their sights on colonizing that planet themselves."

An enormous roar went up in the living room as Bill and John screamed at the television.

"That was the worst call I have ever seen!" yelled Bill.

Buster ran over to the TV and began yipping at the referees on the screen. When Bosley raised his head and barked, it shook the walls and rattled the windows.

"Go back to sleep, Boz," said Bill.

Bosley laid his head back down and was snoring within seconds.

Just then, the doorbell rang and the door opened, with no one moving to it. When Mabel walked in, accompanied by Cal, Celia dried her blue hands as she ran to the older woman and threw her arms around her.

As she hugged her tight, Mabel said, "Careful, sweetheart, you might break me."

Celia giggled and pulled back, giving Mabel

a kiss on the cheek.

"Break you? Somehow I doubt that."

Debbie, Jaxon and Lisa began moving food to the dining room and within minutes, they gathered everyone around the table, holding hands.

Those that believed John didn't have any soft emotions in his heart weren't there to hear the things he said to all those gathered under his roof.

But that's for another story.

The End

I hope you've enjoyed this continuing story about Deputy Debbie, Sheriff John and the dogs and monsters of Prattville. These Cold Shivers Nightmares are meant to be stand-alone novels, but there will be ties between most of the stories.

I would appreciate it if you could turn to the next page and send a rating to Amazon. Obviously I would love to get 4 and 5 star ratings, but more than that, I'd like to get honest reviews so I can see how these stories are being received. Thank you for taking the time to read my stories.

Coming in late 2022
Sister Clarice: Vatican Demon Hunter

A new Campfire Story

Tonight was especially dark, much quieter than usual. Only the sound of her heels clicking on the sidewalk broke the silence as she made her way home. The snick snick snick of her heels seemed to echo off the walls of the surrounding buildings.

Getting off work at midnight each night, Suzanne had grown accustomed to this walk. This part of town was not the worst, but it also wasn't the best.

Clenched in her fist was the small can of mace that she prayed she would never have to use. So far, after seven months of living here, she hadn't deployed the weapon even once. There was no reason to believe tonight would be any different.

Until it was.

Without warning, the calm in her chest evaporated into a cloud of terror, as if something had reached out of Hell and wrapped its cold, evil fingers around her soul.

Feeling the grip of malevolence wash over her, she almost stumbled and had to reach out to grab hold of a railing to keep her balance. As she fought to catch her breath, the mace canister fell from her fingers, clattering to the ground in front of her.

"Oh, no!" she stammered as she bent to pick up the small canister, causing the dizziness in her head to amplify.

Just as her fingers reached for the mace, it rolled away and she had to let go of the railing to reach it.

A wave of wooziness washed over her as she fought to catch hold of the small black cylinder. Each time her fingers came in contact with the plastic tube, it moved away, as if something was trying to keep her from getting her fingers on it.

Fighting the feeling of nausea in her gut, she lunged for the mace canister and wrapped her fingers around it and picked it up.

When she stood up, it felt like she had done so too fast and a wave of lightheadedness washed over her. Beginning to sway on her feet, she closed her eyes and she took a deep breath. Reaching out to grab hold of the railing again, she found it wasn't there.

Opening her eyes, she saw the railing was ten feet away. Stumbling toward it, she reached out, hoping she would get there before she passed out. When she could grasp the cold metal of the rail, her body swiveled on her heels and she collapsed onto some stairs.

Even though her mind was cloudy, she found herself thankful that she had at least fallen into a sitting position. The last thing she wanted was to be mistaken for a drunk laying on the sidewalk.

Especially when she didn't even drink or use drugs.

As she bowed her head and took deep breaths, trying to clear the fog clouding her mind, she heard a door open behind her.

"What are you doing here?" she heard a gruff, male voice behind her.

"I'm just ..." she started, but wanted to breathe, rather than explain herself. Not that she could explain her condition at the moment, anyway.

"Go on! Get out of here! We don't want none of your lot in this neighborhood."

She turned her head and glanced over her shoulder. The man was easily seventy-years-old and looked like he hadn't missed a meal in all those years.

Fighting the feeling of passing out, she said, "I don't feel well. I can't ..."

"Probably from all that booze you drank or the drugs you took. Now get out of here before I call the cops."

He didn't give her a chance to answer. Turning back, he slammed his door with a note of finality, completely dismissing her as a fellow human being.

She took another couple of breaths and felt a little better, so she pulled herself up and got steadied on her feet.

I need to get home and get something to eat or get some water. I'm probably just dehydrated.

Just then, she heard the door behind her open again and she decided to just ignore the guy and get moving. It was only about a hundred yards to her garden apartment.

"Here sweetie."

She turned at the sound of the woman's voice and saw a woman, obviously about the same age as the man. She was wearing a worn housecoat and had her gray hair bundled underneath a night cap. In her hands, she held an open bottle of water.

"Oh, thank you," said Suzanne softly as she took the bottle. It was ice cold.

"Don't pay no attention to Marvin. He'd step over your dead body before he would ever help you."

Suzanne took a sip of the cold water and let out a sigh.

Looking at the woman's sparkling eyes, she smiled.

"I don't know what happened," she said. "I just got dizzy and had to sit down."

She looked up at the door and saw the man standing there.

"And I'm not drunk."

"Marvin, get back inside!" said the old lady.

"You get back inside, Esther. You shouldn't be out here like this."

"I'll come in when I'm ready! Now leave her

alone!"

Marvin just harrumphed, turned and pushed the door closed.

Esther turned back to Suzanne and just smiled.

"Like I said, pay no attention to him. Do you have much further to go?"

"No," said Suzanne before taking another drink of the Heaven-sent water. "Just a few more buildings."

She pointed down the street.

"Come on, I'll walk with you," said Esther.

"Oh no! Please, I feel much better having gotten this water in me. I think I was just dehydrated. Anyway, I'd be a nervous wreck thinking about you walking back here alone."

"Dearie, I've lived in this neighborhood for the past forty years. I've had nothing bad happen to me here and I don't think it will start tonight."

She reached out and wrapped her arm through Suzanne's arm and started walking with her down the street. The younger woman looked down and saw Esther was just wearing a pair of house slippers and was thankful it wasn't cold out tonight.

As they walked, Esther talked about how she and Marvin moved into their apartment when Ronnie was in the White House. And about how their only son hardly ever visited anymore or even called.

"I'm sorry to hear that," said Suzanne. "I used to call my mama at least once a week when she was still alive."

"She passed?"

"Yes, about a year ago, just a few months after my daddy passed away."

"So, are you all alone in this world now?"

"Oh, no. I have a younger brother, but he lives in California. We talk now and then, but we don't get to see each other much."

"Well, stay in touch with him, dearie. Family is all we have worth anything in this world."

"That is so true," said Suzanne as she patted Esther's hand.

"Well, this is me," she said as she came to a stop outside the small apartment building.

"That's my apartment down there," she said, pointing to the garden apartment just below ground level.

"Are you going to be okay?"

"Yes, I'm feeling much better."

Without realizing she was doing it, Suzanne leaned over and kissed Esther on the cheek.

"Thank you for looking after me."

Esther just smiled and said, "Wouldn't this world be a much better place if we all looked out for each other?"

"Yes, it would. Now, I'm going to stand right here on the sidewalk and watch as you walk back to your place. I'm not going in until I know you've made it safely back."

Esther looked up at her and smiled.

"What is your name, sweetie?"

"Oh, Suzanne. Suzanne Kelly."

"Well, Suzanne Kelly. You be careful. There seems to be something in the wind tonight and it doesn't feel good."

Suzanne snatched a quick breath, but before she could ask Esther what she meant, the old lady had turned and started back toward her own apartment. Suzanne watched her go, but couldn't shake the feeling that she had given a warning to her. A warning she did not understand.

A couple of minutes later, Esther reached her own door and turned and waved to her. Suzanne waved back and watched as she climbed her steps and disappeared into her home.

Walking to her own apartment, she stepped down the four steps that led to her garden apartment. It sat about halfway below ground level, with some small windows that looked out to the street in front of the building.

As she fumbled with her keys, trying to balance the mace and the bottle of water, the light over her head began flickering. Looking up at it, she just shook her head.

Have to ask Charlie to check that light tomorrow.

As she slipped into the apartment, she pushed the door closed and set the contents of her hands on the small kitchen table. Turning back to the door to lock it, she felt the same wave of dizziness wash over her again and fell to her knees.

"Oh God," she cried out. "What is wrong with me?"

As she brought her hands up to her head, she squeezed them together, trying to drive the pain from behind her eyes. She leaned forward until her forehead touched the floor.

Clenching her eyes closed so tightly, she didn't notice the dark figure push the door open and step into her apartment. It was only when the door clicked closed, she opened her eyes, looking through the pain.

And screamed.

To be continued ...

Other books by D Glenn Casey

Beware The Boogerman
A Cold Shivers Nightmare #1

Where it all began.

How do you fight the thing monsters are afraid of?

After Deputy Debbie did her tour in the Army as an MP, she returned to her hometown, marched into the sheriff's office and demanded a job. Her daddy is the sheriff. Now, you can call her Deputy Debbie -- or if you're really brave, Dinkie.

Her hometown of Prattville isn't like other towns. It's where monsters go when they retire. The sheriff's job is to keep the peace between the human folk and the vampires, goblins, werewolves and other scary residents that call Prattville home.

But when a tragic past re-emerges, Debbie's best friend disappears -- again -- in the midst of a spate of attacks on monsters, Debbie fears the worst.

What's killing monsters? Where is it hiding Debbie's friend? And how is one little human woman supposed to fight something that can shred a goblin, decimate a vampire and put two large trolls in the hospital?

All she knows is she has to try. Her best friend's life depends on it.

More demons. Lots more demons.

Shattered Prisons

Cold Shivers Nightmare #2

If things go bump in the night, maybe you should just sell the house and move.

For the last few months before her death, artist Julie's beloved Nana started to talk about strange things - evil demons, dark angels and bad humans. Julie let her prattle - it was just harmless talk, wasn't it? Wasn't it?

Now on her own with her grief in a big empty house, Julie's beginning to think that maybe there was something to Nana's wild talk. Most normal families have skeletons in the closet. Julie's family is a little more unusual ... her closet has demons.

Demons are on the loose, a friend is in peril, and a family legacy has been thrust upon her surprised shoulders. Can Julie transform into a badass demon fighting machine or will she cower behind her easel?

With the forces of evil on the prowl - released from their prisons by a clumsy friend - Julie must scramble to train and take her place beside Templar Knights, demon-fighting monks and a feisty Dominican nun who has an obsession with cherry pie.

Want another story about demons? And angels?

Into The Wishing Well

Welcome to the afterlife. Please take a number.

Melanie lived a good life. She played by the rules, loved her friends and neighbors, and was always kind to strangers. But when an "accident" sends Melanie to the Pearly Gates, she's shocked to find Heaven is closed for new arrivals! How was she supposed to know she needed a number to get into the afterlife?

While she waits for a spot to open up, Melanie discovers she isn't the only spirit walking around her old town. A diabolical demon also walks the earth. And this sinister entity has made it his mission to capture Melanie's soul for his master. A war is brewing between Heaven and Hell, and poor Melanie is caught squarely in the middle.

With Angels and Archangels sworn to protect her, and Lucifer's own minions eager to take her captive, it seems like death is only the beginning of Melanie's problems. And the fate of both Heaven and Hell may rest in her ghostly hands.

Crossing The Veil
A Cold Shivers Nightmare #3

They heard voices from the other side. Perhaps they should have ignored them.

Carol Hamilton is one of the most brilliant, quantum physicists in the world. Her mother and father were smarter than her, but they disappeared into one of their experiments, leaving her to try and figure out what happened.

When she opens a doorway to another part of the universe, it draws the attention of the military, the politicians and everyone else that wants to have a say in the matter. Realizing she may have found a way to bring her parents home, she sets off a chain of events that could have dire consequences for the entire universe. Or did those events start when her parents went missing?

The Army is tasked with the impossible mission of bringing her parents back and Carol isn't about to let them go without her. But, when the general places two mysterious strangers on the rescue team, the others have to figure out what's really going on.

Why are the strangers going with the team? Why does Carol keep hearing her father's voice in her dreams? And what will happen when she realizes she may be bringing about the end of the universe?

Wicked Rising
The Chronicles of Wyndweir - Book One

by D Glenn Casey

Garlan has finished his trials in the Land of the Dragons and he is heading home. The only thing he can think of is being reunited with the woman that has stolen his heart.

But, there is evil rising in the Eastern Desert and war is on the horizon. Everyone he knows is expecting him to rise up and be a leader and vanquish this evil. He'd rather they find someone else.

The Tales of Garlan
Prequel to the Chronicles of Wyndweir

by D Glenn Casey

Garlan went to live with the old wizard, Sigarick when he was eight years old. Now, in his twenty-third year it's time to prove he's actually learned something.

These four short stories tell of wizard duel, clearing thugs from villages and facing a final set of trials that could very well kill him. All in a days work for Garlan.

Printed in Great Britain
by Amazon